Praise For Karl Drinkwater

"Drinkwater creates fantastically believable characters."
On The Shelf Reviews

"Each book remains in my mind for a long time after. Anything he writes is a must-read."
Pink Quill Books

"Karl Drinkwater has the skill of making it near impossible to stop reading. Expect late nights. Simply outstanding."
Jera's Jamboree

"An intelligent and empathetic writer who has a clear understanding of the world around him and the truly horrific experiences life can bring. A literary gem."
Cooking The Books

"Drinkwater is a dab hand at creating an air of dread."
Altered Instinct

"A gifted writer. Each book brings its own uniqueness to the table, and a table Drinkwater sets is one I will visit every time."
Scintilla.info

THEY MOVE BELOW

KARL DRINKWATER

ORGANIC APOCALYPSE

Organic Apocalypse Copyright Manifesto

CONTENTS

TRANSMISSION (PART 1)

Have you ever viewed the night sky, so vast and black and cold, and wondered what's up there? Take tonight for instance. Rural area, so little light pollution. You could exit the leafy country lane, wander up the drive. At the rear of the stone cottages are big oil tanks partly obscured by a trellis. Plastic deck-chairs and a table conveniently left out on the lawn. No movement in the house: everyone is asleep. So you put your bag down, hear the tools within rattle against each other, and plonk your arse on one of those seats after tipping it first to spill off the rainwater that has pooled there. Stretch and look up at the space between the stars, thinking about blackness.

It's mystery, you see. The unknown always cloaks itself in that colour. The horrible, the grotesque, the supernatural (if there is such a thing – I'm not convinced, myself, and believe me, I've thought about it a lot). That's why places of blackness and shadow are such a good fit for anything nasty. Caves splitting down through the earth; damp cellars; cobwebby attics; underground car parks; the dead of night; deep water that light never reaches; even our worst memories, sometimes.

It takes about thirty minutes for your eyes to adapt properly to darkness. That's retinal darkness adaptation, rather than pupil dilation, which only takes seconds. Hey, you know something funny? Kids growing up in cities nowadays don't even realise that you can see the Milky Way with the naked eye as a pale river of light in the sky. Yep, all that permanent city neon and fluorescence making its own never-ending twilight and stopping you seeing the real world. Takes a three hour drive from the suburbs to get the view I'm seeing now. City cowards think all that light makes them safe. It just highlights a target, if you ask me Not that anyone does.

It's not empty out there. Looking up you see the moon, stars, Venus (at its brightest), constellations, speckled galaxies, nebulae. All spread across the black blanket backdrop that could be hiding anything.

Danger is another thing I associate with that colour. Well, that absence of colour really. That darkness.

I've already noticed the deadly bushes nearby. It's rare to have one of Europe's most toxic plants in your garden. It tells me that whoever lives here doesn't have children. The bell-shaped flowers have a faint, unforgettable scent, but it's the berries I like – they ripen to shiny-black and contain a fun compound of tropane alkaloids. It's effective poison – just ask the ancient Romans – a small handful of berries can kill an adult. Six will usually do it. Another connection to darkness: one symptom of nightshade poisoning is dilated pupils. Like a panic, to let more light in, fight off the blackness inside (isn't nightshade a great name?). It's where the plant gets its other name from: belladonna. Italian for "pretty lady". Because women used to put drops of the poison in their eyes to make their pupils bigger and darker. They'd go blind because of it. The things women do so people find them attractive, huh? It's right up there with foot binding and plastic surgery. Some sicko stuff.

Well, the full moon's winking at me. A white pupil in a black eye. Reverse of life down here. That's because anything out there would be the antithesis of life. I know it. This planet stands alone, a negative version of the usual template. Each star that shines is watching us. Each gap between the stars could harbour anything.

I can't help but shudder. It's creepy shit. But night's waning and I've got stuff to do. I pick up my tool bag, feel it sag from the weight of the implements. Visits wouldn't be half so much fun without them. The lock-picks. The drills. The full syringes. One last look up at the night sky, so vast and black and cold. Yeah, sometimes I truly wonder what's out there. Watching us move below its gaze. And waiting.

If That Looking Glass Gets Broken

Her son. Her son! He was the best one in the world. She knew. She had a few, and had known others; she could see and hear, not senile yet, she had her senses. She loved him.

"He's so good," she said, almost purring satisfaction while slurping tea in hands still steady enough not to spill it into the saucer.

"Shut up mumbling, woman," said her husband, an automatic snap, like a leg-hold trap buried in leaves. Couldn't resist catching her words, teeth digging in and weakening them.

So she just nodded while he read the newspaper; she smiled, let words run through her head instead of from wrinkled lips and across the cracked lino surface to his hairy ears.

Best son in the world? Maybe best *listener* in the world was more accurate. *He* never made her shut up. These words in her, wriggling below the surface – they always welled up and had to spill over. That good son! He let her speak. He didn't stop her as words flooded out, crimson and shining and alive. Yes, old woman nonsense her husband might call it, but *words must flow*; mouths are cuts in our faces aren't they, blood flows, it has to. Her son was a lifeline.

She looked at the clock, lovely big grandfather clock, dark stiff wood that perseveres, keeps on ticking and tocking, feet darkened from years of mopping, only a few minutes now.

Oh, her boy!

Of course it's natural that sometimes when you're talking your child seems distracted; momentary thoughtlessness crossing a face as if they're not listening, just making the noises. You can't hold it against them. Times when they're not really there, bound to be. Still, a good listener.

The best of all her sons.

The clock would chime the hour soon. She was excited. She wanted to say so. She slurped cold sweet tea instead, noticing the taste less than the moisture of it, and watched her husband over the delicate cup's rim. He shook the paper dismissively, he hated crinkles in it, crinkles and wrinkles, yet he was so frinkle-frowny, grumpy puss, ooh she wanted to say that, quick, another sip of tea, drain the dregs –

The clock gave a ting, such music in one note!

Not too eager, can't be, he'd say no just to be stubborn, old frowny face. Wait, calm the hands, count: one, two, three.

"I'll go and feed him," she said. "I've finished my tea."

He stared at her, pierced her, those murky grey eyes weren't soft, they were hard, could see every detail. Could he perceive the trembling excitement inside? Would he crush it with hammer words, bludgeon her enthusiasm into submission, oh unbearable if –

"Okay," he muttered, returning to the printed words with another rustle of the paper. "Soup. He shouldn't have solids."

"I *know*," she said, pretending to chide and moving before he changed his mind.

As she warmed the soup she felt safe to hum part of a song, her husband wouldn't hear it from the parlour. The sweet, sweet words rose and fell in her mind, a natural pulse to flow with the notes.

"Hush, little baby, don't say a word, Mummy's going to buy you a mockingbird."

The soup was warm now, and she sprinkled in some of the powder they kept in an old spice jar, stirring until it dissolved.

Oh, son! Best of all her children. She would tell him. She would sing to him. Oh, baby!

She unbolted the cellar door and balanced the tray in one arm while she switched the light on. It really needed a clean, she thought, eyeing up cobwebs and coal dust. Baby didn't mind, though.

She took each step down carefully, the smell of damp tickling her nostrils.

God wanted people to have children. The priest said so. She knew anyway. It was obvious. The shops full of baby things. Children on the TV during the rare times her husband could put up with the noise. The government, helping families out with money and nice laws. Oh yes, everyone knew. Children were from God. Praise God! He gave her another son, the best of all sons! He *listened*.

She opened the door to the fire room, and saw her son, lovely son, squatting near the crunchy coal pile; he tried to stand because he was well mannered but the chains stopped him moving much, so good, and he made noises but without a tongue they were quiet ones, now it was healing, like the ragged calf-wound from the trap, and she began to talk, to tell him everything, and maybe his eyes glazed, not tears, no, he was a good son, he would last longer than the others, and she wiped dried blood from around his mouth and wondered if she should shave him and cut his matted hair again, and she sang to him, "Hush, little baby, don't say a word," she would spoon him soup, oh, her son! The best of all her children so far.

THEY MOVE BELOW

She ignored his swearing as he fixed whatever was wrong with the sails. Instead she looked out at the undulating blue which glowed in the sunlight. A shimmering surface. Unknown what lay below.

"I shoulda knowed he'd stiff me. Typical damn chink furreigner." He banged a tool against the deck, making her flinch.

You only discover what's underneath after you've dived in. And then it's too late.

"We Burmese. Not chinks."

"Chink, gook, burmen, same thing." Damp patches spread under his arms and down the back of his short-sleeved shirt. He was clumsy, the spanner often slipping from the corroded bolt he was trying to tighten near the mast, something he had called a bird neck ... no, gooseneck. "Don'tcha mean ta say *Myanma*? Ain't you all proud nowadays?"

"That is literary, not spoken."

"Just mincing words." More cursing as he used brute force to adjust the fittings, kneeling and surrounded by tools. "Hey now, you just go on and enjoy yourself there," he said, with a tone she thought might be sarcasm. "Nothing else ferrit, right?"

The anger steaming from him made it impossible to relax and enjoy it.

"I would help but I do not know much about boats."

"You're telling me you grew up by water without learnin' a damn thing about boats? You gotta be shittin' me."

"My *ah phay* ... my father ..." But her voice faded out, and she looked up at the sky, shading her eyes with a forearm.

A dot which grew in size; it resolved into a speeding jet, low in the distance, roar of engines reaching them across the water. A machine's screech breaking the natural peace. He stopped to watch it too. Soon it faded to a dwindling streak on the horizon.

"Military. Jest sabre rattlin', pay it no mind," he said. "We all so impressed now, we shakin' in our boots. Still, 'tis mighty odd fer the M.A.F. ta be this fer away from Pathein. Wonder what's got them all riled up? Lookin' fer something?"

She gazed down at the water. A few strands of seaweed floated past, twisting hypnotically in motions caused by the boat's passing. It was more calming to gaze at those than the clumps of plastic bottles and bags that had marked the surface as they'd first left the coast.

Her camera was heavy on its strap around her neck. She raised it to her eyes and used the viewfinder. Had to increase the shutter speed to cancel the boat's motion; a small aperture; then focussed on the seaweed a few metres away. A click, and the wide-angle lens captured everything to the far distance in focus. This would be her remembrance.

"People are disappearing again," she said, satisfied with what the small screen displayed. "Some say it is poisonous insects that live in *jet suu* – you call castor oil plants? Everyone is nervous lately. Others say it is the army. There have been lots of soldiers around, very busy, like angry click beetles."

"Yep, that's so."

"Will other countries do anything? About missing people?"

A snort. "With all this demand fer Burma oil and gas, tain't likely. They all know ifin Burma gets snubbed, they'll jest cozy up even more to China. Ya dreaming, girl."

"That's why you are here?"

"Plenty of contracts once there's military running things. When the tide rises, all the boats float higher, so they say. Hey, reach me that there." He gestured at a tool. It was not far from him; he could reach if he stretched. She picked it up, heavy metal, adjustable teeth for gripping, and held it out.

"Don'tcha worry none, I ain't gonna bite ya." His hand brushed hers as he took the implement.

She retreated, while he scowled at the mast and returned to his adjustments. "This here boat is a piece of shit, that's fer damn sure. Gotta be forty fuckin' years old, ifin it's a day. You can knock me over with a feather ifin that engine works 'tall. Better be hoping we don't ever need it."

"If it is so bad why did you take it? Did Maung intimidate you?"

"Na ... don't reckon Maung and his midget goons could bother me none." He yanked hard on the sail, tightening something until his knuckles were white. "Jest ... it was available. Anyway. What were you sayin' about your papa afore?"

"He died at sea," she replied. "Almost ten years ago today. We never found his body."

He sighed. Looked down. Tightened another bolt. "And?"

"I was scared." She leaned on the rail again, felt the boat's movement as her own. The sea was always in motion. Restless, her stomach rolling with it. "But you get older and do not want to be scared any longer. They say you should face your demons. And now I am here it is not so bad. I am not superstitious, but ... my mother talks of *nat*, the spirits. We make peace with them. Perhaps I am here for that."

"You got on with your papa?"

"We ... argued."

"So you come all the ways out here to apologise?"

He would not understand. That topic was not for him, not for now. Another one. "I respect the sea," she said, softly. It was so big, dominating the view on all sides. Bigger than land, deeper than mountains, darker than night in its secret depths. "So there is no hurry. I will take photographs. That is why I not mind sail problem. This experience, this time out here. I wish to save it. No, sorry: savour is the word I mean."

He looked over his shoulder, caught her stare. Grinned. Stood and stretched. Wiped sweat from his sun-reddened brow. Stepped heavily over ropes and fishing tackle to reach her. "I hear ya. You and me, we're out to sea, jest the two of us."

She took a step back but her waist was against the metal handrail, could go no farther. He gripped her upper arms, slick skin on skin, leaned in and put his salty lips to hers before she unfroze, turned her head and twisted, struggled to move away. A look of annoyance on his face when he saw her angry expression. He let go.

"Oh, I see how it is. Teasing ta get what you want, then leaven a man high and dry. Don't that jest take the cake. Leaves a man kinda aggravated."

"It is not what I thought, what you said. You are old enough to –"

"Mebbe you'll be a changing your mind along the way."

Beware of a man's shadow and a bee's sting.

She watched him until he turned away. He held a finger to each nostril and snorted outwards, clearing his nose on the deck. It made her feel queasy. She noted the spot where he was stood. She would be careful where she stepped.

His anger was back as he snatched different tools. "I reckon you took me fer a fool. That ain't respectful," he said, without looking at her.

"I thought of you like an uncle." Though he sounded like a child.

"Uncle!"

"That is a kind of respect. Just not what you mean."

"And there was me, bein' all sweet on the shy woman in the bar, spending wads of kyat on drinks and boats. Fooled me twice, girl. I should learn to read what's really goin' on behind those black eyes. And what you hidin' under all them clothes when it's so darn hot." He flexed his meaty hands. It would be better to change the subject.

"Earlier you say you do contracts, big business. So you have a lot of money?"

"Depends on what you would call a lot. I've paid $20,000 ta hunt a lion in Zimbabwe, but there's no way I could afford a black rhino."

"You hunt the rare animals?"

"Don't give me that look. Hunting is hunting. They're all going anyway. The clock's ticking on the greatest fire sale on Earth, and ifin I didn't get in there I'd miss out. Jest like business. You seize opportunities when they come, or you lose."

"You are not like I thought. When I met you."

"Out at sea, in the wilds – that's where a man's a man. Pretty words don't mean nothing. Actions speak louder then."

"I liked the pretty words. Kind words."

"Hardly likely ta get me all famous with those. Shit!"

Something had snapped off. He nursed his hand, red in the face. Tools and pieces of metal lay around him. It didn't seem like he'd finished – in fact, everything appeared more broken than when he'd started.

She turned back to the sea, though she kept an ear on his movements. Unable to relax as she watched the ambiguous waters. Scary yet calming. Salty yet clean. Clear yet obscure. She was disoriented from the gentle undulations. The horizon seemed flat, but her body felt the motion, dissonant sensations. Always movement out here. Always things moving below.

Another clump of seaweed, larger, floated past. A green tangle like a sea giant's wig. Ripples on the sea where it caressed the boat. She took more photos, wide views where the whole world seemed to be made of liquid. She noticed that the shade was brighter here, azure transparency – beyond, some distance away, the sea was darker.

"The water is a different colour," she said.

"What?"

He wiped his palms on a rag and scrambled to the edge of the boat. Looked out across the water. Cursed. "We've been adriften."

"How?"

He didn't answer.

"It's like a river of pale blue colour," she said, pointing towards the horizon.

"We must be in a current. Warm stream, water of a different temperature, hotter'n the rest of the ocean. A sorta gyre. But there shouldna' be nothing like this. No warning of one." He looked off at the clouds which skidded along the horizon. "Damn, how long've we been driften?"

"Fast," she said.

"Yeah, that I can see!"

"Is it bad?"

"Once in a while boats are found, everyone on board dead – some think they get pulled out and caught, lost in one of these currents washing into the Indian Ocean."

"You are joking me?"

"Wish I was."

"Do you know where we are?"

"Mostly." He scratched his chin. "Hell, I didn't realise the current was so strong. I shoulda dropped that anchor."

"Should have dropped ..." Her skin was clammy with sudden sweat. The boat seemed to be turning round. "You told me you know these things! Know boats."

"I got us here, didn't I?"

"Is this a problem?" She realised she was rubbing the camera. Had to stop her hands from fidgeting, but felt her own sea of panic churning inside. "You can point back in the right direction?"

"Not so simple. Depends on the wind. Ifin we have ta resort to the engine we're limited, and unless we're spot on ... Well, with the compass we can't miss land eventually, but it might not be where we want ta be. Depends how fer we've moved, what direction. It'll make distances a guessing game." He picked up binoculars from amongst the tools. Scanned the horizon. She did the same with her naked eye and realised there was no sign of land.

"I don't normally come out this fer," he mumbled.

"*What?*"

"I assumed we'd be fine, jest head back in the direction we came. This day-sailer's not meant fer more. I swear I think we're taking on water – don'tcha reckon we're riding a bit low? Gotta be more than the usual bilge, or mebbe there's a crack ... Hey, don't look at me like that. You're jest as guilty here as me! You were only interested when I mentioned going out to sea."

"I thought it would be safe!"

"This is jest bad luck." He kicked the fishing rod he'd been using earlier, it tangled up in some netting. "It's not my fault."

She followed him to the cabin. There was only room for one at the controls unless you were willing to be very close. She stood nervously outside, arms folded. He checked the thing she knew was a compass, looked out of the window in one direction, frowning. Referred to his maps (no, *charts*, as he'd corrected her earlier), a thick finger drawing lines across them. She asked what he was doing but he swatted a dismissive hand in her direction, picked up the radio mouthpiece, turned it on, rotated a dial. There was a crackling noise. He spoke into the microphone, asked if anyone received him.

The radio hissed with static. He thumped the display, tried different channels, repeated his message; then after a few minutes banged the mouthpiece on a metal part of the cabin, hard, and let it drop.

"The darn thing must be broken. Or the battery's failing."

"You are rough with things. *You* could have broken it. You said it worked before?"

"Well, it did when I tested it on shore."

"Can we use our phones?"

"Girl, you know nothing! They don't work out at sea. No cell masts. That's why boats *have* radios. Except this one ... Mebbe it's a question of range. What do these things work over? Fifteen miles max? Could be we're further out than even ..." He gazed at the horizon, long seconds passed; then he said with certainty: "No. It must be broken. Like everything else Maung rips me off with."

"You blame luck. You blame Maung. But like many Americans, you do not blame yourself."

"Could be true that I ain't hit the right blame yet." He narrowed his eyes. "But not me. *You.* You're a Jonah. A curse that runs in the family. Bad luck ta have in a boat."

"My father is nothing to do with today! Do not bring him into this."

"I thought you'd be up fer a bit of superstition?" He tried the radio again. Repeated names and words. Almost frantic. Betraying himself.

"What if ... there's no-one to answer?" she asked.

He licked his lips. "Why you spouting off nonsense?"

"But it is so quiet out here. And the sky, it does not look real. You could imagine we are somewhere else."

"Jest pray ta Buddha it stays quiet."

"Why?"

"Pirates could be a danger if they were listening in. At least we're not further West – or mebbe we are now? Godammit!"

He pushed past her, observed the sea. Huge bunched-up clouds sailed ahead of them, casting shadows onto the water's surface as they piled up white and grey, towering over the world. Then she noticed that amongst the shadows were even larger patches of floating seaweed; it might be possible to walk on it in places, it grew so dense, apparently liking something about this strange liquid.

"Cumulus. You get them above warm waters. This ain't normal. Not a good sign. We need ta get out." He licked his lips again.

"You are scared, aren't you?"

"I told you, you silly chink, I'm not scared of nothing! Your pissant army, your rip-off dealers, your silly fat gods, they can all take a flying fuck fer all I care. Ifin anyone should be scared, it's you. Jest stay quiet and stop pissing me off."

He checked the compass again. Barged past. Considered a small flag at the top of the mast as it fluttered, tendril-like, the material snapping back and forth. "Wind's the wrong fucking way." Back into the cockpit, turned on the engine. It erupted on the second try with a sputtering roar, deafening after the peace. The boat lurched forward, he looked through the front window and guided them around even greater masses of seaweed, inverted forests that reached down below them, falling into the gloom. He craned his head forward. Squinted.

"What in the hay is that there?" he asked.

She followed his eyes. There was a shape in water. Not seaweed this time. The texture was smooth. It was as big as some of the clumps though. Enough to dwarf the boat.

"Is it a whale?" she shouted over the noisy rattling of the diesel engine, watching the curve as the object moved and undulated lifelessly.

"No." He changed direction to guide them nearer. "But I don't know ... fishing net? They're often cut loose." He pulled back on a metal lever and the engine dropped to a thrumming vibration she felt in her feet. They continued to move closer to the shape, slowly cutting through weed. He locked the wheel and left the cockpit to get a better view from the deck.

"It looks like a parachute," she said. "It is flopping. Like a plastic."

"Yep!" A crooked smiled, ugly but relieved. "That would make sense. Mebbe that's what the plane was looking fer? Keep your eye out fer someone, in the water or on one of the seaweed rafts. Though they could be under the parachute. Drowned, in that case." A glint in his eye as he regarded her. "Can you imagine that? Trapped underneath, struggling, tied up, unable ta get out as you run out of breath? Knowing you're so close to air but can't break through the tough surface." She moved away from him, but he followed, his steps matching hers. "Then giving in, struggle over, drowning, sinking down into the colder, darker waters until you're suspended, dangling from the canopy and driften till you're eaten by fish."

"Stop it!" She pressed her hands over her ears.

"No burial."

"I said stop! STOP!" She reached the prow of the boat, could move no further, trapped between the water and *him* again, not sure which was worse. Looked for something to pick up, then saw beyond ... and stared, wide-eyed.

"It's not a parachute," she whispered.

He clambered to the cockpit, stopped the engine, and the boat drifted the last few metres to the mound. They looked over the edge as it drew alongside, and her stomach clenched. Her guess had been true. It still didn't make it any easier to believe.

It was more than ten metres across. Floating lifelessly, the gentle waves sometimes submerging it completely until it rose again, thick gelatinous body undulating, translucent under the water, but resembling a gluey putty when it rose above the waves. A stalk-like thread of tissue descended from the centre of the bell, surrounded by rope-like tentacles each thicker than a man's arm. They sank into darkness further than she could see; a sensation of vertigo came over her, as if she was swaying on the edge of one of the tallest apartment buildings in Yangon, a memory she tried to drown because the sensations had terrified her; deep blue you could fall into so easily, ending it all, and light blue above, a sky that can't hold you up –

Suddenly snatched by a big hand, pulled back.

"Watch out, you nearly tipped over the rail!" he said, snapping her back to mindfulness.

She looked down in horror at the bobbing giant as the boat's sides brushed the edges of its bell, a dry rasping of compression. Once, a few years ago, she had looked at death. It was as empty as she was. In the end she had not leaped into it. She had chosen life instead. Face it, do not run. But it was always just a step away.

He had already turned his attention elsewhere. "Have you ever seen ... I didn't know they could grow ... Must be one of the deep sea ones, died and drifted up. Unbe-fucking-lievable." He grabbed a long pole with a hook on the end. Leaned over the boat's rail and prodded. The rod pushed the jellyfish's skin down so even more water washed over the surface. The skin was thick and didn't tear, and immediately buoyed back up again, sloshing at the edge of the hull. "What do you know? That's some thick shit."

"I don't like it," she said, shaking. "This is not a natural thing. It is not."

"Could be that's what happened to your papa, huh? Eaten by a jellyfish?"

"Don't say that!" she screamed, tears in her eyes. "You know nothing, you foreign, you cruel man!"

"Lost your Eastern cool, eh? Now who's the scared one? Not me."

"You should be scared."

"Of a dead jellyfish?" It sounded like water slapping against plastic sheeting as the rippling jellyfish body dipped and rose in the current. "I'm not scared of anything," he said. "It's jest ... awesome." He slapped his palm on the rail, making her jump.

"Pics! Proof! YouTube!" He grabbed her camera, lifted the strap off her neck. She didn't struggle. He jabbed at the button for recording video, then held it up to face her. "Say cheese!"

She span away, wiped her eyes, but he had been teasing, had already swept the camera over the edge of the boat, filming the bobbing horror, like a thick plastic sheet with body parts hanging from it. He was laughing, describing the size, saying it was the world's largest jellyfish. "Ifin it hadn't died it might have grown even bigger!" he added for emphasis. "I'm gonna be famous. Ya'll will know my name now! Never bagged nothing this big afore. Wonder ifin I can tow it back?"

"Leave it!" she yelled. "It is part of the sea, not yours!"

"Yeah, yeah, princess." He stopped recording. "You're right though, in a way. They're made of sea too. Over ninety-five per cent water. It'd break up ifin I towed it. Can't see how I'd get a rope around it anyways."

She could not take her eyes off it. The horror and fascination of nature. A terrifying creature that lived and died in the sea; was mostly made of sea; only existed in this environment ... an agent of the sea.

"I don't want ta swim with it," he continued, as if to himself. "Even dead, it might still sting. Shame I'll jest have video, it doesn't show the scale of it. Damn, this falls into my lap and I have ta leave it!"

"Yes, leave it."

"Shut your trap, you ain't the boss of me."

"It is so big."

"Yeah, you said that. Wait a minute ..." He picked up the rod in one hand while the other kept a hold of her camera, prodded the thick skin again. "Shit. That would be kinda awesome."

"What?"

He didn't answer. Opened a locker and took out a wetsuit and boots. Stripped down to his underwear and put the new gear on in the cockpit. She looked away while he puffed and strained; then he was done and came clumping over. The rubber was tight on him, curved around his too-large stomach.

"What are you doing?" She was nervous enough to grasp his arm but he just smiled, a wild look in his eyes.

"Gonna set a world first record. Get some scale to it too. You're gonna film me."

"What?"

"I'm gonna walk on that fucker. Won't that be grand? I'm only in this mosquito-filled backwash country fer a few more months, why not do something *no human has ever done before*? I'm thinking that'll have ta get me on international news! Walking on a jellyfish! The world's largest! Wow!"

"There is something wrong with you! You are crazy!"

"Stop getting hysterical. You only gotta do one thing, and that's press the record button. I jest need to take two steps, let go of the rail. Guinness Records, girl! I'm a darned genius!" He was speaking fast, unfolding the rope ladder while she stared in disbelief. He hooked it over the edge of the rail. "Need to do it now afore we separate. Good, it's still there, see? Caught against the hull I reckon. And that thick pinky bit's underneath it. Woo." He took deep breaths through his nose. "Pick up the camera." He sat astride the rail. She didn't move. He suddenly seized her forearm, dragged her to him. She struggled but he was stronger. "Don't fuck this up," he hissed, holding her precariously near the edge. "And don't get any funny ideas, or I won't take you home. You'll be swimming with the jellyfish instead." He let her go, a switch flicked behind his face and it became a smile, as quick and false as that. She steadied her hands, picked up her camera, pressed the correct button, pointed it at him, trying not to think of what was floating nearby, it was nothing, just the sea, the open sea, blue and blue on blue ...

"I'm the captain here, and I'm gonna to make history!" he said into the lens. "Bravest man in the world shit about to happen!"

He climbed down the ladder, placing feet carefully on each rung, a hairless gorilla with a red face. She had to lean on the rail to keep the image centred on him. The jellyfish rose and fell, rose and fell, its dead bulk the immense backdrop behind him. He hesitated at the last rung. Looked up. "Gonna be like walking on the moon," he said, then swallowed. "Armstrong had it easy. One giant step ..."

He tentatively reached out a padded boot, prodded the jellyfish skin, put more weight down. It sank, and he seemed about to change his mind but looked into the camera again. Clenched his jaw and inhaled. Let the water rise to his knee – then it stopped sinking. A look of pleasure on his face. "I got it," he said to himself, lowering his other leg into the water. His arms gripped the rope ladder, taking some weight, but the water still rose to his groin. "I can do this." He took a step back, still holding on. Let more weight go onto his legs. The jelly ballooned around him but held. Her throat constricted, breath trapped, feeling faint again but also mesmerised, morbidly fascinated, this was not *the* world, this was another world, another's madness, but she could almost believe in it.

He let go.

Stepped away from the boat towards the centre of the jellyfish, and as he did it became more buoyant, more supportive, and he whooped for joy as each step got easier until it only sank as far as his calves and there he stood, a few metres from the bell's centre. Gelatinous translucency surrounded him, pinks and blues and greens. He had done it. She watched his triumphant expression through the camera. An insect on a giant sea flower.

The camera moved, sending him to the edge of the viewfinder. Maybe it was the boat's motion. It was difficult to know what stillness meant any more. She glanced over the top, past the long black lens. No, not the camera or boat – *he* had moved. His expression changed to fear, and she realised there was a pulsing motion. One vibration. Small. Then another, bigger, and the surface shimmered. He sank to his knees, slipped sideways, and tried to stand again, arms reaching out for the ladder, only two metres but the uneven moving surface gave no purchase, he sank into the water, up to his chest now. Another tremor in the jelly – it was rotating from the boat, starting to turn. He cried out, slid away from the ladder as the jellyfish tipped, scrambling and splashing in panic as he screamed that it was alive, slipping but moved by something bigger, something that weighed tons, a mass against which the man was nothing, and she felt madness pulling at her, watching the slow performance of the horror below. He reached up to her, called for help, words that hardly made sense as she watched the ripples lapping against the boat, waves caused by the monster's convulsions.

She glanced around. The hooked pole was nearby. She picked it up, could hold it out to him, pull him in, perhaps.

Mebbe you'll change your mind afore we get back.

Beware of a man's shadow and a bee's sting.

He reminded her of her father; the night-bed visitor who died before she could tell him she hated him as much as herself. Spirits harbour grudges but so do the living.

She laid the pole back on the deck by her feet.

Many seconds of frantic splashing passed, then the creature pulsed again and the bell contracted and expanded, enough to throw him into the water in front of it; his voice cut off as he gulped liquid in panic, tried to swim around the jellyfish but it was too big; a few mammoth contractions and it passed him, forced him under its bulk, but she could still see him struggling, kicking, mouth and eyes open in fear until she lost sight of them amongst the giant fleshy underparts which tangled him up. And the behemoth began to sink. She realised she too was screaming, and she dropped the camera, still recording; it plopped into the water and span down in a spiralling dive away from the light, beyond which the pale ghostly transparent mass sank, into darkness; she thought there was a glimpse of legs, or arms in the mass of tentacles which streamed behind it; the jellyfish's weight sank down, the surface light making its body luminescent for a few seconds before it faded, a raw mass of beautiful alien sinking under the sea, under her.

She stared down at the nothingness that went on forever, blue, beautiful blue, home of ghostly giants, it went on forever in beauty, blue on blue on blue, like floating in the sky above Yangon, only a dive away from ending it all and discovering what there is in the black. She realised she'd been leaning dangerously far over the rail again, hypnotised by the pulsing, the depth, the vertigo. No. It was not her time then, and not her time now.

Deep breaths, eyes closed, she squatted and held the rail. Tried to calm the pulsing inside, the convulsing heart that reminded her of something else as it squished liquid inside her. Be practical. Be brave.

The sails were still in disorder after he'd been messing with them. "Unsafe," he'd said. She didn't understand how that all worked anyway, just a confusing tangle of material and cables. Luckily, she would not need them.

She walked to the cockpit on shaky legs and tried the radio. Still the hissing. A faint smell of burnt electrics.

The compass worked though. If she headed north or north-east she would surely reach land somewhere; if the radio wasn't broken she could get help then. She had seen him work the engine and steer. It seemed easy enough.

The boat drifted fast, creaking as it turned in the current that trapped it and dragged it along.

She reached down to turn the key and start the motor. She would soon be on her way home. But the key wasn't there. She tried pressing where it said "Start". Nothing. She knelt and scrabbled through the items on the floor, in case it had fallen; then went through the pockets of his clothes. Many items, but no key.

No key.

When he got changed ...

And don't get any funny ideas, or I won't take you home. You'll be swimming with the jellyfish instead.

She rushed to the edge of the boat and looked over the side into that endless depth, depth that seemed closer, *we're taking on water*, and she screamed, tearing her hair; the boat danced faster under the eerie sky, turned and groaned, heavy in the water, carried out to sea and descending slowly with each revolution, as if the seaweed rafts orbited her in endless space, airless, and dark down there with all the night-time dead things that waited, reaching up for company.

CREEPING JESUS

"Ah, this is *borin'*. Museums are rubbish."

"Fabian James!" Mr Jenkins, the teacher, hissed through clenched teeth. "Will. You. Be. Quiet!" A phrase repeated for the third time that day, with more verbal punctuation added each time. "Please pay attention and stop ruining things for everyone else."

Some of the other members of Fabian's class giggled, looking forward to another amusing episode. Fabian looked down and kicked the toe of his shoe against the floor.

The curator showing them round continued.

"And this is the archaeology section, the Bowen Gallery, where we keep historical items that have been dug up. Stone samples, pottery, tools. They tell us a lot about the past."

"Have you got any axes and spears?" Fabian asked, looking up.

"Well, no, but we do have –"

"Just so's I can kill Tommy with one," Fabian interrupted.

"Fabian!" erupted Mr Jenkins. "I won't have that kind of talk."

"I'd kill you first," muttered Tommy, so only Fabian could hear.

"What we do have is something *scary*," the curator continued, trying to get the class's attention back. "A skeleton!"

Some of the class perked up at that.

"It was dug up in Aberystwyth Castle twenty years ago. We have assembled the pieces over here," he said, gesturing towards the glass display case, causing the children to crowd round it, "and –"

Fabian laughed. "Skellingtons aren't *scary* any more! They were only scary hundreds of years ago. Only aliens or zombies are scary now, or axe murderers. Skellingtons are just *sad*."

"Right, that's it!" snapped Mr Jenkins. "Fabian, if you speak again and interrupt the curator you are going to miss out on the school party next week. You will be banned from attending and I'll write a letter to your parents explaining why. Your behaviour has been disgraceful today and I am *very* disappointed in you. It's like you've been trying your best to ruin the day for everyone, despite us being shown around this lovely museum."

"And he touched all the things in the *bwthyn* that said 'Please do not touch'," said Jessica.

"He spilt juice on the carpet in the shop on purpose," alleged Tommy.

"He pulled my plait," added Amanda.

"Fabian stole two of my sweeties and put 'em both in his mouth at once," wailed Samantha.

"And he said a rude word when we went to the top balcony," added little Dafydd Huws.

"So that's your last warning," shouted Mr Jenkins, red-faced with exasperation. "DON'T SPEAK AGAIN, FABIAN!"

Fabian knew Mr Jenkins was serious. So he shut up and let the curator talk about cannonballs and broken vases. Though he couldn't resist sticking two fingers up at Tommy when Mr Jenkins wasn't looking.

His interest revived at the recreation of an iron-age hut. At one end a life-size creepy dummy of a girl held a stick and stared out. From the other end you could see another dummy squatting over a fake fire, eerily lit by the orange light that made it look like flames. The fake hut was lined with rags, and harboured deep black shadows.

The dummies looked as fake as lots of other stuff in the museum, but it wasn't those that interested him. A devious expression crossed his angular features. He couldn't speak, but he could still have fun. He hung around at the back of the group.

Mr Jenkins thanked the curator for being so helpful. He'd enjoyed the last half hour, looking at the items arranged around the top gallery. The children had all been quiet so he could ignore them and listen to the curator's interesting comments. As the group moved back down to the shop, Mr Jenkins saw that many of the parents were already waiting to collect their precious offspring. Some children joined their families, others ran out of the museum cheering at the end of the school day, some wanted to go to the toilet first, and it was hard to keep track of who had been collected and who hadn't in the chaos.

The museum was locked up for the night. All the staff had gone home. But the museum wasn't empty.

Fabian crawled out from behind the big basket of wool in the iron-age hut exhibit. He was getting hungry but it was worth it, he thought spitefully – Mr Jenkins would be in *so much trouble* when Fabian's parents found out he had been "abandoned" in the museum by a careless teacher. Mr Jenkins might even get the sack! That would be good, Fabian thought, grinning.

Of course, that wouldn't happen for a while. Father would work late, and if Mother went to her aerobics class she wouldn't notice that Fabian hadn't walked home until tea-time (the meal no doubt delayed, as usual). Still, they *would* notice. Eventually.

It was dark in the archaeology room. The only illumination was the amber light from the fake fire in the hut, and a faint glow from the street lamp outside the museum. Enough to see by, though it looked eerie with deep shadows in the room that seemed to move when you weren't looking at them, as if the whole room was a crackling fire.

He crawled out, under the wires meant to stop people from entering the exhibit, and tried the door that led out of the Bowen Gallery and into the main part of the museum. He was sure he would have fun running around and eating chocolate from the shop until a teacher (or his parents, or the police) came back to rescue him.

He turned the door handle and pulled – but the door wouldn't budge. He tried again, and realised it must be locked. He had thought it was just the click of the door closing when a member of museum staff had put the main lights out and left, but he must have locked the door, not just closed it.

"Why lock an empty room?" Fabian murmured.

He jumped when he heard a muffled thump from somewhere behind him.

"Only something I disturbed," he whispered, as if to convince himself. "I'll just wait. Someone will come soon."

He decided to look at the boring stones and bits of rubbish in the exhibits anyway. But as he turned away from the door he caught a glimpse of the strange iron-age girl dummy, the one stood behind him – and he felt that its eyes suddenly flicked forwards, as if they had been looking at him. His heart skipped a beat.

"Only a dummy," he told himself nervously.

He knew he only had to prod the dummy with his finger to prove it was a lifeless piece of plastic ... but he couldn't bring himself to do that. In daylight her skin had seemed dry and plasticky; her hand fake and twisted wrongly; her hair artificial and straggly – but in the weird orange glow she

she?

looked a lot more ... real. Her eyes glinted as if moist. Fabian couldn't bring himself to move within reach of that hooked lower hand.

He moved away quickly.

"Trick of the light," he muttered, like he'd heard in a film once. Though he didn't like the sound of his voice in the otherwise silent room. It felt like it didn't belong there.

He moved over to the cabinet which held clay smoking-pipes, and tried to be interested. He noticed that one pipe was red on the part that goes in your mouth. It reminded him of blood.

Then the hairs on the back of his neck rose. His eyes focussed differently, and he saw there was a reflection of the dummy in the glass panel over the pipes. And the head was slowly turning towards him!

He spun round, heart really racing now, and he noticed that the dummy – although deathly still again – was leaning right against the criss-crossed wires.

"It fell forward, it just fell forward ..." he repeated, like a chant.

There was a click, and the orange light in the hut went out. Fabian knew the bulb could have blown, but it sounded more like it had been *switched off*, from within the display. The thought of the crouching dummy on the other side of the hut, next to where he had hidden, made him shudder. And now he could hardly see anything, despite the street light outside.

He kept his eyes on the dummy. It didn't move. And a horrible memory surfaced in his mind – the game he had liked to play when Granny was alive. He used to sneak up on her when she wasn't paying attention, freezing if she looked his way. She was so short-sighted she didn't notice him if he wasn't moving, until he was almost next to her. And so he would stealthily make his way over while she read, or watched TV, noisily sucking toffees. Then he would say something like, "Do you want a cup of tea, Granny?" in his most innocent voice. Granny would leap out of the chair in shock, hand clasped to her breast, and glare at him until she got her breath back enough to scold him. And he would sweetly claim he hadn't snuck up on her, saying it wasn't his fault she was half-blind, leaving her squinting at him with pursed lips, shaking with frustration and impotence.

So she had nicknamed Fabian "Creeping Jesus", and always said it in a mean way. She called him that whenever Mother wasn't around, right up until the day Granny had a heart attack and died, a year ago.

After that he had felt funny, and had bad dreams for a while in which Granny just pointed at him and ground her teeth together, but said nothing. But then Father had bought him a Nintendo DS and he forgot about Granny.

Until now.

Creeping Jesus.

Maybe they couldn't move while he was looking?

He watched the dummy. It was still. Good. He could keep watching it, and –

The head of the dummy turned a little more, he could just make out the movement in the darkness, heard the strained creak of stiffness, and the clawed hand pulled at the wire while the other reached towards him.

He shrieked and backed away, told himself to be calm, he could run round and round the exhibit: if the dummy was stiff then it would move slowly. Perhaps smash the window and call for help once he'd outrun it, set off an alarm ...

He heard the dummy fall with a crash. Yes! Then the head rose with a creak and the stiff arms and legs began to drag the body.

Walking might be impossible with those limbs, but crawling was doable.

He'd seen enough and broke into a run. Past the window and round the corner. He was approaching the rear of the hut when a hard-skinned arm shot out and flailed for his ankle. He jerked back in panic, just in time, and the fingers snapped shut on air, clicking open and closed, arthritic and eager. It was the second dummy, the one crouched over the fake fire. He retreated from the creaking horror as it pulled itself out, a stiff spidery outline that clicked unnatural joints and scuttled under the wires. He was glad it was too dark to see much, because the way it moved was *wrong*, unnatural, and seeing it clearly would freeze him in panic.

He ran back, skidded round the corner, and saw the shadow of the first dummy. They were coming from both directions.

Nearby was a bench. He was temporarily out of sight. Maybe they couldn't see well, eyes glazed like Granny's? If he could just stay out of their sight ...

He crawled under the bench and held his breath. He listened to the rustling and dragging noises getting closer. Scratchy clothes being pulled along the floor, the dummies not even trying to be stealthy. He had to breathe, took a gulp of air, and held it again. Bumps nearby, as things without proper joints knocked against cabinets clumsily.

He scrunched his eyes tightly closed, curled up in a ball, but in his mind he saw the dummies, and their creepy faces; something below the hardened shells animated them, moved limbs so they could drag themselves along the floor ...

"Oh Mummy, oh Mummy," he whispered as the two shapes pulled themselves nearer. Realised he was whimpering, tried to be quiet again but it was too late.

Cold, hard hands groped for him, succeeded in latching on to one of his ankles. A sudden tug of inhuman strength hauled him partway out from under the bench, and another hooked hand grabbed his wrist and pulled that hard too. He squirmed, heart beating fast, as stiff arms dragged him out.

"Please no please no please no," he repeated, a pleading chant of protection, "I'll be good."

He screamed but it turned into a squeal as the heavy stones hammered against his body, knocking the air out of his lungs; the rocks fell again and again, sickening thuds on his flesh underscored by cracking femur, ribs, mandible, ulna; the dull blows crushed his skull, and from then on the only noise was the regular thumping sounds, gradually shattering and cracking the remaining bones.

Eventually the blows stopped, a respite while creaking and clacking sounds moved. Searched. Found what they needed. And finally the wet noises began; eager, like a boy slurping milkshake through a straw.

Half an hour passed.

In the darkness an impossibly limp shape was dragged into the iron-age exhibition; it was so floppy it fitted into the little gap under a floorboard in the fake hut; and the floorboard was covered by smelly rugs.

The curator made his report and put the phone down with a sigh. He was unhappy at having to come back to the museum at night, unlocking everything and looking around with his torch. Especially in some rooms and areas where the hairs on the back of his neck prickled for no apparent reason, such as near the stuffed animals, or in the Bowen Gallery. Silly to feel that way, but he couldn't help it.

Anyway, he'd checked every room, shone his torch into every dusty corner, and all locked doors were still locked. There were no boys hidden anywhere. The brat must have got lost somewhere else, after he had left. Everything here was in its right place.

Well, almost.

It was weird that one of the skeleton bones had been left on the floor outside the glass case in the Bowen Gallery. The pipe cabinet was open too. Probably something to do with the horrible kid who'd been messing around and not showing the museum its proper respect.

The curator had put the small bone back in the glass case where it belonged.

JUST TELLING STORIES

"Go on. Tell me stories."

"What kind?"

Her eyes gleamed in the light from the bedside lamp. "*Scary* ones."

They were in twin beds facing each other over the gap. There was not much luxury in this hotel, so a single lamp with a worn shade sat on a bedside table between them at the headboard end. It shone in his eyes making him squint if he looked too far to the right. An unspoken barrier of light.

"They might give you nightmares. We've got to be up early tomorrow if we want to catch the first bus back."

"I won't have nightmares. I'm a big girl." She pulled down the duvet, revealing a nightie which was loose enough to expose the edge of her breasts. She covered up again, grinning.

He shifted uncomfortably on the bed as memories hardened into focus. It hadn't been his plan, but maybe it was worth humouring her.

"Okay. I'm short on inspiration, so it'll have to be things from books or films. Since we're in a hotel, there's one I read once ... A book by Dean Koontz. Called *Midnight*, I think. A woman was staying in a little seaside town where people were acting strange. There was a scene in a restaurant where all the locals were stuffing spicy food into their mouths but just staring ahead in silence as they ate, that kind of thing. She was in a hotel, got thirsty and left her room for a soft drink. Her bedroom was in a long corridor with stairs at each end, all the other doors were just to apparently empty rooms. She realised she hadn't seen any other guests. Into the enclosed, gloomy staircase, then down to the ground floor. She put money in the drinks machine and got a can of something, but as it clunked she thought she heard the door she'd come through close, two flights up. As if someone had been waiting for her to make a noise which might cover the sound of them shutting the door. Stealthy. She listened but heard nothing else. Maybe she was imagining it, but she *felt* that there was someone listening to her, somewhere on the shadowy staircase above. If they were hiding and following her it wasn't with innocent intentions. She couldn't bring herself to go back up the stairs so she entered that floor's corridor of rooms, sprinted along it, opened the fire door at the base of the second set of stairs at the other end. That was dark too, maybe the lights were broken. She was about to go up when she thought she heard a click, a door on another floor opening or closing. As if the person had moved along her floor quickly and was now up there. Or, even worse, she suddenly realised, what if there were two people, one at each staircase, and they were working together, going to ambush her? Even now one of them could be coming down these stairs, another could be at the other end of this corridor, having followed her down, and they could be getting ready to trap her, for whatever reason ... Shit, that's scary."

"What did she do?"

"The sensible thing. Got help from the person on hotel reception. And of course, the member of staff didn't find anything, thought she was mad, saw her to her room. But she wasn't mad. I won't say what happens next, but it's a good book to read, especially if you're staying in a hotel. All his books have a good premise. Like the first of his I ever read, back when I was at school, *Phantoms*. I picked it up – it was my nan's, she wasn't interested in it – and started reading. A woman and her sister driving home for a holiday. Got to their hometown after night had fallen. And the weird thing is, lights are on in some houses, but there's no sign of life. No people on the streets. No-one in shops or bars, no answer at doors. She leaves her younger sister in the car, gets out and walks down a pitch-black covered alleyway, thinking she can hear something in the rafters above, almost panicking her, but she gets through okay. She goes into a kitchen. It seems empty at first. But then she realises there are two hands holding a rolling pin, severed at the wrist. Something apparently cut them off before the person could react, while rolling out pastry. No body, no blood. Until she sees a head in the oven and gets out of there. That idea of being totally alone, a whole town wiped out without any sign of a struggle, I couldn't stop reading."

"We've not seen many people in this hotel."

"Yeah. Imagine if they'd all disappeared, or been killed? And the killers were creeping down the hallway towards our room ..."

They both listened for any noise. It was eerily quiet, only an occasional scratch of rain gusted against the window. Then they heard a cough from outside their ground-floor room, presumably someone having a cigarette on the grassy walkway which circled the hotel. She smiled.

"Not all dead then!"

"Not yet," he said in his most ominous voice. "Hey, if this gets too horrifying, do you want to hop into my bed?"

"Not a good idea."

"Why not? Wouldn't be the first time."

"Things are different. We're just friends now."

"No benefits?"

"The benefit is my company."

"Spoilsport. What if I get cold in the night?"

She shook her head. "I agreed to a night away as friends. That's all this is. To make sure we still *can* be. So just carry on with the scary stuff."

He bit back a snide remark. Deep breath through the nose. Then continued. "A lot of Koontz's books start with that kind of hook. *Intensity*, where a woman stays at her friend's house in the country, and can't sleep so stands by the window in the dark. All quiet. Thinking. But then she realises someone has broken in and is murdering her friend's family, and her room is next. So she hides under the bed. The killer comes in, puts the light on. Luckily she hadn't got into the bed, it is still all made up, so the room looks unoccupied. She spots her bag and pulls it under at the last second. But she can't leave people to die and begins to sneak through the house in the dark, not sure where the killer is."

"Urgh. I'd stay hidden."

"Even if your friend was still alive? She'd been raped and tied up; maybe you could free her before he came back?"

"I don't want to think about it."

"Coward."

She picked out a pattern on the bedspread with one of her long fingernails. "Would you come back for me if something horrible happened?"

"Of course."

"Even now?"

"Yes. I think we'd both come back for the other."

She nodded, satisfied.

"Your turn to tell me something," he said, to break the silence.

"Okay. This is true though."

"Yeah, right." He snorted.

"It is! I was looking after my friends' house once while they were in Spain, I was about twenty. They had a cat called Poppy. It wasn't theirs originally. It had belonged to a woman. But she'd killed herself. Hung. And the cat had been locked in the house with her, and it was five days before anyone found the body."

"Really?"

"Yeah. It was horrible. The cat was trapped with her dead body all that time. Poor thing. Anyway, I was staying in the guest bedroom, it was really nice. I liked house-sitting."

"Hey, I could do it for you, whenever you and *whatsisname* go on holiday."

"You know his name. And I doubt he'd want you in the house."

"I wouldn't root through your drawers."

"That's not the reason. And I'd rather you kept him out of the conversation. Okay, house-sitting ... I was a bit scared. I'd watched a horror film, I think it was *The Fog*, so I was jumpy, kept looking out of the windows to make sure there wasn't any fog rolling in, hoping the doorbell wouldn't ring. And then I went to bed, cuddled up to the cat. But in the night I woke for some reason and realised the cat wasn't on the bed with me any more. I switched the bedside lamp on, there was no sign of it, so I got up. On the landing I saw the door to the main bedroom was ajar. It had been closed. I was nervous but I went in, switched that light on ... The cat was sat on the bed, shivering and staring up towards the corner of the room. At *nothing*. But it was as if it could see something I couldn't; for the cat *something was there*, something *hung* there. I freaked out, it was so intense, I got out of there, back to my room, locked the door so the cat couldn't come in, sat in bed with the light on. And when I phoned my friends the next day they said it often does that: just stares up, as if it still watched its dead owner swinging there. They said not to worry, there wasn't a ghost or anything. But I never looked after the house again."

"I don't think I would either." A creak from the corridor made them both glance at the door. It wasn't repeated. "Just an old floorboard," he said.

"Your turn to tell me something again now, not from a book." The light from the lamp was nicotine yellow, gave her skin a sickly tone as she leaned on one elbow facing him, eager for another tale. She looked good in bed. Always had.

"Oh I don't know ... Though I remember something I was frightened of as a kid, some story me and my cousin used to tell about the black nuns."

"What are they?"

"The funny thing is, I can hardly remember many details about them now, or even where we'd heard about them originally. Maybe we'd discussed it with other kids who'd known the legend. I was about nine, I think. I just remember that we got really scared when we talked about them. He would be in a sleeping bag on the floor by my bed when he was staying, and in the night we'd whisper about them after the lights went out. They were called the black nuns, because they wore long black robes and the hood things nuns wear."

"Wimples?"

"Could be. But the nuns weren't alive. Maybe not human, even. They'd all had their heads removed, and others sewn on in their place. Heads that were blackened, swollen, like they'd been poisoned or burned or crushed, or come from Hell – I can't even remember why the heads were that way. We used to know."

"Dementia."

"The heads? Oh, you mean me. Unlikely at thirty."

"I've heard of it. Maybe you're really an old person, senile, unable to walk, trapped in a decayed mind where you think it is forty years earlier and you fantasize that you're in a room with a beautiful woman."

"It would be a nightmare. Turn out you're a vampire, or an axe murderer."

"Charming," she said, amused.

"A cannibal. You wait until the lights're off then ... eat me."

She frowned, perhaps seeing innuendo there.

After a pause: "So these heads, they were sewn on, rough stitches." He drew a zig-zag line on the coarse blanket he'd found in the wardrobe and had put over the duvet to keep out the autumn chill. "And the black nuns would appear around people's beds in the night, have sharp implements to cut off heads and sew these weird black heads on, make more black nuns. You'd wake and they'd be there, staring; then they'd make their move."

"That's nasty."

"Yeah. They could appear anywhere when you weren't looking. In a wardrobe, or round a corner, or in a bathroom. Then get you when you were weakest. They're like a combination of all your worst fears. I think they went after unbelievers, and preferred adults so that the bodies were the right size to sew on the heads. I vaguely remember something about them corrupting a person's blood first, changing their body until they were ready for the nuns to appear."

"I bet you both scared yourselves silly."

"We did. I remember one day he said we shouldn'ttalk about them any more."

"Why?"

"In case it summoned them. It was a silly idea but seemed dreadful yet true to a kid, so we stopped. Never talked about them again. Just in case."

"Great. And now you've told me."

"We were kids. It was just a fantasy."

"Still freaky. Tell me something that *isn't* real again, so I don't get too scared."

"You're insatiable." A pause. "Always were."

She threw one of her pillows at him, an energetic swing that surprised him when it flumped off his head, leaving his hair ruffled. Her aim had improved. Her playful temper hadn't, and it was getting easier to push her buttons towards physicality. "Thanks. You remembered that I like somewhere soft to lie my head. Talking about the black nuns reminded me of a bit in the film *Exorcist 3*. Have you seen it?"

"No."

"I think that film had heads being sewn onto bodies too? Jesus heads from life-sized crucifixes? That's probably why I remembered this. But it's a great scene. In a hospital. The camera is looking down a long hallway with some doors leading off. At the far end of the viewpoint is a desk, and a nurse working there. Night time, subdued lights. Then you hear a weird noise, a sort of crackling. She looks up, in the direction of the camera, past all the closed doors. The noise stops. She goes back to work. Then you hear it again. She seems agitated. Indecisive. You know something's up, yet the sound isn't overtly ominous. Suddenly the big door nearest her desk opens, she nearly has a heart attack, a doctor comes in, he's laughing, finishing his shift. Tension all broken. He takes his leave, goes. She grins. Back to work. *Then the noise, again.* You remember how weird it is, that crinkly rustling. She looks. Works. Again. She leaves her desk to investigate, unhappy about it but not able to ignore it any longer. Walks towards the camera."

"Don't tell me if it's disturbing."

"She opens the first door. Looks in. Nothing. Does the same for the second door. The room is empty. *Creak*. Moves on, obviously spooked. Thinks she's nearer to the noise. Opens the next door, cautious, looks in, and you see it."

His voice had lowered. She inched closer to the edge of her bed, to hear him better. Brushed hair behind her ears nervously. He could smell the coconut shampoo she always used.

"What?"

"A glass of whisky with ice in. The ice is cracking in the warmth. Breaking down. She breathes a sigh of relief. We do too. It's all explained. False alarm. She smiles. Closes the door. Starts to walk back to her desk. Then," he clapped his hands, making her flinch, "*just as she walks past one of the rooms she'd checked the door opens and a man in a gown and mask walks out with a pair of surgical shears at head height.* Decapitates her. Shit, it's so unexpected. What makes it creepier is that she'd checked the room, it was empty. Then he just steps out, no hesitation, just methodical ruthlessness. Brilliant cinema, a masterpiece of tension, all done in one long shot. She thought she was safe from that direction, but you're not safe anywhere." He glanced behind her at the window, eyes slightly wider; she followed his look, nervous, now right on the edge of the bed nearest him. Close enough to reach out and touch. He continued, pulling her attention back. "It's like when I went to the pictures to see *The Blair Witch Project*. I knew nothing about it beforehand. The film was disturbing, but I wasn't afraid – until the final scene when she walks into a derelict room in a house in the woods, sees her friend stood facing into the corner, his back to her, and when she approaches him something gets her from behind, possibly a dead child molester. I thought I was okay, said bye to my friend, went home – only lived in a poky flat in those days – and found I couldn't walk into a room normally: I was terrified that wherever I turned my back, something would be there. I ended up – this is true – going into my bedroom sideways, back to the wall so nothing could get me from behind, edged round the room and got into bed. Left the lights on all night, like you with the cat, sat up in bed, watched the door. Fell asleep sat upright like that. I hate the way ideas get under your skin, stay with you. You can't turn your back on anything. Urgh. After that every noise in the house seemed ominous; signs of things creeping around."

"I've never seen that film. Don't want to, now."

"Probably best." He was close enough to see how dilated her pupils were – fear as much as the sickly light. Once upon a time he'd looked into those eyes as they made love, seen the pupils expanded in orgasm. A stirring down below. Keep it up. "Another film that got under my skin is *The Exorcist*, the first one. It's worse because you know it really happened, but it was a boy who got possessed. I saw the film as a kid, made me worry about creaks in the attic. Many years later I'd told my friends it was good, and they hadn't seen it, so when I found out there was a late night showing at a cinema in Manchester four of us went. I was about nineteen I think. It should have been good but some people in the cinema were laughing, jeering, ridiculing the effects. It killed the mood, making it less scary. Really annoying. So when we came out, my friends weren't that impressed. We got a bus home. But pictures get lodged in your head. The film is known for that, I think there's even a few bits where there are subliminal images, like a monstrous white face flashed over another face for a fraction of a second. And we'd got off the bus, it was all gloomy, just street lights, walking down the road, thinking we were all fine, and I was walking past a car –"

"I don't think I want to know any more if this is going to be awful," she said, but her eyes glittered eagerly.

"It's okay, it's not bad. It's just that as we walked past I saw something, and almost shrieked, because for a second I thought I'd seen a pale face with wild hair rear up in the back of the car towards me, I was so freaked out – but there was nothing there. My friends laughed. Said it must have been a reflection. And I think they're right. But it seemed real, like I'd created or summoned it by *believing* in it. Just a reflection. See, I said it wasn't terrible. I wanted to show that it's only in our minds. Psychology."

"It does creep you out. I feel like the hairs are up on the back of my neck."

"Yeah, it's funny. Sunny day, you never think of these things. Dead of night, you cack yourself. It's your fault, you wanted to tell scary stories."

"I know. I wish we hadn't now."

"Because it affects you?"

"Yes."

He realised they had been talking more and more quietly, voices dialled down. It reminded him of times from the past, things that happened between them, but that was a different intimacy from a different time. This was the intimacy of fear. He looked round the room. It seemed more murky than before. Deep shade around the portable TV, between the large wardrobe with creaky doors and the long curtains which shifted in a draught. The wall corner at the foot of his bed obscured the short hall which led to the bathroom and hotel room door. It could hide anything.

Psychology. Just psychology, he told himself. But it could be used, if you were clever. Only a few more buttons to push.

"It affects me too. Don't tell anyone this, but I hate being alone at night, because I have three fears that always get to me. They're all related, and usually all freak me out at once when I go to the toilet."

"Toilet!"

"Yeah. In the dark."

"Why not put a light on?"

"I'm trying to get over these fears. So I challenge myself."

"I'll probably regret this, but I can't resist if it's toilet-related fear. What scares you? And don't dare tell me it's a giant snake. I know you, remember? Tadpole more like."

"If you're going to be like that ..." He turned away, as if she'd offended him. *Oh, she was going to get it.*

"Don't be silly. Tell me."

"Well, the first one is that when I go to the toilet in the dark I cross the landing; the entrance to the bathroom is right at the top of the stairs down to the front door. And I try not to look down the stairs in the moonlight because I worry that I'll see a man, Michael Myers from the *Halloween* films, stood there in workman's overalls, looking up with his pale moon mask on, a large kitchen knife or pair of scissors in his hands; and as soon as I see him he'll start walking up the stairs, that horrible purposeful stride that isn't a run but still means he'll get to you in seconds. So I don't look, because I think that then he won't be there. Except as I go into the bathroom I can see down the stairs out of the corner of my eye, and because I'm not looking properly I see the shape of the coats on hooks and it looks a bit like a man in the gloom, as if he *is* there, and I rush into the bathroom and then look anyway, to see if I need to bolt the door – not that it would do any good because he would punch his way through, breathing heavy, that eager rasping, slashing with the blade –"

"Fuck, stop it, that's hideous."

"So that's what I expect to see when I use the toilet in the dead of night."

"I wish I'd never asked. Now *I'm* going to think of that too."

"That's my trip *to* the toilet. Fear number one. The second fear is as I leave the bathroom."

"I don't want to know." Rain sheeted against the window like wet scratches eager to get in.

"You do really."

"But this is already going to give me nightmares!"

"Isn't fear good? You wanted it. Don't chicken out now."

"You're a monster." She put her hands over her ears.

"Fear number two."

She sniggered.

"I see what you did there, but that wasn't a joke. No. I leave the bathroom in the dark, and always expect a shove from behind as I pass the top of the stairs, some kind of malicious poltergeist. It will shove me with loads of force, cold pressure, solid air, and I'll tumble down the stairs, breaking bones, and lie paralysed at the bottom, knowing that whatever pushed me is moving down the stairs after me."

"I said I didn't want to know any more!"

"Then you took your hands off your ears. That's my second fear, why I always feel my way to the banister and grab it as soon as I can, grip it tight until I'm past the top of the stairs."

"You're being mean now."

"Only one more fear."

A sudden cracking noise from the other side of the wall, like splintering wood. They both recoiled, looked at each other, wide-eyed.

Then he shrugged. "Just a door banging."

"First time I've heard anyone in the room next to us," she whispered.

"Yeah."

Still looking into each other's eyes. He searched, but all he saw was signs that she was spooked.

"Oh well," he added, "it's not like we've paid enough to have the whole extension to ourselves."

"No, I suppose not." Uncomfortable pause. "Talk to me. I want to hear you talking. No more scary stuff though."

She was really scared. This was it. He reached across the gap between the beds, to hold hands, ready to follow. She touched his fingers ... then patted them awkwardly before moving her hand further away. Retreating towards the middle of her bed, away from him. He gritted his teeth. *Right.*

"I'll tell you that last one. I worry that if I look in the mirror above the toilet in the dark after midnight I'll see the Devil's face looking back at me instead of my own; or maybe it will be behind me, looking over my shoulder."

"I feel upset. Stop now."

"If it's any consolation, I've shit myself up too," he said. "I keep imagining that someone is going to step around that corner from the bathroom with some shears. They'd be on us in a second. Or maybe they're in the wardrobe."

They both looked at the corner. It seemed darker than before. They held their breath and listened.

"That's enough, I really mean it now. *Please.*" She looked like she would cry.

He'd got her all right. Made sure things hadn't gone how she'd expected. He'd teach her to lead him on.

"I'm going to the bathroom first," he said. As she picked up a magazine he added, "Wait ... what's that? A scratching noise?" and pretended to listen.

"Stop trying to scare me."

"What, like pretending I'm being attacked while I'm in there? Or coming out with a pair of scissors?"

"Better fucking not! Do you know why it didn't work out between us?"

"Yes. You didn't love me enough."

"I loved you. But you were too controlling. Always had to get your way. I'm serious."

He was on the edge of an apology, then killed it. Too aroused. "You can only control if people let you."

She gave him an evil look. He grinned.

But in the bathroom he didn't feel so cocky. Checked behind the shower curtain first. Just an empty, stained bath. The room smelt damp but all was safe. He washed his face, avoided looking in the mirror.

"Your turn," he said as he stripped to his boxers and T-shirt. She got up on the side of her bed furthest from him. Typical.

"Hey, it's almost midnight, you know? Don't look in the mirror."

She glared at him before disappearing round the corner. Click of a latch.

Maybe he could hide, jump out on her? He looked round the room for a good spot. Except then he realised that they *were* good hiding places. And he was more nervous than he'd appreciated. He drummed his fingers on the bed, watching the curtains. In the shadows, and out of the corner of his eyes, they looked like they'd moved. Nonsense.

Just psychology backfiring. He turned his back on the window.

Felt as if he was being watched.

He got up and snatched the curtains back. The window was fastened tight, water running down the outside. No-one within the field of light, though that soon faded out to impenetrable gloom that could hide anything.

Taps squeaking in the bathroom.

He opened the wardrobe cautiously. Nothing but hangers, clothes and shadow.

The toilet flushed.

Into bed. Fluffed his pillows. Picked up his book. Lay on his side reading it, turning pages impatiently.

The bathroom door opened. She must have already turned the light out in there. He avoided looking at her as she shuffled over to her bed and got into it in silence, a pale shape.

"No monsters?" he asked. No reply.

Fine. He turned the lamp off. Lay down, fingers interlaced on his chest. Fidgeted. Lamp back on. Got up. Opened the hotel room's door. Looked out towards the stairs at each end of the long hallway. No people. One of the hall lights wasn't working, leaving patches of shadow around an abandoned trolley covered in towels and pillow cases. He didn't remember it being there earlier. He closed the door. Flicked the lock. Stared at it. Then got a chair and propped it under the door handle.

The wardrobe was at the foot of his bed. He hesitated, then picked up the folded suitcase rest and leaned it against the wardrobe door. Looked over his shoulder towards her, pleased. She was under the covers and hadn't moved. He frowned. She couldn't be asleep with all his movement.

Back into bed and turned the lamp off, a click to black silence.

He lay on his back. Eyes yet to adjust to the darkness. Shouldn't be open. Onto his side.

A noise. Creak.

Bedsprings.

Rolled over, stretched his legs out.

A bang from across the room.

It was only the radiator, he told himself. Why did floorboards settle and radiators make strange gurgling noises after the lights went out?

"You hear all those noises?" he whispered.

Silence.

He sighed, frustrated.

Lay on his front, arms crossed under the pillow.

Listened. It was quiet now. The room, the hotel around them, even the wind and rain seemed to have died down. He was just starting to relax when he heard dripping noises from the bathroom. Must be the shower. These old places with their crappy plumbing.

He tried one last time. "Hey, hear that dripping? It might be black nuns forming in the bathroom."

No answer; maybe she really was asleep.

He thought about what he'd just said. Wished he hadn't. Despite his exhaustion from the long day he listened until the dripping stopped.

He scrabbled up from the well of sleep: a noise nearby, creaking in the blackness, movement just below consciousness. Disoriented at first, then realised it was probably her bed springs when she changed position. Maybe she was awake.

He whispered her name, his voice sounding hollow. A movement. Rustling.

He felt irrational fear prickling his neck. Wanted to turn the lamp on even though she'd be angry if he woke her. For some reason he was afraid to stretch out from under the covers. His eyes adjusted to the murky dimness and he saw a vague shape, as if she was sat up in bed watching him. Panicking, he reached out, his hand brushing rough material in passing, releasing a smell of burning; then the lamp came on.

The charred yet swollen face was staring at him from hollow eyes, figure in coarse black clothes, he could see the rough and bloody stitching at the neck where it joined skin discoloured with infection, weeping and raw, holes in flesh pulled taut in attachment; it had been watching him sleep. The bed behind was soaked in blood, some ran down the wall, drying spurts on the headboard. In the periphery of his vision he thought there might be other dark-robed figures in the murky shadows; and on the other side of the bed was *her* body, uncannily stood facing into the corner, shivering but headless above a ragged neck wound; the blood-smeared sharp shears in the sitting figure's hand the obvious cause; then he noticed black string and a long thick needle on the duvet next to a disembodied head, blackened and ready to be sewn.

No.

Two heads.

"Mm-mm-m," he stuttered as the figure rose and leaned over him, eager, focussed, methodical even, opening the shears and cutting his scream short.

CLAWS TRUTH FOREBEAR

A warm breeze bends the grasses and ferns, bringing a dry, dusty smell to my nostrils as I look out over the land which rises in bare hillsides and falls to verdant, moss-filled craters. In the middle is stony plain where the trees are long gone and little now grows, soil blown away to reveal razor-sharp ridges of volcanic rock. A hard land of death with a history of violence. I'm aware of how alone I am, how exposed on this outcrop. And how it was only two generations ago that the hag-ridden natives still ate each other. I've seen the bone pits. I rest my hand on the shoulder bag for reassurance, to stop my fingers twitching, and the outline of the pistol does its job. He'll be here soon.

A volcanic land, tough and sharpened from the heat of the past, that shapes the beings which live upon it. When the molten rock still flowed it rippled with bubbles of gas, fighting to rise through hardening ground, to get to the sunlight. It rarely succeeded. So there were pockets and curved passages deep in the earth; water eroded others, ground quakes opened up fissures. And a war-like culture of humans arose that acted more like rabbits, disappearing down into hidden holes, ancient dwelling caves passed from parent to child as inheritance. In times of blood they were retreats from the slaughter, easy to defend: any invader crawling blind down the constricting tunnels could not dodge a spear or arrow. Or they might fall down a chasm, hit their head, or wander into a poisonous gas pocket. Or, the worst death: get lost, run out of light, starve to death in the almost-air-less blackness.

This is why I need a guide when I go down there.

The jealously-guarded tunnels were also stores for family se-crets and treasures. And every time one of my hosts dies, the secrets they knew about die with them. Gone forever! So many caves packed with irreplaceable treasures!

I had explored one or two small ones, but they had been disowned, seen as abandoned by the protective ghosts of the ancestors, and picked clean long ago. The few baubles within were of little value in themselves: but they hinted at what was likely to be buried elsewhere. As did furtively-shown drawings of items said to exist, drawings traded for the luxuries aboard our ship. Some sketches were no doubt fake, but there was enough detail to convince me that the items existed somewhere, hidden from eyes, hidden from sun. I must get into these archaeological time chests and recover the priceless riches to send back. Elgin had the right idea. The clues to the past should be in a museum where knowledge can be preserved, rather than left in the hands of sickly tribes that change and fade when confronted with the civilising force. Damn their primitive superstitions. And dou-ble-damn the fools who tried to use force to claim the mysteries, and just ended up with more dead, and more lost secrets. No, that approach does not work. If they are to bend to us then we must be as gods to them.

Not as difficult as might be presumed. Many are already in awe of our expedition. All it takes is some basic medicine for common illnesses. Some knowledge. Suddenly I am a witch-doctor, a white-hair with supernatural powers. Once one native claims this, the rumours spread, and become true through repetition.

Not all can be fooled in this way. There was a feast last week. A communal meal of fish wrapped in *taro* leaves. Chief Atahan was silent for much of it, but I felt his eyes boring into me and my team. I listened to tales from the natives in their broken English; they warned me against going into more tunnels.

"There is death down there," I was told.

"Strange beings," another said.

Of course I pooh-poohed all that superstitious tripe, leading to many hurried warding-off gestures. Only then did the chief interrupt. He did not stand – did not need to, his people view him with more awe and fear than they do me – but his voice rang out slow and strong.

"I forbid you to enter the tunnels."

Everyone went quiet, natives and crew alike. I looked at him, with his weathered brown skin. He was unadorned, not some painted chief. It was his manner that proclaimed his rank.

"And why is that, Chief Atahan?" I asked, up to the challenge.

"Because I know you and your kind. I see you as you are, White Hair, not as light shows you."

"And what does *that* mean?"

"You pretend to help. To be caring. Yet I know that my people get sick when your kind come here. The coughing sickness and burning blood that we never suffered before these visits. It is you that *brings* the sickness, not you that *cures* it."

Since that night we've been shadowed everywhere we go. I feel the eyes on us.

The sun is setting when I see the figure stealthily approaching. I open my bag, ready to snatch at the revolver if necessary, and wish I'd brought one of my most trusted team members with me: Tom the wireless operator, with his sharp eyes, or Ed with his prodigious strength. They could have hidden out of sight. Impetuous of me not to. Foolish. But I must appear calm. Gods do not get flustered by shadows, and one does not gain great things without risk.

"Señor?" a voice whispers.

"It is me," I return.

Tepeu approaches, glancing back all the time. He shakes my hand then squats on his heels, as the natives do.

"You are shivering, Tepeu. Shall I light a fire?"

"No, Señor!" He looks around nervously, the whites of his eyes visible in the last of the light.

"Do not worry, my friend Tepeu, no-one followed me."

He seems to warm at that. "Am I your friend, Señor?"

"Of course you are. My special friend."

None of the villagers from Ahu are particularly bright, with the exception perhaps of Chief Atahan; but Tepeu was even simpler and more easily dazzled than most.

"And here, I have some gifts of friendship for you to prove it." I remove a small sack from my bag, careful to keep the gun hidden. He takes the sack eagerly, looking through the treasures within. A handful of local coins, some cigarettes, some alcohol.

I swear there are tears of gratitude in his eyes as he thanks me.

"It is nothing, friend Tepeu. Only a taste of the rewards you will receive if you help me. You would not believe the wonders I could shower on you. *If* you help me. And all I want is some worthless old trinkets from the caves, things that only superstitious people would care about; and that is not modern men like you and I, is it?"

He strokes the golden label on one of the bottles of whisky. "Would you ... take me with you?"

"To the caves? Of course. You will be the guide."

"No, Señor, I do not mean that. Can you take me back to your world when you go? To this place where there is so much?"

"Of course I can, Tepeu." I smile at him, make sure he sees my teeth. "It would be nothing."

It isn't a lie to say that I *can*.

"I am not superstitious, Señor, not like my brothers ... but still, if we go down there, it is against the wishes of the ghosts of my ancestors, and –"

"Tepeu. My friend." I hold up a hand. "I know you are a modern man. Trapped in this place with people you do not resemble. These are just tales. And you know that my white-hair powers would protect us."

He nods. Then suddenly grips my hand, hard.

"You must tell no-one here I do this, Señor."

"I promise," I tell him, and the shaking in his arm seems to fade.

Three days later and the preparations are done. It is to be myself and Tepeu alone. He was adamant. That or "no old caves, Señor, no old trinkets". I judged he was too simple, and too frightened of everything for it to be a trap. So I will go with him. If there is more than I can carry then all I need is to explore a bit and mark the entrance: later the whole team can come, and take everything before setting sail. At that point it won't matter how much stern Chief Atahan disapproves – their wars are fought mainly with spears, arrows, stones and clubs. He knows how pointless it is to argue with a rifle.

This works out better in another way too. Even at night we know we are being watched by the chief's most faithful. But if we split up they cannot watch all of us, all the time. My team found reasons to spread out through the village. Ed is sleeping with the native girl Marianna, who told him she likes big men. If he isn't bothered about dirty beds and lice then so be it; at least his contribution to the expedition has some agreeable qualities. Dooley is staying out drinking and playing cards; Alvaro in his own hut, developing photographs; and Tom has set off to camp by the lake nearby, taking tools with him in a way that is sure to attract suspicion and attention. So it wasn't likely that I was seen climbing out of the open rear window from my hut.

I wait at the agreed rendezvous. An almost full moon, washing everything in cold blue light. The grassland sighs when breeze ruffles over it, making me wonder if anyone is approaching, hidden from view. But it is silly to be jumpy like this. I distract myself with checks. I have everything with me. Pistol, bags, torches, light tools. It is entirely possible that he's changed his mind, has let the fear of his ancestors' spirits and other dark imaginings dissuade him from what might count as sacrilege in their base religion. Or maybe even fear of the living could be enough to make him stay away.

I am returning things to my bag when he appears. One minute just shadow beneath the treeline, the next he is there, a silent ability that the natives seem to have perfected.

"We must hurry, Señor," he whispers.

"Indeed we must, my reliable friend."

We walked for a long time. At one point he led me in circles amongst boulders and dips in the shadow of a massive rock outcrop coated in scraggly vines, seemingly lost, or perhaps trying to disorient me; I stayed patient, letting him think he was being sly. When I checked my pocket watch it had been over on an hour.

"Are we almost there, Tepeu? The moon has most definitely shifted."

"Oh yes, Señor, almost there."

I let him know my impatience with sighs; before long he stops, and says, "This is it."

I can see nothing but jumbled rocks.

"Where is this cave?" I ask angrily. "Are you playing me for a fool? It is very easy for us to leave, you know. Leave you all behind and go somewhere with more hospitable people."

"No, this is it, Señor, I swear on my family's name! See!"

He kneels and scrapes away at loose plants, leaves, earth, using his bare hands. It is rock beneath. But then he slips his fingers into a crack and heaves; a huge slab lifts, and he lays it to the side. At first I am astonished at his feat of strength but when I examine the rock it all becomes clear; it is a form of lava rock rich in bubbles, dark and foamy scoria far lighter than normal stone. How cleverly he's concealed it. No wonder we'd had so little luck when we explored this area on our own! Without a full surveying team the chances of us stumbling upon one of their hideouts is a million to one.

"You clever rascal!" I say, pleased. Then I feel less pleased upon eyeing the entrance. A black hole into the earth. I gaze down but see nothing. "How do we descend?"

"It is not deep, Señor. Just lower yourself in."

"Shouldn't you go first?"

"Then you would not hear my directions. It is very specific, only one way to do these things. Also, how could I pull you out if you got stuck, Señor? I must be behind you."

"Stuck?"

"You have to trust me, Señor. Like I trust you. I am your special friend here, no?"

I nod. Sit on the edge, then hold on and lower my legs; slide forward, rough rock scraping at my spine, and still feel no ground, only the rock of the entrance tunnel guiding me down.

I bite back my fear. The role of the Great White Hair demands it.

"Jump, Señor."

So I do.

The drop is over as soon as it begins, my feet hit stone at the base of the narrow shaft. I feel around, but there seems to be no way on. It is a pit. Up above, Tepeu's head is slightly darker than the sky which displays his silhouette.

"What is the meaning of this?" I ask, trying to keep the edge out of my voice.

"It is good, Señor. You do well. The cave is near your feet, very low. You must sit, put your legs into the hole."

I only just have enough room to crouch; I feel around in the loose earth, hoping for little but then finding that he tells the truth after all – a small hole seems to be the start of a side tunnel, which splits off at almost 90 degrees. And so I edge my feet into it, then extend my legs as I lower myself into a sitting position. It feels like I am sat in a coffin which is bent at a right angle. An unfortunate image, hardly conducive to fighting back the fears that whisper in my mind. My legs are now stuck out straight, thighs enclosed in rock.

"Now you must move feet-first, Señor. And this is very important – leave your arms above your head. It makes you smaller, like a snake. Then you will not get stuck."

I hadn't thought of snakes until now. This land is rife with them. Poisonous too. They like nothing better than crevices to slither in, curl up in, coiled and ready to spring when disturbed – no! Cease such thoughts. Whether intentional on Tepeu's part or not, this is a test. If I do not have the courage to proceed at this point then it was all for nothing. An expedition in futility. I take a deep breath. Feel better. Edge my hips forward, back bending uncomfortably, and wiggle my way gradually down into this side channel, remembering to leave my arms stretched up over my head. It seems to take an age before I am lay on my back in the small horizontal duct, face up, like a stone sarcophagus now. Getting back will be just as complex. I repeat in my mind that I can do this, get in or out, it is nothing, it is nothing. It matters little that I cannot turn, or get my arms to my sides. Tepeu's voice assures me it gets better, I just have to go on, I will reach the cave.

So I slither feet-first in this tight space, rock grit falling in my eyes. I shut them, realising it is no use to have them open now the moonlight had faded. It is intense dark. I take deep breaths, not thinking about the rock against my chest, how it presses; the sounds of the wind become a moan, as if saying goodbye. I hear Tepeu scrabbling behind me. That is good. The nightmare image of him covering the entrance again with rock can fade away. Though, as he stretches into the tunnel just above my head, I feel another panic; being unable to breathe as we both gulp down the limited air in this cramped space. Or, worse: Tepeu dying, maybe a heart attack, and me being unable to pass the lump of his dead body, unable to get out.

Calm. Breathe. Calm. This is no good. If I give in to such thoughts I am no better than a native. Our minds are trained by education, by civilisation. I have to just keep moving.

If this is the worst, I can cope, I tell myself as I am funnelled downwards, into the earth.

I drag my bag behind me. It is too tight to have it over my shoulder. Something tickles my face. It feels like web. Of course, spiders are another denizen of these spaces. There are probably some on my body even now, crawling or being squashed by my movements. I hope they are not biters.

At which point I notice it is getting tighter.

"Tepeu, is this right? I can barely move!"

The only response was muffled, incomprehensible. I try again, raising my voice; he seems to be telling me to go on. What if he has found the wrong entrance, and this is a dead end, a trap? By now I desperately want to change my position, to contract my stretched-out body, but can't. My inhalation is tight, breaths laboured. I stop, try to edge back to the sound of gritty shuffling behind me, but sandals connect with my head, refuse to budge; I feel them tapping on my skull, trying to push me forcefully, and I resist, panic rising in me while blood pounds in my ears.

"Go back! Go back!" I say, shoving against the blockage.

"It widens, Señor!"

"I can't breathe!"

He kicks more forcefully now, it hurts, and I retreat.

"Push through, Señor, next chamber soon! No go back!"

He will not budge. I remember that I have to trust him if he is to trust me. I take more struggling breaths, try to calm myself as the very rock seem to push against me, crush me, thousands of tons above and around; I relax my muscles as much as I can and feel the pressure recede slightly. It has to be onwards. I wriggle my hips and use my shoulder blades to continue, trying to focus only on the idea of space, a cave, an opening, somewhere I can turn or stand; struggling just makes me feel more trapped. I have to use every part of my body, digging my heels in for purchase in the loose grit, and moving inch by inch, every one a victory. Tepeu has stopped kicking, our progress excruciatingly slow but steady. And then I realise my knees can rise slightly. With renewed enthusiasm I move, find that half my body is out of this confining tunnel and into something wider, larger; a few more energetic twists and I can breathe again, a flood of relief filling my body and lungs, every sound taking on a different quality in the larger space around me. The sweat of exertion soaks my clothes, but I am through. I huddle away from the entrance as Tepeu makes his own final push to join me. We have done the barely possible.

Sweat chills me as I realise I will have to do it again to get back out. And dread when I wonder if there would be anything worse ahead.

Kneeling in the dark, I feel in my bag for the items we'll need. Our breathing seems loud in this confined space. I do not stand yet, for fear of breaking my head on the rock. There is another noise, high pitched and nearby. At first I think it is wind blowing through a fissure, but when I ask Tepeu he says: "No. It is only the rats, Señor."

I work more quickly.

Soon the paraffin lamp is lit, and feeble illumination shows we are in a small chamber of rough lava with several side openings, some too small for human passage, others would be a tight squeeze not much wider than my shoulders. I examine the small objects amid the rubble on the ground but they are just shells and fish bones.

Tepeu's eyes flash in the low flame, his face looks troubled. "Not here, Señor. We go further. It is not so difficult as long as we do not grow lost. But first I must do something." He reaches into his loose-fitting trousers and withdraws a jagged knife. I back away though I am still within easy striking distance; there is no room to go farther. But Tepeu does not attack. He makes a small slit on his thumb and squeezes a drop of blood, letting it drip to the floor. Then he passes the knife to me, evidently intending me to perform this primitive act. I hold out my hand and touch the tip of the blade to my thumb, seeing the skin depress, resist. It does not want to split. My hand begins to shake. I still it. Tepeu is watching like a hawk. This won't do. I am a Great White Hair. I look up to the sky – though of course, it is not there, just crumbling rock – grit my teeth, and cut. A sharp pain, blood welling up from the slit and dripping to the floor. I return the knife and suck on my thumb, which stings. Perhaps I cut too deeply. Too late now.

Tepeu bows his head down to the ground. Not at me, but at a small drawing on the wall that I had not noticed in the flickering shadows, something angular and abstract. It is faded by time, originally a deep black or red. He mumbles words in his native tongue, then smiles at me. "It is good. We can move on now."

He leaves the knife below the sketch on the wall, and sets off down one of the tunnels. I see he has torches tied to his belt, the kind one sets fire to, but he seems content with my lantern for now. We have to crawl, sharp stones digging into knees. I have a tricky time of it, only being able to use one arm because the other holds up the steel-plated lamp, but crawling like this is better than the experience of entering the cave system in the first place. A lot better. I freely admit that I am no spelunker.

At the next junction I use chalk to draw an arrow on the wall. Tepeu immediately tries to take the chalk off me, saying we must not mark the walls, but I insist and tell him that any educated man would do this; if he intends to come back with me to civilisation, surely he knows this? He relents, though I can tell he is unhappy. Still, this is my way back if anything happens to him.

And my way back in, later, with others.

We can stand now, moving along a passage with a sandy floor. It has been disturbed by previous footprints. The routes we take undulate up and down, which adds to my disorientation. I am also losing track of distance and time – ten yards or one hundred, ten minutes or sixty? It is as if those things don't apply in the underworld. I resist the temptation to keep removing my pocket watch. The acoustics are equally confusing. Sometimes I seem to hear sounds ahead, or down a side passage. Tepeu tells me they are echoes of our own movements.

There are further narrow passages. In some of them I turn the lamp off on the tight sections. It makes no sense to waste ten minutes of light when there is only one way to go. Still, it is always a relief to turn the flame back up, or re-light it; to banish the blackness and give colour to things again, even if the colours are dripping greys and rough browns flickering in shadow with every movement. We often have to stoop and my limbs are stiff. I dream of big, open spaces. When I leave the caves I will appreciate the airy sky like never before.

The passage slopes deeper, and moisture runs down the walls then trickles down the centre of the path. It smells of stagnation; and when I kneel, my fingertips feel it forming slime during its sluggish route. I am careful and only slip once, bashing my arm and adding to the hundreds of scratches already received from the rock. Tepeu always moves sure-footed, even here; he helps me up. My first concern is the lantern, but it seems undamaged apart from a solitary crack in the glass. Perhaps I should have brought a spare. I hadn't realised how big these legendary warrens were. I will need to be more careful. I have spare fuel but it will be little use without something to put it in! Oh, how vital light is to life. This, indeed, is my lifeline.

I feel such relief when the passage widens again into a larger cave, perforated with holes that could be further tunnels, or just big cracks. The water runs down a carved channel in the centre of the floor, forming a pool to the side which looks remarkably clear, though when I dip my fingers into the icy water I see small pale things skittering within crevices beneath the surface. I quickly withdraw my hand. There are other passages leading on, but this is not just a featureless junction. Ledges are gouged out of the softer rock, which house small stone and wooden sculptures; elsewhere wood shelves have been fastened between outcrops, and hold even more items.

"This is my family's cave," Tepeu says sadly, as I move from item to item, eagerly turning them round, using my fine brush to stroke dust and dirt from indentations which reveal further carved details. It is an amazing haul. Ancient stone sculptures of fish and birds, stylised but recognisable. Black rock carved into the semblance of entwined snakes, that could represent yet another culture independently mythologising the ouroboros. Wooden mammals I do not recognise – fantasies, or creatures as yet unknown to us? Or even the only record of extinct beasts? These are indeed ethnographic treasures that would be priceless to art dealers and academics.

I spend an hour examining items, measuring with my ruler, weighing with the lightweight scales, and cataloguing them in my notebook. The lamp sits safely on a ledge. Tepeu seems miserable, resting his head in his hands as I carefully pack items into my bag, each wrapped in cloth.

"Cheer up! You will be rich!" I tell him. It does not help. He only perks up when I mindlessly prattle about home, with tales of motor vehicles, aeroplanes, telegrams, ballroom dances, and beautiful refined women who speak English, French and Italian.

My fortunate discoveries almost come to an abrupt end as I lift one flat carving, only to discover that the shape beneath is not more carved rock, but a live scorpion which arches its evil stinger. I pull back so quickly that it has no chance to impress me with its venom. A rock soon puts paid to the vermin, and it is pleasing to see it squirm the last of its life: as I would have done were I not so quick in my reflexes! The thought of dying in these caves makes me shudder.

Tepeu allows me to pack many items; occasionally withdrawing permission for others, which seem to have more sentimental value to his family. Unfortunately, they are often the oldest and most interesting relics. Nonetheless I acquiesce, because it is becoming clear that I cannot carry all the items I want, even with the spare sack I had the foresight to bring. I will need to come back later, with my team: and without Tepeu's knowledge.

I heft the bag and sack, but they are too heavy. Even if Tepeu carries one, I do not fancy the final squeeze to escape from these tunnels if I have this weight pulling me back, refusing to let me go. Now that I am decided on returning it makes sense only to remove a sample. I tell Tepeu that I do not need so much after all. He seems relieved as I pile items neatly back on the shelves.

"If this is your family cave, what is down that passage?" I ask, nodding towards the largest of the fissures. While making my notes I had experienced a cool breeze which seemed to gust from it occasionally.

"More tunnels. They connect with other caves, other family shrines. And go deeper into the rock."

"Other caves like this?"

"Yes. But I never go far. It is bad luck. And you need luck in places where there are spirits."

"Never mind the spirits!" I am excited, because Tepeu's family are one of the poorer members of the tribe (though this is such a pitiable land that it is all relative). Other caves might have even richer finds! I wouldn't favour exploring further when I return; it would be unsafe to have us bumbling around beyond my chalk marks. But if I can find at least one more cave then this could move my expedition from a resounding success into another sphere altogether. Riches, certainly. World fame, probably. A lasting place in the annals of history? Possibly that, too. "Could you show me?"

"It is not a good idea, Señor! Bad air! Bad things!"

"A little further, Tepeu. That is all I ask. We won't take anything. Won't even touch anyone else's precious artefacts. Just look. I will store it all in my mind, and it will help me when I write papers about your great culture. You understand academic papers, don't you, my special friend?"

"Yes, of course," he says quietly, kicking at some dirt with his sandal. "I am a civilised man too, Señor." Ah, the native's

sullen refusal to admit a weakness in front of those they admire.
I depended on it.

"Then we will go on, just a bit."

He does not argue this time.

I take the lamp. It needs refilling, but I have plenty more oil
in my metal flask. We will not want for light. And since we are
only going on a little way, I can just take the few items I might
need in a much smaller bag, then collect the rest on my return. I
transfer my chalk, some tools, my notebook, and the spare oil. I
am careful with my final item, try to shield it from his view, but
in this small space Tepeu's beady eyes grow inquisitive, and he
sees that I am also taking a gun.

"Oh no, Señor! That is very bad luck!"

"It's only a pistol. No civilised man would go into caves without one. What if there were large snakes, or a bear?"

"No bear! No gun!" He is tearing at his hair now, stamping his
feet in frustration, as if about to have a fit.

"I am sorry, my friend," I tell him in my most soothing tone.
"I had not realised it would be such an issue."

"It is not for me, Señor, but it is cursed for a stranger to bring
weapons! It means we are invaded, in war, and family spirits
will come out! Only we who worship in the caves may have
weapons." He has calmed a bit, but is now sulking. He will not
go a step further under these circumstances. Sometimes they can
be bent, sometimes they are rigid as stalactites. There is only one
thing for it.

"I will leave the gun here, Tepeu."

"No! It is still a sign!"

"What if you carry it?"

At that his eyes brightened. "Me, Señor?"

"Yes. I will trust you with it. And the spirits will accept you, because you are of this land. Then all is good, and we can go on a little more. Then it is all over. I will look, we will come back. In fact, if you agree to this, I will leave all the items from your family cave. I will not take a single thing!" I dig out my notebook show him the pages of records that are no doubt only squiggles to him. "This contains all the information I need, after all. So why take your treasures? No need. No need at all."

"Really, Señor?"

"Yes! We will look, then go out as we came. No harm done, nothing taken, no spirits rattled, eh?"

"And if you leave my treasures you will still take me with you when you ship out?"

"Of course! I would not abandon a special friend, would I? Not one that has been so helpful and uncomplaining; a friend who understands the value of knowledge; a brave friend, who did all he could to help me?"

By now he is beaming, teeth glinting from that dirty face.

"Good. We go on. Only a bit."

"Only a bit. And in return I will give you many presents."

I hand him the gun and he cradles it as if it is magic. Good. It might prevent him being tempted to play with it, and accidentally blowing a hole in one of us. He tucks it into his waistband and leads on.

The passage curves and passes through irregular rock, the likes of which I've never seen. Networks of domes, presumably fashioned by huge gas bubbles in the lava. The ground is curved and uneven, with pools of water forming in the indents. Some look deep, dark, and are no doubt freezing. I am very careful to hold the lamp high and watch my footing.

Soon this rougher, less-trodden route reaches a junction where stone walkways cross, polished by generations of feet. Tepeu cautions me to move quietly. I am creeping behind him when I remember that I have not left a mark. I take out my chalk. Tepeu immediately grips my wrist and shakes his head.

"No, Señor. No signs here."

"But this is my protective mark," I tell him, thinking quickly, and aware that I have adopted his hushed tone. "It ... adds power. Prevents spirits from finding us."

He glances left and right, obviously wanting to depart this ancient throughway. "Okay," he whispers. "But make the sign small. And low. Very low, Señor."

I do as he suggests. I also change my arrow to something like a curved pentacle, to look more mystical. I am careful that its tip points the way back. We move on, and I make my "power marks" at each junction. There are many forks – it would be so easy to get lost. Or wedged in, since numerous routes clearly became inaccessible to humans as the cavities shrink to head-sized, or smaller. I shiver, only this time it is from external causes too – the damp, frigid rock slowly passes that iciness into my own body.

In one wide passage I tell Tepeu to halt for a second, after seeing something interesting in the shadow of an overhang. Tepeu makes it quite clear he is not happy about this but I ignore him and squat to examine the curved items.

They are bones. Hominid bones, browned and crumbling, patched with green. I notice that what I thought was gravel is actually human teeth littering the floor I crossed. Could it be people who crawled here to die in the past, when injury or illness was going to finish them? Or a place of entombment for dead relatives? Then I realise that I've seen such piles before, and in that case they had suggested cannibalism. Suddenly I am certain of it. Many ancient cultures consumed all around them; and eventually themselves.

Once we are far enough from the crossroads Tepeu lights one of his own torches and I am glad of the additional illumination, even though the thick black smoke his torch gives off seems to stick in my throat, and I worry about the flames consuming even more of our precious oxygen. He tells me we needed it and I see why presently. Our path is split by fissures of unknown depth, some wide enough to swallow a man. Who knows what moves below? We advance slowly, making sure of the solidity of each bit of rock we place our weight on. But he promises me we are near our goal; and I know I could be on my way home soon. After enduring so much already, what is a little bit more caution?

And we are through. A new tunnel to our left, but it is the angled crevice in the rock that Tepeu leads me through, into a medium-sized domed cavern that had partly collapsed, perhaps millennia ago, in some seismic disturbance. He places his torch in a cleft at head height, and I hold my lamp high to behold the find.

I thought I'd found treasure before but this is something even more amazing. Resting on frozen folds of lava are items large and small. Some are covered in web and dust, others seem polished and pristine. It is not their number that strikes me, or the obvious gleam of precious and semi-precious stones, but the carvings.

Like a whole different cultural stratum, perhaps much older than the items I have already seen and catalogued.

Tepeu is angry when I pick up the first item reverently.

"You promise!"

"I'm just looking. I'll put everything back carefully, exactly where it was. No-one will know."

"We should not have come." He sulks, but stays with me as I make my preliminary examinations.

It is as I thought. Carvings from mad imaginings. Their oldest myths, many probably forgotten and only existing as these remnants of history. Almost all of the stones portray strange hybrids, as if different creatures had been knitted together. The most common are bird men with toothed beaks, long like a crocodile's snout. Possible correlation to Egyptian gods, though how it could come about when they were over 9,000 miles apart would be fuel for many a paper. Other distorted figures are even less clear about their contributing parts: generic monsters, devils, skinny things with too many arms or eyes. Many are male, as shown by the huge phalluses they sport, reminiscent of Greek *herma*.

"Have you seen these before?" I ask Tepeu, showing him one of the more horrific items, where a wide-toothed humanoid seems to tear apart a child. "They are obviously made up, but quite consistent."

Tepeu flinched away from the stone, then made signs of warding. "Not made up, Señor," he whispered. "They *live*."

"Live?"

"In the deeper caves. No-one goes there now. If they do, they never return."

"Preposterous! If they never return, how do you know it was the fantastic creatures portrayed in the carvings?"

"They used to talk with my ancestors, Señor. Then we did something bad, disappointed them, and they left us, went deeper. But I know they were real, because when I was a little boy I saw the skull of one of them. Not a fantasy. Very real."

His superstition leaves me annoyed. Partly at how primitive minds hide the truth, and partly because – against my nature – I am disturbed. The base parts of our secret minds love to play "What if?", and I find myself listening out for scratchings from the passages leading into this cavern.

I scribble more notes but it is pointless, since it would take days to describe all this. Besides, it is getting difficult to focus my eyes. They are no doubt strained from staring so intently for long periods in poor light. Even the air seems stuffy, stale as the dust which coats my hands and clothes. I feel we have spent enough time here. I know how to return later, and how many sacks I will need to take it all. When I stand and stretch, my back creaks alarmingly. My wife always told me off for getting too absorbed in something, so that while my mind was active, my body seized up. Perhaps she was right for once.

When I first hear the faint noises I think nothing of it until I see the puzzled look on Tepeu's face.

"Rats?" I ask.

The noises grow louder. Scraping movements and high pitched sounds like distant squeaks.

I try again. "Lots of rats?"

Tepeu shakes his head, eyes widening, and I instantly know that it is not beings from the genus *Rattus*. He grabs his torch from its place in the wall and extinguishes it in a pile of sandy grit; I follow his lead, turning off the lamp, snatching up my things and cramming them into my side bag.

It is impossible to tell how close the creatures making the hooting and screeching noises are, because of the echoing distortion that plays havoc with all sounds down here; but I can say with certainty that they are increasing in volume. And therefore, presumably, getting closer.

I feel a hand grip me and pull, resist at first until Tepeu tells me I have to follow, we need to get away from this room. He pulls me off-balance in the pitch black; I have one arm out, hand on the rough walls to help, and the noises grow louder still. Hoots that make me think of bird men. Tepeu runs, and I trip, fall hard. I scrabble in the darkness, reach out for Tepeu's leg, hand, but he is gone, only rock abrades my skin. I follow the wall as the passage curves, suspecting we are moving away from the direction of the exit, but fear is infectious and panic multiplies in darkness; I am being chased by beasts, the echoes of their cries all around me. I have to keep moving, though my mind's eye fills every invisible step with pits, icy pools, creatures, traps; torn between caution and the fearful need to flee, groping ahead, blind.

I must have cracked my head on a low roof because I am on the floor again, stunned, nearly passing out from pain in my skull. I do not even know what direction I face. The sounds of the things pursuing me still echo around. Then I hear water trickling nearby, and use that to navigate in the dark, keeping the sound to my left, praying it does not lead to an underground waterfall. I have heard of bottomless vertical shafts. I stay crawling this time, though at a frenzied pace, and distract myself from the pain and discomfort and terror by dreaming of dazzling sunlight, of open fields, of fresh breeze. Not an easy thing to adhere to as the ground softens, and I find cold mud plastered to my body from each time my legs or hands slip. The noises are fading behind me though. Then I hear a loud crack, which reverberates towards me. A gunshot? If only I'd kept the pistol.

I can think of many another "if only".

I am truly exhausted by now, but it is quieter. I seem to have reached an opening that is off the vertical plane, with boulders and stones piled near the bottom. I curl up among them gratefully. I could worry about what is in the caves with me, whether I am still being hunted, and how I will get out; how parched I am, so even my tongue feels like dried leather; and how lances of rock jab into my ribs; but I am too tired. So I sleep.

I wish I could say I feel refreshed when I wake, but it would be a lie. I am lost for a moment, unable to explain how I got here, and why I can see nothing at all; but that bliss is dissipated all too soon by cruel memory.

Every joint aches, feels fused to the rock that has been my bed. I fumble for my bag but it is not over my shoulder. In fact, I cannot remember checking it before I slept.

I groan. It must have fallen during my escape. Perhaps the strap snapped on a jagged protrusion. I would not have noticed while my heart hammered and my breath came in ragged gulps.

That was my lifeline. Amongst other things it held the kerosene lantern and fuel.

There is nothing for it. I will have to try and find my way back. Hope I pass it in the dark and a randomly-groping hand lands on that worn leather. Or that I will find the caves I have been through, somehow recognise them in the dark, and reach the narrow squeeze to freedom. Even that would be a relief now. What will I find if I escape? I have no idea if it is day or night, how long it has been since I beheld the sun or moon. Only that it is too long.

I move, hoping I have remembered the way accurately. Yes, over these boulders. The floor flattens slightly. Yes, this seems correct. I stay crawling because it increased my chances of recovering the bag, but fail pitifully at stifling my pained moans. My knees and hands are bleeding, this I know. But the only cure is to get out.

There is a scuffling sound up ahead. Not my own echo, but another creature. I clamp my jaw shut and freeze; it seems to do the same, as if studying me. I dare not breathe even. What things we imagine in such circumstances as these: they are all terrors. Then the voice whispers.

"Señor?"

Oh, how the relief floods through me! I crawl towards the voice, babbling nonsense, affirming that it is me, that I am happy to hear his loyal voice! I hear scratching sounds, which give me pause; but then I am blinded as he lights a match, the flare making me cover my eyes like a child facing the sun. Tepeu ignites his torch and it is minutes before I can look at him.

He is bleeding from many wounds and tears in his clothes. Obviously terrified. In the light from below he seems deformed, inhuman, his chattering teeth visible. They remind me of the teeth I had found on the floor earlier, which is not a reassuring association. I look to his belt but he carries nothing apart from his torches. So, the gun is gone.

"Do you know the way out?" I ask, unable to keep the beseeching tone from my voice.

"Yes, Señor. But we cannot go that way yet. Is not safe."

"Those things – what were they? Are they still here?"

As if they had heard me, an alien call echoes from a tunnel ahead of us. Tepeu and I both cower back.

"I said we should not have gone deeper, Señor."

He will answer no further questions, only lead the way swiftly, taking passages I am certain we had not traversed. At least with the torch held up we can move at a great pace, with little risk of injury. Even crouching is a luxury after so long on my battered hands and knees.

"Follow. The air is bad here," is all he will say.

Yes, I can smell it, and do indeed feel rather dizzy. Volcanic domes are known to trap all sorts of gases.

At each junction we hear calls again; Tepeu leads me away from them, yet the sounds seem to be closing in, distorted voices pursuing our every progress.

I lean against the dank cave wall. "I cannot go on, Tepeu. There is nothing to be done for it. We must hide."

The fear in him sharpens, makes him feral. "No, master! We cannot! They will be here! And they eat souls!"

"I do not know what they are, but I don't think they can take our immortal spirits."

"Then they will kill."

His torch is burning low now.

"And what is the point of running? We will be ever farther from the exit!"

He keeps glancing ahead and behind, as aware as I am of the closing pursuit. Then a sly smile crosses his face. "No, Señor! There is a way! A way out! I know where I am now. I would not choose it, because it is difficult, but I know it has been used before. Tight, but not dangerous if we stay calm. Of course! We go down the passage, we get out!"

I scarce dared hope.

"How far?"

"Very close. This now, I think we must be under Panau, the big rock over plains, runs to sea. There are holes in the cliff face, ledges. Birds nest there, but they are also tribal caves. Other family secrets. I am sure this takes us to them! Come."

He snatches my hand and leads on speedily. If what he says is true then there could be an end to this nightmare. No doubt it could involve a dangerous climb, but I was never scared of heights. Just to feel sea spray on my face would revitalise my whole being; the thought of cold salty air blowing through my hair makes me wish for such a miracle. I do not hesitate. Anything to be out of these infernal caves. Anything.

The passage is rough, and narrowing. We cross scree, scramble down a slope, and reach an apparent dead end. But Tepeu wedges his torch between two rocks and claws with his hands; what I had thought was shadow is actually the beginning of a hole, which grows with each second of frantic scraping at the gravel.

The screeches from behind us have gone silent. I do not know if that is good or bad.

"You go first, Señor."

I eye the small hole with distrust. And bad memories. "Why?"

"Because I can push you if it gets difficult. I push you through, then you pull me out. It is the best way."

"Is it far?"

"Not far, Señor."

I sit on my rear, extend my legs into the hole as before.

"No, Señor. Lie on your belly. We go head first this time. Arms out in front. It is easier to pull then, you can grip onto rock, slide through. Yes, much easier."

That made sense. Going in feet-first last time had seemed unnatural. I position myself. Am gazing into the blackness before me when Tepeu extinguishes the torch and everything disappears.

"No fire, or I burn you, Señor. We will need it at the other end, but not for long. Just feel and crawl."

The wild screams begin again somewhere behind us. Tepeu smacks my legs as encouragement and I crawl low, get a few feet before I have to lie flat and wriggle. He was right, my arms can pull me in further. Tepeu is right behind me. I am soon enclosed in the rock, sounds changing as before, feeling like my heartbeat is outside my body, and Tepeu's panting breath is somehow within it.

"It slopes down, Tepeu. Is this definitely the correct tunnel?" I ask, worried.

"Yes! Go on. We must get far ahead of them!"

I move as quickly as I can, hoping my next handhold will find the lip of an opening, space beyond. Not yet, though. And then, as the stone seems to bite hard against my shoulders, I reach out and touch solid rock. My head swims, panic rising as if it would disgorge itself from my throat.

"It is a dead end, Tepeu!"

"No, it cannot be!" He seems to panic too. "Feel around for a way on! A bend, maybe, Señor?"

I bite down on my tongue, explore with my hands. Jagged rock, mushy soil, something slimy, and – yes! – there is a sharp turn, as if the rock had slid to the side in a great shift, forming a zig-zag. I need to be calm. If I am calm I can bend. If I am calm I can fit. I twist my body, glad for once that I cannot see what I am doing; try to imagine space around me. I am a snake, able to fit. I am a child, only wrapped in soft blankets. Nothing can stop me. I will be free.

And so I move into the corner, thankfully less than a right angle; it bends again immediately. I am aware of the face at my heels, helping to push. The rock digs into my spine as I arch my back, and I push against Tepeu's shoulders. I can hardly breathe; have to keep things shallow to free up precious inches for my ribs, contracting them with every exhale and using it to slip forward another inch. I know there will be no way back. Tepeu had warned me it would be bad. But we need not go far and we will be out. I tell myself this. Other thoughts buzz in my head, making me want to laugh out loud, to shout, to scream; voices like madness, always there, in my ears, and a repeated chant of "No way back!" as if from schoolchildren, all in my head with me, but I push, though it seems tighter, hotter.

"The chamber is ahead," Tepeu reassures me as my legs finally follow me around that bend so I am once more straight, arms extended; straight, bleeding, agonised, but able to move on. This will be it, he promises. Only a bit further.

"Are you certain?"

"Yes!"

It slopes down. I have trouble hearing what he says, my body muffles his voice to me, mine to his.

"I want to turn around, Tepeu!" I call, mouth full of dirt.

"You have to go on, Señor, it will be okay." All or nothing. Tepeu pushes me on, reaching around the bend I had traversed. "Big chamber soon," he declares, but it does not help my rising panic, because I want to believe, but am terrified of what would happen if I really got stuck, as it feels I must if it does not open out soon, shoulders almost lodged in place. I now have to push with my toes, so little purchase for anything else, blood rushing into my head, breathing so tight I have to respire fast just to get enough air into my lungs to keep dizzying unconsciousness at bay. It must be soon.

And that was it.

I am stuck. It has got narrower not wider, and by the time I realise it for sure, I am well and truly lodged, my feet higher than my head, squeezed tight and funnelled down, rock closing round my body which drips with sweat.

"Tepeu! Help me!"

And there are other noises now. Muffled but loud and close, the noises of monsters, triumphant monsters, echoing from the very mouth of our tunnel. They were following us!

I hear Tepeu begging, feel him grip my ankle but he is pulled back, screaming, and I hear his voice fading into weakness, gurgling; I need to get away from his dying cries but cannot move an inch. I listen; and after long minutes of ominous silence I finally hear scrabbling in the tunnel behind. Getting closer. I imagine long-toothed snouts, wide mouths, stabbing beaks. What is this? How has Hell established itself in this remote place? I am trapped with death, and it is crawling towards me.

More inhuman whooping and hooting behind. But this time something in my brain interprets it differently. It sounds familiar.

"Hello, White Hair," says the voice from behind me.

My chest tightens. Chief Atahan!

"What did you do to Tepeu?" I gasp.

"We killed him. For helping you. But when we caught him we persuaded him to trap you here first. A penance. We told him there would be mercy."

"Animals! Savages!" I try to kick back, strike his face, but I am jammed in tight, and cannot extend enough. I only succeed in sliding another inch down the rocky tube. He laughs at my helplessness.

"Are you going to kill me too?"

"Oh no," he says, calmly. "We won't kill an important man like you."

I want to shout at him. I want to curse, but I can scarcely pull in enough air to breathe; the straitjacket that holds me is too crushing.

"I know you, White Hair. Your kind. You lie. You trick. You use words like 'natives' as if it is a bad thing, we below you. Now you below us. You say 'primitives' but it is not us who steal. This is not your history to own or study! You have no right to it! You want it for your people? I tell you of your people. We are losing

our land to tree cutters and machines and roads. You find out all
the medicines made from our plants, then take them. We have no
say! We can't even have the medicines you make with our secrets!
Your law is no help. Law is for money. I spit on money! This –
this is all we have, and it will stay ours, and when we are all gone it
will be lost because it is the only way we can stop it being stolen.
You people want to take it all. And this time – this one time! –
you will take nothing."

My anger is gone now. I do not want to curse any longer. I just
want to beg.

"We killed Tepeu. Punishment. And it *was* a mercy. We not
kill you because your punishment is worse."

He laughs again, but it fades as he crawls backwards, ignor-
ing my almost-silent pleas. I listen so carefully, wanting them
to relent, to come back, to tell me it was a prank, to teach me
a lesson. More whoops, but they move away. I yell until I am
hoarse, crying now, barely able to breathe, mouth choked and
dry, half buried in sand.

I am alone in the black.

And the air is getting stale.

I urinate. The hot, stinging liquid rolls down my body, soaking
into my shirt. Then, in time, it cools.

No way back. No way on. No light. No sound but the blood
pounding in my ears.

I will die in the darkness, trapped below the earth's surface
and buried alive. My only question is how this will end. Oxygen,
thirst, or going mad? My chest is so constricted in the vice grip
of rock that when I start screaming, the loud cries of horror in
my head come out only as a shrill, wheezing whistle. I am empty.

BREAKING THE ICE

DC ILLINGWORTH: Before we begin I need to formally caution you. You do not have to say anything unless you wish to do so, but what you say may be given in evidence. Do you understand?

NATHAN TAYLOR: Course.

DC ILLINGWORTH: Everything said in this room is being video and tape recorded.

NATHAN TAYLOR: Startin' now?

DC ILLINGWORTH: Yes. And can you confirm that you chose not to have a solicitor present?

NATHAN TAYLOR: I don't need one. I'm only goin' to tell the truth.

DC ILLINGWORTH: I understand that. Okay, I am Detective Constable Gene Illingworth of the Serious Crimes Investigation Team. Would you introduce yourself with your name and age, please?

NATHAN TAYLOR: Nathan. Oh, you want the full name? Nathan Taylor. I'm 17.

DC: Nathan, can you tell us where the others are?

NATHAN: I can't. The bodies were taken.

DC: For the record, this is the second attempt at an interview. When Nathan was first brought in he was hysterical and under the influence of as-yet-unidentified prohibited substances.

NATHAN: You'd be hysterical if your friends got dragged off and you -

DC: Maybe it's best to start at the beginning. I would ask you to account for

your movements last night. Describe to me everything that happened.

NATHAN: I thought it would just be a normal party.

DC: Normal?

NATHAN: You know, chill out, then put up with people braggin' about who they'd got off with. Or tryin' to keep quiet about who they'd got off with. The usual. I never thought all this shit would happen … That so many of my friends would be …

DC: How did you get there?

Nathan: Walked. Not far from my place.

DC: What time did you get there?

NATHAN: About nine? I didn't look at my phone. Was all a bit hazy. I'd been workin', see. I'm behind at college and don't want to get chucked. Studying. Or tryin' to. To be honest I just kept thinkin' about the party and didn't get much done. I ended up on the Xbox.

DC: Can we see the work you did that night?

NATHAN: Sure, if you wanna know about style sheets and web design. It'll still be on my desk. Obviously I've not been home since you lot brought me in.

DC: Can you recall what mood were you in?

NATHAN: A bit down. Maybe 'cause it was drizzlin' and I was sober. I had a bottle of cider under each arm, but I'd not drunk any. And a bit annoyed about going to the party alone. Why are you lookin' at me like that?

DC: So you were angry? Depressed?

NATHAN: I wouldn't go that far. I'm not whacko!

DC: I never said you were.

NATHAN: You were implyin' it. It was just that my mates didn't wait for me. They'd wanted to get there early. Marcus was after some girl.

DC: This was … Marcus Jaffere?

[Silence.]

DC: For the record, Nathan nodded. Can you describe Marcus?

NATHAN: Cocky. Black. Sporty. He was into free running, could do fancy flips and jumps and stuff.

DC: Maybe he is still into that.

NATHAN: Yeah. I meant that. His body wasn't found, was it?

DC: So you walked to the party. What happened next?

NATHAN: What about Teia? Please, at least tell me if you found her?

DC: That was the name you were screaming when we found you. Is she your girlfriend?

NATHAN: No, but she was the reason I was going. To the party.

DC: Go on.

NATHAN: I hoped she'd be there. She's in the college but on a different course. Knows some of the same people.

DC: What was her surname?

NATHAN: I never found out … oh fuck!

[Crying.]

DC: It's okay, Nathan, take your time.

NATHAN: It's okay. I'm okay. Just … Right.

[Pause. Deep breath.]

NATHAN: Okay. Back then I was thinkin' about the way she looked. She was gorgeous. Fit. Sporty. Always in good trainers. Hair so blonde it was white in the sun, usually tied in a pony-tail. Brown eyes. Like, real soulful ones.

DC: Any other distinguishing features?

NATHAN: Do you mean, like, to recognise a body?

DC: Just for the record. For now.

NATHAN: Why won't you tell me which ones you found? They were my friends, for fuck's sake!

[Silence.]

NATHAN: She had a mole on her left cheek, is that the kind of thing you want? I liked it. When she smiled it moved up. I didn't stare in case she got self-conscious. She was nice. Popular with everyone. I didn't see how she could be single, but Marcus swore she was.

DC: Did you see anyone while you walked? Anyone suspicious-looking? Perhaps someone you'd seen before?

NATHAN: No. It was dark. It's like, winter, y'know?

DC: And you got to 6 Partridge Avenue around 10pm.

NATHAN: A bit earlier. You're not tryin'
to catch me out are you?

DC: No. Just finding out facts. You
weren't making sense earlier.

NATHAN: What do you expect! After what
I'd seen!

DC: After what you *said* you had seen.
Let's just be logical so that nothing gets
missed out. You arrived at the address.

NATHAN: I had to wallop the door, music
was so loud. Their system's a beast. Denee
answered it. She's Australian.

DC: Denee …

[Rustle of papers.]

DC: Brogan?

NATHAN: Yeah. She was drunk and tried
to kiss me. Usually that's followed by a
grope combo so I headed for the kitchen
and she followed, asking me to dance.
She's a total man-iser, doesn't stop.
Sorry, that's not relevant.

DC: Every detail might be relevant. I'm impressed by your recall. It really helps. Carry on.

NATHAN: Managed to cram my cider in the fridge after pourin' a big glass first. Big table with crisps and butties and stuff. A group of lads stood round like they were guardin' it. I didn't like them. They went all sly if a girl walked past, showin' off, you know the type: cocky pack animal type as a gang, but quiet on their own. I was desperate for a fat munch so had a look to see what there was.

DC: Fat …?

NATHAN: Hungry. They looked at me like I was invading their territory, and that pissed me off. It was my mate throwing the party. The food'd probably been made by Tony's little sister. Susan.

DC: Tony and Susan were the ones hosting the party?

NATHAN: Yeah. While their parents were away. So I munched some mini sausage rolls. Then one of the lads leaned over, and said, "You hungry, mate?" He was the biggest in the group. His eyebrows met in the middle like a caveman. I'd seen him round, a retard from the maths retake group. I ignored him but he said, "You want this?", picked up a ham butty and held it out to me, but squidged it up all greasy between his fingers. I didn't want a fight, not with all them, and not in my mate's house. I said I was stickin' to liquids, and he laughed and said I was all right and held his other hand out for a shake, but in some daft rap way. I shook anyway. It's best to pretend scum like that are mates. He was called Patrick. He went on about "scopin' the ladies, better to browse before you buy, innit?" What an arse. I tried to get away but one of them with lank hair over his face and a Cattle Decapitation top asked me -

DC: Cattle Decapitation? A picture of a cow having its head cut off?

NATHAN: Kinda. The band. They're gore-grind. You okay?

DC: Things are different from when I was a teenager.

NATHAN: Well, he asked if I was after anythin'. Started listin' off what he could get me.

DC: You mean drugs?

NATHAN: Yeah. I was surprised they were dealin' there, but guessed Tony was all right with it. I didn't buy anythin'. Just went in the living room. It was hot and packed to fuck.

DC: How many people would you say were in the house at that point?

NATHAN: Hard to say. Thirty or so? Big room, long as the house. Used to be two rooms but I'd helped knock out the dining room wall last year. They bricked up one doorway so a new kitchen could be fitted. That means just one door in and out apart from the French doors to the garden. I didn't know that'd make it a deathtrap. I saw Tony dancing and went over. He was either pissed or on somethin', not making much sense, but happy enough. We sat on one of the settees in the shadowy end of the room. Smoky too. People there were monged on weed. I shared a spliff.

DC: Did you see any other drugs being used, apart from the cannabis?

NATHAN: Not at that point. Just weed.

DC: Describe Tony, please.

NATHAN: My best mate. I think he's been mithered by his hair recently, 'cause he's goin' a bit bald even though he's only my age. He never says anythin', it's just what you pick up on. Not slap-head bald, just thinner, y'know. Kinda like you. No offence. Marcus saw me and came over for a toke. Then he pulled out this little brown medicine bottle. Didn't have a label on. Looked sus. When I asked what it was he just said, "Summat special, bwoy." I hated him callin' me that. He was black but he was from Sale, so all that street cred stuff was bollocks. He told me it was somethin' they'd all tried, would chill me out. He unscrewed the top and took out one of them pipette things. It had yellow liquid in. I thought it was poppers. Told him you're not meant to drink it, an' it's for gays anyway. But he said it wasn't poppers. I let him put some drops on my tongue. It didn't taste of much. Just fizzed and popped a bit.

DC: You have no idea what it was?

NATHAN: No. I was just hopin' it wasn't piss. Maybe somethin' with a bit of acid in?

DC: Have you had acid before?

NATHAN: Once. At school. I don't think this was the same.

DC: At school …

NATHAN: Yeah. I wasn't the only one. Anyway, the music picked up. It was like loads of conversations finished at the same time and everyone wanted to dance. Denee appeared and grabbed my hand, said "C'mon, spunk". She never understood how dodgy that sounds in this country. Denee was fairly pretty, a bit chunky, and totally drunk. It was obvious she was after someone for the night - I mean, she was doing the Lambada to every song. I kept looking round for Teia, worried that she hadn't come, and tryin' to keep Denee from slobberin' in my ear. I got away, and was chattin' to someone when I saw her. Teia. She was looking straight at me and smiled and I just burned up. How can eyes do that? If it hadn't been for the drink I dunno if I could have walked over like I did. She was sat on the floor with some girls I didn't know, right in the corner, sort-of hidden by one of the big armchairs. I plopped myself down, chatted with her, trying to act the cool dude and hoping I wasn't coming across like a dick. Wasn't comfy, arse was against somethin', and when I checked it was a brown bottle, empty.

DC: Like the one Marcus had?

NATHAN: Yeah. Dunno if it was the same one or not; though I did wonder at the time how many people were on that shit. The room was spinnin' and my mouth felt dry, which must've been to do with it.

DC: You realise we didn't find any bottles?

NATHAN: I can't help that.

DC: **What about people's behaviour? Would you say that many people seemed to be drunk, or maybe on drugs?**

NATHAN: Quite a few were wasted, or just actin' weird. But that coulda been normal. It was a party. Even Teia - she seemed to be two people. One minute she was laughin', enjoyin' herself; the next she was sayin' she nearly didn't come out that night. That she'd got a strange feeling - I remember, 'cause she touched her temple with a finger when she said that - but she'd felt it was … I think she said it was "important that she came". She asked me if I thought she was weird, because she sometimes got those feelings and always followed 'em. She smiled, and I wanted to lean over and kiss her. Wanted it so bad.

DC: **Did you kiss her?**

NATHAN: Not then.

DC: **How did you answer her?**

NATHAN: Uh?

DC: She had asked you if you thought she was "weird".

NATHAN: I told her she wasn't. What would you say? And it's true. Most people don't pay attention to gut feelings, which - well, it's sad. I told her I liked her for it. She seemed chuffed. I remember the moment really clearly. Actually I remember the whole evening clearly, nearly every word people said, it's really strange. Teia. That's a weird name isn't it? Foreign or somethin'?

DC: Possibly.

NATHAN: Or maybe her parents were hippies. But it fitted her. Slightly different, but pretty. Her friends moved off. I reckon they felt like gooseberries, because me and Teia didn't stop talking. She was into big stuff, fate and shit like that, I didn't follow all of it but I loved listenin'. It was like no-one else was around, just us in bullet time.

DC: Bullet time?

NATHAN: Erm, like in *The Matrix* or *Max Payne* when stuff slows down and it goes quiet and you just focus on one thing. Did you think I was talkin' about guns?

DC: No. We're just defining any terms we don't -

NATHAN: Whatever. I felt like I'd known her for ages and we just sat and talked. For hours. It was … breaking the ice, I guess. Get through all those barriers between two people, two worlds, just chip and melt away until you can get through.

DC: So, going back to what you said about time slowing down, do you mean to imply your perceptions were altered?

NATHAN: The room spun a bit but it was fine while I was sat down. A weird buzz. I wasn't high, or hallucinating, just … it's hard to explain, y'know? A bit out of it. My head was hot. But that could just have been Teia. I could imagine really liking her. Any guy would. She was sweet. It could have been so perfect … but that was when …

[Pause.]

DC: It's okay, Nathan. Take your time.

NATHAN: I noticed there was less people.
Some must've gone home. Quieter music too.
Then a girl squealed.

DC: In distress?

NATHAN: Nah, more like girl-shrieks to
get attention. A big moth was fluttering
around the room. When it went near a lamp
it made these huge shadows that flickered
across the ceiling. Must have come in
when someone left. One of the girls was
panicking, flappin' arms and shit. Funny
for about two seconds then borin'. Some
guys tried to catch it to shut her up
but it kept flyin' off if they got near.
Moths must have good eyes. That reminds
me, I said it was big, and at one point
someone tried to sneak up on it when it
was on the wall, and it opened its wings,
and it was like it had a big pair of eyes
on them. Freaky. It flew off again. They
should've left it. But there was a guy
called Baz. He was always doin' stuff to

get attention, like dropping his keks in front of girls.

DC: Barry Preston?

NATHAN: We called him Baz. Baz the Spaz. Some people thought he was funny. He was older than most of us, his parents were rich and he just seemed to hang around college doing different courses, or Students' Union stuff. He was fat and sweaty, but his reflexes were quick. He reached up as the moth passed him and caught it in his hands. I remember he said, "It tickles." One of the girls asked him to put the moth out but he shook his head. "I'm hungry," he said. I think it was still sinking in when he put the moth in his mouth and swallowed it. Then it was mad, set everyone off. Some of the lads thought it was funny and cheered – the dicks from the kitchen had come in – but most people were disgusted, said Baz was sick.

DC: What did you do?

NATHAN: I'd been on my way to the kitchen to get another drink. The idea of anything

bein' eaten alive makes me feel ill. So I
shouted at him. He told me to calm down,
that it was only a bit of fun, but that
just made me angrier. I flared up.

DC: You attacked him?

NATHAN: Nah. Just shoved him. Because
he wasn't expecting it he fell over. Cue
laughter. That's not an attack is it?

DC: So you restrained yourself?

NATHAN: Yes! I mean, I felt like jumpin'
on him, pummelling his face. But I didn't.

DC: What stopped you?

NATHAN: Teia. I saw her and stopped
being angry straightaway. She made me
feel good. So I ignored Baz, even though
he was slagging me. I knew he wasn't
impressing anyone with big talk, and I
just went into the kitchen. I was on my
own and my head was poundin'. Coulda been
anything causing it. Even the flickering
of fluorescent lights can set me off
sometimes.

DC: Migraines?

NATHAN: Yeah. I just wanted to be back in the dark again, with Teia. And my cider was gone from the fridge. That pissed me off even more. But Teia followed me in, checking if I was all right. Only good people do stuff like that. And then … never mind. That's when the lights went out.

DC: You were going to say something else.

NATHAN: No, I … What does it matter anyway? What does any of this shit matter?

DC: Please sit down. We're just trying to -

NATHAN: I want to know what happened!

DC: So do we, Nathan. Calm down. You're doing well.

[Sigh. Chair scraping.]

NATHAN: I didn't think it was important. I didn't want to say.

DC: You can't do that, Nathan. Hold back. Everything you say is important, that's why we pay so much attention. There may be some detail that comes to your mind, it may seem trivial, but we need to know, since it might be a clue or a key. That includes private things you might not feel like sharing. This is too serious to be coy. And if you hide things - that doesn't look good.

NATHAN: But I didn't do anythin' to them! They were my friends, for fuck's sake!

DC: So help us, and yourself. Don't hold back.

NATHAN: Okay. We kissed. Happy now? She moved close and started issing me. It's the last good thing that happened and even my headache went. There! Nowt held back.

DC: Thank you.

NATHAN: You're smug, you know that?

DC: I don't think I am. Do you want a drink of water?

NATHAN: No. I just want to get this over with, now we've gone this far. So the music next door started jumping, then it went slow and deep, then stopped, and at the same time all the lights blinked out. Teia pulled close to me, I told her it was fine, just fuses. Led her by the hand and when we got to the living room everyone was swearing, laughing, yelling at Tony to "Fix the fuckin' lights". All pitch black, had to feel my way round, kept touching people's clothes and just trying not to trip over. There were thumps and crashes as people knocked into stuff. Tony shouted that people should stay still until he sorted it out. I got Teia to sit in a chair and made my way to his voice, got hold of his arm and told him it was me. He asked me to check the fuses with him. I think he was worried about the place gettin' trashed.

DC: It doesn't sound like panic.

NATHAN: It wasn't. Just shits 'n' giggles at that point. We went to the cup-

board under the stairs. I banged my head
on the frame, gave myself a right proper
crack. Could hear something clickin'.
Tony said it was weird, but the emergency
torch wasn't working. Then he rattled a
box of matches and put 'em in my hand, told
me to keep him lit. Long matches, didn't
know they made 'em. I got one going and
held it near the fuse box. He checked and
said the trip switch was fine - if there'd
been an overload or blown fuse it would
be off. He started checkin' each fuse.
I realised we were whispering. Don't you
think that's weird? There was no reason
to whisper. We kept doin' it though. I
lit more matches and Tony said it must
be a power cut. It was easy to check by
looking out of a window - there wouldn't
be any lights at all. Even the street
lamps would be out.

**DC: There wasn't a power cut last night,
Nathan.**

NATHAN: Look, I'm just tellin' you what
happened. I thought you wanted that?

[Pause.]

NATHAN: A match burnt down to my fingers and I dropped it and lit another. Tony joked about me bein' a danger to myself. I told him to go fuck himself. He said he might have to, 'cause the party was over. Back in the living room there were a lot of questions. Someone said their phone wasn't working, so we all tried ours. Yep, all dead. Couldn't be a coincidence. That's when I felt somethin' cold all down my back, like I was spooked. I pulled back the curtains to look out. Couldn't see a thing out there. Really, nothin' but black. Even in a power cut you'd expect to see *something*, right? Even just different shades of black. It's hard to explain, but looking out that window, it seemed like there was *nothing*. Some people were getting freaked out about the phones, others telling them to chillax. Tony told everyone to head to the front door. Lots of shuffling, holding each other, a fucking creepy conga. I went back though, found Teia, held her hand. I figured I'd walk her home or somethin'. Then someone said, "What the fuck's that?" Everyone froze. Moaning. Upstairs. It put the shits up me. Others too, I could tell. Then someone - I think it was Baz - said,

"Who's havin' a good time, eh?" That set
people off giggling again, wonderin' who
was up there, but everyone was definitely
quieter than before. Tony was pissed off
that someone was shagging in a bedroom,
started to go upstairs. Everyone was
waiting for a scene, or at least to find
out who was up there for gossip. Teia
whispered that it didn't sound like nice
moans and I squeezed her hand, I knew what
she meant. Tony's footsteps crossed the
landing. And then …

DC: You're shaking.

NATHAN: I can hardly believe it.

DC: What happened?

NATHAN: It kicked off. Totally. There
was a scream from upstairs, more like a
woman's, then it stopped suddenly, and we
could hear Tony yellin' for help. There
was summat about his voice, sharp and
scared, it didn't sound like a joke. Then
his yelling was muffled by somethin'.
Fuck, those seconds of quiet were like
a knife in the guts, man. And there was
this surge of fear, people started yelling

and shoving. You couldn't see anything and panic spread faster because of that; people trying to run, falling over, a stampede; I knew it was chaos near the front door so I stayed back with Teia, trying to make sure she was all right. Shouting and banging from the front door, I couldn't understand why they hadn't got it open yet. Maybe the catch was on and they didn't realise in panic, or the weight of people pushing meant the door couldn't open in. Then the people in the hall started yelling … there was a noise … weird noise … followed by screaming and thumping, like on the stairs.

DC: What was the weird noise you heard?

NATHAN: It was … I dunno … like a whip cracking in the hall. There was no way I'd go out there to investigate. No. Fuckin'. Way. By then the living room door had swung shut so those of us inside listened. Like cowards. Just stayed frozen until the screams stopped, and the people begging for help stopped, and the banging stopped, and the house was quiet again. But what could I have done? Teia clung to me. She was shiverin' but she was the only warmth that I felt right then. I had to say something, to try and make things seem more normal, to stop me goin' mad, you have no idea what you imagine when you're in the dark. What was going on? Was there summat in the hall? In the room with us? I asked who else was in there. I whispered it. We were talking and -

DC: How many people were still there? In the room with you?

NATHAN: Three. Apart from me and Teia.

DC: Who were they?

NATHAN: Denee. She was scrikin', trying to get her arms round my neck even though I was holding Teia. There was Patrick, the idiot with big eyebrows I'd run into at the start of the party. I heard him rustling paper and sniffing - maybe the wanker was snorting somethin'. Whizz, or coke, or bloody glue for all I know. And there was a guy called Adam, some nerdy bloke from my ICT course I hardly knew. I'd thought there were more of us but no-one else spoke. Adam was frightened, too loud, I kept tellin' him to keep it down. He was scaring us all, saying that the first scream wasn't human, and there was summat else he'd forgotten, something very wrong - freaky shit like that. I was trying to be calm for Teia but I just felt like running or going mad. Then Denee joined in with it. Said that when the lights went out the telly came on for a second. She didn't think everyone saw it, but she said there was a big eye on the telly, and it was watching. Then she'd forgotten about it until the screaming started. Adam agreed - too loudly again - and said he'd forgotten too, it couldn't have been on the TV for more than a second. Patrick told him it was probably just white noise, but Denee and Adam both swore it was an eye. I'd never felt so scared. Couldn't see a thing, same as bein' blind I guess. It was only Teia bein' nearby that let me keep it together. It was like everyone depended on me. I wriggled out of Denee's grip, tried my phone again, still nowt. Adam said it was … some letters. An A.M.P.? No, E.M.P., that's it. He said an E.M.P. burst could knock out electronics. That you got them with some bombs. Nuclear ones. Denee started

to cry again, really fucking irritatin'
because it didn't help.

**DC: Only five of you? Where was everyone
else?**

NATHAN: Maybe they'd gone into the
kitchen or ended up back in the hall
when the screaming started? How should
I know? I couldn't even see anythin'!
But I told them to keep calm. We could
get out the French doors. I left Teia
and made my way there, trying to remember
the layout of the furniture, tripped over
something, a cable or bag, and landed
hard on the floor. But then I found the
long curtains in front of the French
doors, felt my way to the middle where
the handles were. Tried to get them open,
but they wouldn't. Remembered the bolt,
undid that, but they still wouldn't open.
Locked. No light outside, and no key in
the keyhole. I ran my hands over the
floor, just in case. Nothin'. But I knew
where the key was. Tony always carried
a big bunch of 'em. He'd probably locked
the doors up so people wouldn't go in
the garden and piss off the neighbours
- they'd've complained to his parents.

But the problem was getting the key. I didn't want to go upstairs to look for it. I told the others. Denee and Adam were going to pieces but Patrick said we were all bein' mard arses. "It's bullshit," he said. "A joke. They're probably all having a laugh at us." I wished I could have believed him. That he'd been right. Hey, I will have a drink of water after all. I'm really gaggin'.

[Movement. Sound of water dispenser.]

NATHAN: Thanks.

DC: So Patrick thought it was some kind of game?

NATHAN: Guess so. He even started shouting that they could give over and stop fucking about, he didn't believe it. Denee was trying to make him be quiet but I guess he pushed her away. I heard her fall over, just lay there sobbin'. I think Adam went to her. And, fair play to Adam, he did stick up for her. Told Patrick if he really believed it, why didn't he go upstairs and get the key rather than just shouting about it? That called his bluff. He went quiet for a minute. Then we heard it. Noise. Upstairs. Creaking, like people sneakin' around. That sound made me feel sick. But Patrick laughed, saying it was proof. I don't know if he fully believed it, 'cause he didn't move for ages, and there was something in his voice that didn't sound as brave as he acted. But then I heard him shuffle to the living room door, and go into the hall. He said we were pussies as he went out, just before the door shut. Teia's breathing had been hot on my neck, and I noticed she was holding her breath now. And that I was. The noises upstairs had stopped. Patrick began to walk up the stairs. We could hear each creaking footstep. And could tell he was getting slower as he got near the top. He said, "I know it's you over there, you bastard, come out from behind …" Then nothing. The living room door swung shut with a click.

DC: So he didn't come down straight away?

NATHAN: Listen: he didn't come down period. He was *gone*.

DC: Where?

NATHAN: Into space! Up his arse! I don't fucking know!

DC: Calm down, Nathan.

NATHAN: Well you ask me stupid stuff! I only know what I heard. And right then Denee started whining again, saying we should break the glass, that it didn't matter any more, that she didn't want to die. She was begging. We'd gone well past believing it was a joke, yet admitting it was real … that's terrifying. The patio door was double-glazing, small panes of glass. I wasn't sure if you could break that but Adam was on the edge. He found a chair I guess. I knelt down out of the way and hugged Teia. It was all too quick, too unreal. I was tryin' not to think about Tony and my other friends. On top of all that I kept seeing weird … well, I don't know what to call them, ghost images?

DC: Just to be clear, this wasn't things you were seeing in the room, or with your eyes?

NATHAN: No, it was pitch black still. But in my mind I was seein' these images of people dressed in white whose faces you couldn't see. It was so weird. They were all holding knives and standing in front of a huge dirty white cake, grime or mould or somethin', with red cherries on the icing. No, not cherries, it was more like blood, blobs of it congealing. It was so vivid yet made no sense, like I was losing it. The colours flashed, and sound whispered like when I had tinnitus as a kid – the voices wouldn't go away, they terrified me, but they made no fuckin' sense …

DC: Like interference on TV?

NATHAN: That's it! How'd you know? A fuzzy TV picture in my head. I let go of Teia and just covered my ears. She stroked my hair, as if she understood. And it did calm me a bit. Despite the pain I felt so much for her, like she was meant to be for me.

DC: And the door?

NATHAN: Nothing. The chair bounced back with a crack. I think Adam hurt his arm, and the chair hit Denee. More cryin', but she started saying weird stuff too. Adam told her to shut up but it wasn't even like her voice.

DC: What kind of thing?

NATHAN: She said we'd lost our chance and would die now, we'd made too much noise, that it had heard us - whatever "it" was - and that it was coming back. She was hysterical, was scaring Teia, but you couldn't help listen, in case there was a clue or somethin'. And in a way I could believe she was seeing stuff because I had. And she kept going on. Summat about wooden floorboards in a cave, all broke, and you could see a lake underneath, freezing black water deeper than the world, with things squirming below … stuff like that. And Adam dragged the chair to the front of the room and tried to smash the big windows there, but even they wouldn't break, sounded like the chair just splintered and he was swearing, out of breath. That was it for Denee. She said we had to go now, get to the back

door before it came, that it saw us and
was coming back. That would mean going
through the kitchen.

DC: **Wasn't the front door nearer?**

NATHAN: Yeah, but people had tried that,
hadn't they? And that was at the foot of
the stairs where all the screaming had
been. At least you only had to run past
that point for a second if you were going
through the kitchen to the back door.
Anyway, she persuaded Adam. I heard them
making their way to the hall door.

DC: **You and Teia didn't join them?**

NATHAN: I wanted to be outside, sure.
I wanted the back door to open and to
breathe fresh air again, not the dead air
in that house. But I was too terrified
to move. I had my arms round Teia, like
I was reassuring her, but really I know
it was just as much for me. And there was
somethin' else.

DC: **Go on.**

NATHAN: I kept thinking about the eye in the telly. And then it clicked. It was the centre of everything, had to be. Lord of the fuckin' hobbits. Eyes see. What you see, you remember. And the eye was only there for a second - well, yeah, sure, it might never have been there at all, just mad bollocks - but the thought gave me hope because the eye saw the people in the living room. But me and Teia were in the kitchen when it looked. *The eye hadn't seen us.* So long as we didn't draw attention to ourselves we might be okay.

DC: But it had seen Denee and Adam?

NATHAN: Yeah. And they were making noise. Fucking up our chances. Don't look at me like that. I was afraid for my life! Denee had said noise was a bad idea, and I believed her, like an instinct. So I told Teia we would just wait for a minute. Listened. The living room door swung shut. We could hear them though. Muffled sounds. Pegging it down the hall. Into the kitchen, Denee's heels clackin' on the lino. And something moved suddenly - like they bumped into a table and summat smashed, a glass or a bottle. Heavy scraping sounds. I thought I heard keys jangle, somethin' else banged. Then it was quiet again. Teia asked if they'd got out, and I didn't answer. Just pulled her arm gently, found my way to the settee which was against the wall. Crawled behind it. She followed. The space was tight. At one end of the tunnel was a bookcase where our heads were. At the other end it was open where our feet were.

DC: So you were making sure you wouldn't be seen if - something or someone - came looking?

NATHAN: I can see why they made you a detective.

DC: We need to make sure the statement is clear.

NATHAN: There didn't seem like any other choice. No way out of the house. Light was what we needed. Maybe if we could wait until it was day we would be okay. Everythin' would be normal then. I was pushed tight against Teia. I could just move enough to stroke her face. It was wet. Tears. But quiet. I gave her a kiss, only meant to reassure her, but she kissed me back. I know it seems strange to kiss at a time like that, but it *helped*. She tasted sound, like warm vanilla in the dark, taking our minds off the house.

[Crying.]

DC: Take your time, Nathan.

NATHAN: Do you even believe me? Anything I say?

DC: We'll compare your statement against the evidence later. It's irrelevant whether I believe you.

NATHAN: Not to me it isn't. I bet you think I'm making it up? Or the drugs I'd taken made me imagine stuff?

DC: What happened next?

NATHAN: The house was totally quiet. And I felt a bit of guilt. I knew we'd let them go in the hope that we would live. Like a sacrifice. We lay still in the dark, waiting. Teia stopped shivering. I moved down a bit and rested my head against her

chest. Dunno how long for. Her heart beat
in my ear, sounded strong. It was getting
nearer to morning with every beat. That
was the thought that calmed me. And there
was somethin' about Teia, an aura. She
stroked my face. I'm only telling you this
so you know how gentle we were; know that
I wouldn't hurt her. Remember that. When
we did speak we whispered in each other's
ears. That tickly breath, but it was good,
because every quiet sound meant we were
still alive.

DC: What kind of thing?

NATHAN: Just askin' if we were okay;
saying it wouldn't be long until morning;
reassuring shit. I was knackered. I mean,
we must have been awake for most of the
night. Then even Teia went quiet. I could
tell from her breathing she was asleep. My
arm was dead but I didn't want to move it
in case it woke her. Her chest was like a
pillow, gentle up and down, and I couldn't
stay awake any more either, just hoping
we'd wake to bright light and safety and
normal life. I know I slept because I had
dreams - I can't remember them but I think
they were about being suffocated. I woke

needing air really bad, tense and stiff and alert, as if I'd heard somethin'. It took a few seconds to realise where I was, but then it sunk in. Teia flinched too. I must've woke her. Then we both heard it. A noise from upstairs. Couldn't tell what it was at first. But I was ready and listening and it came again. At the top of the stairs. Every few seconds there would be another sound, like summat heavy flopping onto the next step. My skin tightened, prickled. Even though we'd been quiet *something was coming*. Maybe we'd made noises in our sleep? Or it might have known about us after all, and was just lookin' to see where we were, since we hadn't wandered off like the others … maybe it had got bored waiting. But I had to hope it was just doing a last check for survivors before going away, and then we'd be okay. I hugged Teia hard. In my head was an image from a horror story I'd read as a kid. It fit the sounds. A body, no arms or legs, flopping its way down towards us. The image was horrible. Then the dead weight, whatever it was, reached the bottom. Near the living room door. It slithered, rubbing the carpet. I held my breath, but it

moved past our door and into the kitchen.
Teia's arms hurt me, she was squeezing
so tight. I could hear kitchen cupboards
opening and closing. Usually a normal
sound, a good one, but right then it was
horrifying, 'cause I couldn't separate it
from whatever was doing the opening and
closing. Even bottles in the fridge got
rattled. "I'm so scared," Teia whispered,
shivering again, and I put my hand over
her mouth. We had to be quiet, see? She
started to struggle, I think I frightened
her, but I had to shut her up. Noise would
be deadly, tell the flopping thing where
we were … and then the living room door
opened. Whatever it was came in. A chair
or something moved across the floor. A
noise came from near the settee. I thought
we would be able to keep quiet, it was the
final test - I kept telling myself that
if whatever it was knew we were there, it
wouldn't have been searching around the
kitchen. That makes sense, right?

[Pause.]

DC: Go on.

NATHAN: But … Teia struggled. The more I clamped my hands on her the more she panicked. Maybe she couldn't breathe properly, but I was terrified she would make a noise. I was tryin' to save us both, you see? If she just stayed still and quiet a bit longer we would be okay …

DC: Did you kill her, Nathan?

NATHAN: No! That's what I'm saying! I was trying to help us both but she was so terrified … I know that because I was too, but it must have been too much for Teia, I don't blame her but she tried to scream, made noise … that was all it took. The settee was heaved away from the wall. There was a cracking noise. Teia suddenly shot away from me - her grip torn off. I could hear her screaming. I tried to back away but something thin wrapped around my ankle. It was strong. I was yelling in panic when it yanked me out from the settee, across the living room floor and towards the stairs. It was too quick. I banged against the doorway, smashing my shoulder. My shirt was dragged up by the carpet - that's why my back's burnt. It was so quick, the pain was too much. I

was being hauled up the stairs then, so
fast that I was near the top after a
few seconds, battered in the darkness.
I heard another shriek from Teia as she
rounded the corner and saw somethin'. I
shut my eyes. I didn't want to see it.
I knew I was gonna die. I smacked up
the last few stairs. Across the landing.
Through my eyelids I could see light, and
that was a surprise after so long, and
I opened my eyes. I was in the first
bedroom. Something that looked like a
dirty rope was around my ankle, or some
kind of veiny, lumpy tentacle, I don't
know. Teia was being dragged the same way
- straight up a wall in the corner of the
room towards nothing except a cracklin'
brown spot there. Blue light came from it.
She was hanging upside down, screamin' my
name and tryin' to reach out to me, but
you've got to understand I wasn't thinking
straight - the pain, the fear - I crashed
into the wall and was pulled upside down
too, and we were both being lifted to that
hole that the rope things came out of,
a break in the patterned wallpaper that
shouldn't have been there; they'd broken
through from somewhere else, got through
whatever barriers there were, melted them

to get to us. The thing is, I loved her, but instead of saying so, or trying to hold her hand … [Crying, voice breaking.] I prayed that she would be taken instead of *me*! I wished I could live no matter what, even if the others died, even if Teia died … Can you believe that? I was saying out loud to take her, not me, to let me live, and she could hear me as we were dragged up to that impossible hole but I didn't care … In that moment I was just thinking of myself. And the worst thing is that if I could go back I would change it; I feel like puking but it was the *fear* - I even pissed myself I was so scared; I loved Teia, I should have protected her, oh Christ …

[Muffled crying.]

DC: So you were pulled up that wall, what did you see, Nathan? What happened to Teia?

NATHAN: I blacked out! Next thing I knew was waking up to you lot!

DC: And you're still sticking to that story? The same one you tried to tell us

when you were still high on something?
You really want that to be your statement
when telling the truth could help you to
be understood?

NATHAN: It's fucking true! That's why
I'm sticking to it!

DC: Sit down, right now.

NATHAN: You're wasting time, I told you
everything, we've got to look around the
house more and –

DC: Sit down or you will be restrained.

NATHAN: It's true, you fuckin' pig!

DC: True? You admitted you were under
the influence of drugs at the time in
question. You were practically incoherent
from the effects when you were found. Sit.

NATHAN: That wasn't drugs, that was –
shock, fear, something like that!

DC: And you kept things from us. Prior
history. Sit the fuck down.

[Chair scraping.]

DC: Good. Nothing backs you up. Your phone? Worked fine. No "E.M.P. burst" shit. So let's move on. Why didn't you tell us you've been in trouble with the police in the past?

NATHAN: Not trouble as such …

DC: Smashed windows at the shopping centre a year ago?

NATHAN: That wasn't me, that was a stormy night, the wind must've broken the big pane and I didn't notice, I was just sat on a bench nearby with my mate.

DC: A fight six months ago in the Arndale?

NATHAN: That didn't seem relevant.

DC: Of course it's relevant! Did you think we wouldn't check the records? See a pattern of violence?

NATHAN: What do you expect? I didn't mention them because they're nowt to do

with *this*, and I knew you wouldn't believe
me if I told you, and I need you to believe
this since it's the truth.

DC: You're the prime suspect and your
made-up tales of - whatever they are -
don't cut shit. Eight people are missing Nathan. *Eight people!* All traced
to that party. Another three were found
dead. Why'd you squash their bodies into
the kitchen cupboards, did you think we
wouldn't find them?

NATHAN: Cupboards? God …

DC: Don't pretend to be surprised. The
question is, where did you put the others?

NATHAN: Teia?

DC: Give it up. You know that she was one
of the strangled ones we found. Strangled,
you see? That's one of the aspects of
your delusion you nearly admitted to. So
don't persist in these stupid stories,
and snivelling won't help you. But listen
…

[Voice quieter, as if leaning forward.]

DC: We don't think you did this all on your own. Were the missing eight in on it? They ran away afterwards? Or someone else? It's in your best interests to tell us.

NATHAN: Strangled …

DC: This isn't the first case like this. But we have you now. You were involved in this. You and others. The pressure on us to get answers is nothing to the pressure you're going to be under.

[Crying.]

DC: You'll talk, Nathan. Trust me. We always get a confession in the end. That's the termination of the interview.

NATHAN: Why are you covering -

[Tape switched off.]

HOW IT GOT THERE

White lines running through his head, focus on them, crap lasers in a bad sci-fi film as they disappeared interminably beneath the car. His eyes drifted and so did his hands and so did the lines, merging in from the right but he only noticed what had been happening when he glimpsed red and pink guts, flattened roadkill, squirrel or rabbit, which snapped him conscious again, pulled too hard on the steering wheel, shook himself to alertness as the car swung back into the lane. It was the area's fault. Dark, impenetrable trees walled the road, made it seem unending, hemmed in. Anything could be watching from between the trunks. Yes, he'd watched too many horror films. Maybe going to the stag do in no man's land last night was a bad idea. And maybe, if he avoided falling asleep, he'd make it home in one piece.

He snatched up the coffee cup from its holder, a reminder of the service station which had been the last sign of civilisation for twenty miles. It had been pretty disgusting when he bought it; now it was tepid and just tasted of plastic. He was on a straight so lit a cigarette and opened the window instead. Rental cars didn't even have ashtrays any more. He didn't really feel like a cig after the over-indulgence of last night, but it gave his hands something to do, distracted them. Might keep him awake. A few drags of it and he gave up, let it fly; tasted as bad as the coffee. Must be his mouth. The breeze and drizzle had woken him up though as it flipped his hair about, moistened his face. He shut the window and drove through more damp puddles on the badly-kept road. You had to be careful. Totally eroded in some places; every patch of water could be shallow or something deeper, coating the old undersurface like a scab.

He noticed her clothes first, then her body. Beside the road, one arm flung out. He slowed. He'd seen no houses. What was a woman doing out here on her own?

It was easy to drive by in a city. You were just one car among thousands. But she was already waving frantically, looking at him, some nebulous connection but enough to make you feel like a shit if you drove past. Plus, girl. Plus, alone. He decelerated, but not so much he couldn't get moving again.

No visible companion hiding nearby. And she was short. Only up to his chest. Non-threatening. Dressed a bit goofy. Already picking up her duffle bag in expectation, walking out into the road, making herself obvious. Crunch time, 3 2 1 ... He pulled over and stopped. She grabbed the passenger door handle, yanked at it, but it didn't open. Locked. He lowered the electric window a few inches instead; in turn she lowered her head to speak to him, and he got a good look.

She wore a purple knitted hat like a cross between a baggy tea cosy and a crocheted crash helmet; it seemed to be an attempt to control wild hair that spilled out. She had thick eyebrows and a jutting chin.

"Can I get in?" she asked.

"Where are you going?"

"Anywhere that isn't this shit hole."

Not much to say to that. He unlocked the door. She climbed in, threw her bag onto the back seat. Slammed the door shut, said thanks. She smelled of damp. Her baggy blue jeans had been darkened by rain, the black and white canvas pumps muddy. The car beeped at him until she fastened her seatbelt. He put the heater on low, then pulled out too quickly, wheels spinning on the slick surface.

"Sorry," he said.

She removed the hat, threw that in the rear too. Roughly tied back a wild tangle of thick curly hair. He took a few sidelong glances. She had a high forehead and a slender neck and seemed to be in a bad mood. Was a few years younger than him. He drove in silence until she said, "I appreciate you picking me up. Thought I was going to have to walk."

Her accent was Welsh. "You live round here, then?"

"No. Bangor."

"So that's where you're going?"

"If I can."

"All roads go that way. Eventually."

"You?"

"Chester. I'll drop you off."

"Thanks."

"How come you're in the middle of nowhere?"

"Journey ended prematurely. Like everything else."

"Been there long?"

"Ever since I dumped the wanker. Look, can we not play twenty questions?"

He was surprised at the anger, risked a glance, she was facing him. Two weird things about her. Her eyes were violet: a freakish mutation. And her teeth seemed sharp.

He suppressed his instinct to suggest she get out. Her appearance was too striking. He returned to watching the road, which had temporarily left the trees behind and now coursed through scrubby hillside. There was no fence separating the cars from the sheep which stared at him as he drove past. Last thing he needed was to hit one.

"You do know nothing will happen?" she asked.

"Happen?"

"Don't insult me by pretending to be naive."

"Okay. I didn't know. Thanks for telling me. It's always nice to get turned down for things you haven't even thought about."

She folded her arms. Faced forward.

"For the record, I didn't assume anything," he added. "I don't try it on with every woman I meet, gorgeous or not. I don't have that much to offer."

"Don't be silly. If you were single, I reckon most women would eat you up."

"Sounds nice; yet to happen; wouldn't believe it if it did."

"You want me to eat you up?" she asked. He caught her looking at him, assessing, with a surprising shine in her eyes. He thought of her teeth. Didn't answer. Just stared at the flat black tarmac which crumbled at the edges, becoming part of the fields where the bracken died back, brown and crinkly.

Out of the corner of his eye he saw her reach behind, take some small item from her bag. He tensed, ready to swing the steering wheel to the right, fling her against the door at the slightest sign of something sharp or metal. She jabbed, pressed a button, then threw the item onto the dashboard in disgust. A mobile phone. It slid to and fro as he straightened the car out.

"Not even a message," she said. Then: "Shit. I'm really sorry. It's not you. Please can we start again? I'm not usually a prick. What's your name?"

He realised he'd been holding his breath. Snorted with relief. "Glenn. Glenn Comewell."

A part of him always expected to hear the usual joke that had haunted him at school: "Do you?" Instead she nodded. "A friendly name. Like 'Welcome'."

"I've never thought of it like that. You?"

"I'm Fflur." She held out a hand. He crossed his arms, shook it gently. Her palms were surprisingly cool.

"That's a pretty name."

"I think so."

He hadn't bothered checking his phone's sat-nav for a while. No need with these roads: most of the turnoffs seemed to be forestry or farm. And he now recognised the route from the way up yesterday. He was at the highest point; it would follow a switchback descent to the coast before turning south towards the mainland. It might be drier down there. He turned on the windscreen wipers, let them do their rubbery squeaking thing.

"Nearly two hours," she said.

"Sorry?"

"How long I was waiting. You asked before. I bit your head off. Two hours since the wanker I was with dropped me off in the middle of nowhere in the latest episode of Argument City."

"Boyfriend?"

"Ex. I learnt something today. A true hypochondriac is a vindictive person who would rather say 'I told you so' than find out they were wrong. Anyway, I don't want to talk about him ever again. I was just answering your question."

"The past is past for a reason," he said, then wondered where the hell that had come from. It was like an echo from somewhere else.

But she nodded, seemed to approve. "Hope I've made up for being so rude to the knight in shining Ford Fiesta."

"Glad to help. Could never leave a damsel in distress. You looked so vulnerable with the massive trees all round."

"And because I'm small you mean? Works out sometimes, makes people protective, gets me into places. Downside is being eight inches shorter than most men. Spend half your time looking up nostrils. Believe me, it's not a good view."

He rubbed his nose self-consciously, and heard her laughing. Saw an infectious deep-cheeked smile, first time since she'd got in, and found himself smiling back.

He passed a sign reading Pen y Coed and began the steep descent. Straights alternating with super-tight bends. He would go slow on the way down. Last thing you needed was someone speeding towards you on this kind of terrain, in this visibility-smudging drizzle.

"What do you do?" she asked.

"The ultimate in boring. Records management."

"Music?"

"No. Corporate records. Content management systems. Please, don't ask, I really will fall asleep. What about you? Student?"

"I was. A few years ago. Fine art. Now I illustrate."

"What?"

"Children's books, mainly."

He glanced at her again. For some reason he'd have assumed she was too young.

"You look like you disapprove," she said.

He returned his gaze to the road. "Not at all. That's just my face. I'm impressed. Anything creative, it's a world away from what I do. I'm always in awe of people who can do something that makes a difference."

"Drawing?"

"It's art, isn't it? How'd you get into that?"

"A friend who was a kids' writer, she saw some of my projects and got me to sketch for her. Coupla months later it ended up working out, the book took off. I never imagined it's what I'd do, but I love it. I was into painting with bright colours anyway, hyper-real, lots of quirky details, seems like a good match. Little spider on every page kind of thing."

Another tight bend, had the steering wheel on full.

"Do you have anything I could look at? If I pulled over, obviously."

"I have a portfolio but it's not with me. They're mostly online now."

"You could give me the web address."

Conifers on each side, darkening the road, that enclosed feeling again, concentrating on what was in front. She was getting something from her bag.

"Yes, I could."

"Look at that," Glenn said without looking at her, slowing the car.

The trees opened up, revealing the broad sheet of grey sea being thrashed by wind and rain. Dark clouds poured sheets of leaden water on everything moving below. An island in the distance sat in the sea, looking forlorn and slightly creepy. Gorse-covered hills sloped down, rising to cliffs on each side of the road that had been cut into the stone.

"Glad I'm not out there," she said.

"Me too."

It was pummelling the car now, rattling on the roof, making it feel like the vehicle was a tin box to be played with. Wind blasted sheets of rain horizontally at him; on this exposed stretch of road if buffeted the car, tried to wrench steering out of his hands. She was looking at him, had something in her hands. Rainwater sloshed out from the car's wheels. He risked a glance. Paper. Pen. Sketching.

"Me?" he asked.

"You look really intense. I'll call it Heroic Records Manager Saves The Day. Might get me an exhibition. Stop grinning, you'll ruin the mood."

"I just want to ask," Glenn said. "Your eyes ..."

"Contact lenses. When I was –"

"Hold on. What's this?"

He pulled up.

A tree lay across the road, angled away from them. The base of the trunk rested in the thick bushes at the edge of the road, a high verge backed up by more trees. Yes, some of those were tilted or fallen too. Not surprising if they were regularly hammered by this weather.

"Shit."

"Can you go round?" Fflur asked.

"Not on the right. And it looks pretty flooded on the left." He drummed his fingers on the steering wheel, a tattoo matching the rain on the roof. "Wait here."

He got out before his courage failed. Immediately blasted by the rain and wind, had to lean against it. Headed to the narrow end of the tree. Gripped it in both arms and tried to push. A few feet would possibly be enough. Strained with all his might, heaving, blinking water out of his eyes, legs like a power lifter.

Didn't move a fucking inch.

His body sagged. Shirt already soaked. He ran back to the car, slid into his seat, wiped the water from his face. Giant fingertips continued to tap the car.

"That was impressive," said Fflur.

"Thanks. I practise every day."

"What if I helped?"

He shook his head.

"Can you nudge it out of the way?"

"I could if I'd hired something big and sturdy. Should have thought of that, coming to Wales."

"Turn back?"

"It would be a massive detour. And there's no help round here, it's so isolated on this stretch of coast." He kept his gaze on the tree, assessing. "Maybe you were right and we can go round."

"What if we get stuck?"

"Ring for a pickup. Worst case would be waiting till they come – no longer than the detour. Best case is we're on our way. I think it's the top option."

"Then I guess it's over to you, Elfyn Evans."

"Who?"

"Welsh rally driver."

"That's why I've not heard of him."

"You're full of shit." But she was smiling.

He edged the car forward in first. In some parts he could see mud and grass, in others the brown water was the only visible surface. The car bumped as he took it off the road onto the low flooded area in front of the trees; room to spare, but he kept as close to the fallen tree as possible, letting the branches rub across the car, and grimacing when he heard the scraping that suggested impromptu paintwork decoration. It was hard to see what he was driving on, tried to get the feel of it. The tyres spun, he'd over-revved, so he eased off, then stuck, pushed down on the pedal and lurched forward with a splash, the car lower than before, but almost round the tip of the tree. He began to spin on the wheel and moved another few feet, but it seemed harder to grip; the car slid, he braked, car jerked to a halt; tried to tap the accelerator but apart from juddering it went nowhere; looked in the rear-view and saw mud spraying up behind. Reminded him of a nature documentary he'd seen once where hippos were having a shit, spraying it with their tails like ... well, a shit storm.

Yep. He was being a hippo and getting nowhere. Stopped. Tried again. Seemed even worse, no purchase, the car lower. Too late to turn around or reverse. Kept trying, taking the wheels one way then the other hoping he'd shift it, engine sounding pained, but it was no use. The car wasn't even flat, tilted at a slight angle. Well and truly stuck.

He stopped. Turned off the engine. Let the sound of the rain reassert itself.

"Oops," he said.

"So. You're telling me that it's pure accident that you've ended up alone with me, in a parked car, with hours to kill?" Fflur said.

"Yep."

"Isn't that convenient?"

"You backed me up. Maybe *you* wanted to be stuck with *me*."

She smiled, showing those pointy little canines again, eyes seeming more violet than ever in the subdued light. There was an intensity to her when she looked at him like that, something that awed and excited him at the same time; a personality that had been totally hidden when she was just Morose Passenger. "I do have something in my bag that could pass the time," she told him.

"What?"

"Travel Scrabble."

"Are all Welsh girls weird or is it just you?"

"All."

"I have an idea. I can chuck some stuff under the wheels. Sticks, stones, gravel or something. If I get enough under them I might be able to get going. It was just a little deeper than I thought. A bit of purchase could be enough."

"Can I help?"

He opened his car door. Saw that he would get out into ankle-deep mud and water. "Nah. No sense both of us getting soaked and covered in crap."

"I said you were a gentleman, see?"

He laughed and entered the squall again. Then stopped laughing when his feet sank into the cold and gluey sludge. Trouser legs dragging in it. Lifting his foot almost lost him a shoe. Yuck. Slammed the car door, made his way towards the trees, lifting each leg like he was either walking on the moon, or incredibly pissed. Mainly concerned about falling forwards. He had to squint against the rain lashing his head, whipped to a frenzy by the gale. Water in his mouth, water down his back. It was a relief to get below the cover of the trees where the ground was only slightly squidgy, and the worst of the rain held off. He looked around. Yes, lots of branches had come down. He could make a pile here, then take an armful and place them in front of the tyres. A couple of stones too – there were plenty lay around on the uneven needle-strewn ground between the mix of pines and more native trees.

He soon had a small pile. His hands were filthy, his nose full of the smell of earthy rot. Body soaked. Glanced at the car. Fflur was waving at him. He waved back. Dragged over an unwieldy branch that could work well, fallen from a diseased tree covered in sickly black and yellow circular patches. Thunder rumbled out to sea. The trees creaked around him, bending as they were pummelled by gusts. He picked up an armful, waded into the mire, realised Fflur had her window down and was shouting at him, her voice carried away by the wind. He gestured to wait, ignored her until he'd split the branches between the back tyres, then got into the car, which was mercifully warm.

"There's someone out there!" Fflur said, before he could speak.

"What?"

"I was trying to warn you! I saw someone over where you were. And then on the other side of the road I thought I saw something in the trees."

"What did they look like?"

"I don't know! Only saw for a second. Dressed in brown. But they were sneaking. I know what it looks like when someone tries to hide. They were getting near to you!" There was a real fear in her voice. He looked out, alert for any movement, but it was almost impossible to see through the rain-smeared glass.

He pressed the central locking. "I doubt if that's enough, but fingers crossed." Started the engine. Rocked the car forward. "Why would anyone be hiding out here in this? It's the middle of nowhere."

"Unless they knew someone might get stuck," said Fflur.

Glenn looked at the fallen tree as the wheels span. You couldn't see the base of it. Couldn't see if it had been cut. "Come on you bastard!" At one point the car lurched forward a foot or two, then slipped to a halt in a fresh patch of deep muck.

"I need to put the last branch under," he told her, "that might be enough."

"No! Don't you dare get out of this car!"

Motion outside, more than the wind. He slammed the car in reverse for the little good it would do, but saw the rock come down at the last second, shattering his side window, held by a thickly-bearded man in a black jacket and wearing a hat tightly fastened round his head. The man reached in with the rock, striking at Glenn's arms as he tried to block, aware of Fflur screaming next to him, struggling, her window shattered too, someone leaning in with a wickedly-serrated knife. Glenn grabbed at the arms attacking him, managed to seize one, wrestling the stone out of a hand that held it like a vice, both of them grunting as they struggled furiously; he pulled the man's arm onto a piece of the glass, making him drop the stone. Fflur was being dragged out of her window now, seatbelt cut through; Glenn tried to grab her legs and hold on but there were two men outside, both lifting her as she bit at one of the hands restraining her, when something hard struck the back of his head. It must have only been seconds but Fflur was already being pulled through the mud by the two men, and his assailant had retreated a step, nursing a bleeding arm. Glenn opened his car door hard, slammed it into the bastard's body, knocking him flat on his back in the mud, a splash followed by water covering his body as he struggled. Glenn planted a kick against his head, wanted to kneel on him, smash that hairy face in, hold it under; but Fflur needed him. That intensity pulled at him; a sudden realisation that if he'd just turned round this wouldn't have happened; he punched a few more times, stood, staggered after her, wishing he had at least a rock.

Fflur was fighting like a demon, biting and twisting and dragging her feet, it took two of them to make any progress. One was tall and thin, the other short and strong-looking, in scruffy camo trousers. He grinned confidently beneath deep-set eyes.

Glenn splashed after them, they were already at the trees, he had to get to her, and too late he saw a fourth figure step from round a tree, a ginger-haired man in an oil-stained shirt, striking with something metal, heavy-duty spanner maybe, and Glenn went down heavy too. His face on the ground, pine cones, mud, heavy workman's boots, rain running down his face hot, red across his nose, not rain, screaming and pain and hatred and sorrow ... and then nothing.

The rain had stopped.

The tree had been moved.

The car was heaved and rolled forward over the branches, onto dry ground. Pushed along a few hundred metres to a turn-off, a muddy track. To its side was a shadowed dip, thick with tangled plant life. The car was released to roll down the loose scree, ploughing through brambles, coming to a crumpled halt when its bonnet smashed into an outcrop of lichen-covered rock. The bushes were fanned out, leafy branches placed in gaps. You'd hardly know it was there if you drove past. A faded old sign was likewise obscured by foliage. The sign simply read:

Penrhyn

Peninsula

Beyond that was Stawl Island.

WEB

This country is three things to me. I list them. First, it is cold. I shiver. I think I have not stopped shaking since I was made to come here. Two, is dark. I have lost the sun that watched me grow up. This one is small and mean and is so far away it has no interest in the people here. Three, is damp. I know heavy rain, yes, but not this always-water thing. Black mould grows along tiles in the bathroom, even if I scrub, scrub a lot, it come back quickly. There is a thing in the kitchen (cupboard? But it has no cups in?) and it is not wood, it is made of something like pieces of wood, all mashed together, baby-food furniture. And where it touches ground it gets bigger, splits, crumbles, and I sweep up the bits. That is what I mean! Damp!

And things you call creepy-crawlies, they like it. They always here. They run in lines along the edge of the carpet. I get up in morning to make Husband breakfast, I see curvy slug trails drying on the worktop.

And every day I clean up thick old web. So much. This, up in the corner. I have to use long duster, it try to hide from me. I push it in, turn it, and all the sticky grey and dead bits wrap around. It remind me of something I see on your television once, called candyfloss. Your fairgrounds make people smile, but this is like making evil candyfloss as I twist sticky horrible onto it.

I would not eat this.

Many spiders in this house. Especially when it rains. That is often. And they hide from me. Leave webs in corners and cupboards and wardrobe and shelves. Laughing, saying, "This is more work for you to do! And you cannot see us!" Their voices would not be squeaky, like a fly. Spider voices are serious quiet, go straight into your head, when they watch you with all their eyes. But you can find them if you are clever. I know woodlice. We have them in Somalia too. They crawl into cracks. And there is a spider here that eats them. Easy to find – look for a pile of dried-up, dead, grey woodlice. Then look above. You will find a spider, with long legs that are fragile like hair, and mouth that can go through shell.

I squat down to see this one. I blow on the spider, let it know I won, I found it; and it go all angry, shaking its legs, shaking the web, like child having a temper tantrum. It has something in its mouth. I think it may be eggs, but no, it is dinner. A woodlouse. The spider is sucking on its face. I look more closely, my eyes are good. There are things on the woodlouse. I think they are parasites at first. The world has rules, and it is common that big things hunt smaller, but smaller ones live on bigger – danger from above and below, outside and within. But these are not parasites. It is baby woodlice. Teeny, yellow, trying to move on their mother insect, alive but trapped in strands of web, stuck to a parent that is having its juices sucked out. A noise outside startles me, like I am guilty, and I hit my head on the top of this cupboard. It is only the postman, pushing all the papers junk through letterbox. I will not look at the baby yellows again, it makes me sick.

I cannot sleep. I keep thinking of what I find hidden in this house. I am getting to know every inch. Cracks, holes, corners, shadows. Always little eyes watch. In the morning I sometimes get strands of web in my hair, from across the doorway, when I get up first. I comb it out. But that tickle, I feel it now. In the bed. Husband is sleeping. He snores when he is on his back like this, rumbling through his nose. Not aware of what is in the bed with us. But I feel that tickle, near my ankles. In the dark I can imagine the things creeping. They are getting brave if they are coming into my bed now. They must know I am awake. I do not like that they invade here. It is my last place. And now I cannot sleep because they crawl up, wanting to go up my legs, my belly, maybe to suck my face ...

I move too much and wake Husband. He sounds angry.

"What is it? Why must you be fidgeting? I need my sleep, woman."

"Please, there is something in the bed," I tell him. "I feel it crawling on us."

He grumbles but puts a light on. Pulls back the sheets. I brace myself to see the things moving below them, staring up at me, all cold eyes ... but there is nothing. He shows me, his hand jabbing at the clean sheet.

"But I felt it."

"It was just the hairs on my legs," he says.

I look at them. They *are* hairy. Dark, hairy legs. I shudder.

"Your legs seem thinner," I tell him.

"I must be losing weight," he say. "I work too hard, not like these bloody English. Or you do not feed me enough. Not feed me right. I need my sleep."

The light is out. Only the dark. I imagine little eyes watching me. Laughing at me.

Next morning I find a nest of spiders. (Is that the word? Like birds? English is confusing.) They are hatching out of an egg. There is a brown spider in a small tunnel nearby, watching them, watching me. She is much bigger than the woodlouse eaters. Her little ones crawl out, all over the web.

I fetch Husband. "See. Hundreds of them, all from one. This is what I was talking about. Everywhere in this house."

He leans in close and looks at them. Husband's nose is fleshy and big, points his eyes at what he wants to squint at; and there is dark hair in his nostrils, hiding whatever is further in those holes.

"They are beautiful," he says, as they scuttle over each other. "Just babies." He looks at me, and although there is rarely a smile in his eyes, this is different, and I feel it is accusation. I am hot inside, because I want to accuse too, or to defend, but I cannot. There would be scoldings. So when he is in work I cut things up hard, and it makes me calmer as the knife chops, chops, and pieces become neat and tidy, in a shape that I choose.

I take a nutmeg. We called it *joss* at home, but nutmeg is a good word too, funny. Like a nut. And more. Because nutmeg is like a brain picture, and I think it makes me clever. Also it is egg-shaped, and is the seed of the tree. Everything about it is tidy and solid. Hard and round, but it will not sprout legs and crawl away. It stays with me all my life. My family traded in it, and many other *xawaashka* – spices – and resins, such as myrrh and frankincense. Our name was well known, and I was allowed into the warehouse where everything was stored, all that hardness, all that flavour, all those scents. Maybe this one, which I bought in the shop run by the Sikhs, maybe it was one that we sold, come back to me? Nice to think.

I grate it. The smell makes me happy. I am cooking *halwa*, and the sugary water is boiling when I add the shavings, lots of them, stirring in that sweetness, brown mixed with saffron-gold. I always loved nutmeg more than my sisters did. My *hooyo*, she said I eat too much, it is bad. No, Mother, it is not bad. It is something of home, even here in this grey country where I only live with things that have too many legs. I grate some more and put it on my tongue.

We eat *cambuulo* beans and corn in silence. Some nights we talk, and that is all right, though he speaks to me formal. And I speak to him formal. I miss other talk; miss talk with friends. I do not call him by his name, Sharmarke, though I know other people do.

People in this country are not formal. They talk like they know you. It is difficult to understand when they are friendly and when they take pee. Sentences that seem kindly can still include insult words. Women act like they are free. To do, to say, to wear what they want. They would be called sluts back home. Looking for men, like a prostitute. It is very different, and I have been told not to make friends with those women.

But there is no talk tonight. He is thinking about things. In his work. It makes his eyebrows pull together, and I never interrupt him then, he has a bad temper at those times, little shakes that rattle this webby house we live in, send out bad feelings, pull in victims. He will take his sleep pills tonight, so he does not turn and turn all night, and go mad with those bad feelings.

I just watch. He eats noisy. Slurps. His moustache wiggles if he chews, one side then the other. The bristles are like salt and pepper, light and dark, because he is much older than me. A sweeping brush, like to keep the house clean. I smile at that. He sees – always sees, with those eyes, dark and serious, that always watch, especially if we are out of the house, when they watch me even more closely – and his lips curl up too. It is a smile back, which surprises me. Also, in that second, I see his teeth, and they remind me of fangs, curved fangs that could sink into your face and suck it off, while you are paralysed in the web, lifted from the ground you felt safe on into this other world where every movement just tightens things around you. Perhaps that is good. It would be quicker. I know my smile is gone now, and he goes back to his eating. I am not hungry.

His face is on mine in the bed, and it is dark, always dark when he does this. His bristly whiskers on my face, rough, like the mouth parts of a creature, mandibles is I think the word; I do not know *dibles* but I know the first bit, the man bit, the bit he is putting in me.

I normally feel nothing. Sometimes hurt, but I ignore it, and he moves and makes noises and has his pleasure. The bristles make me feel something this night though, and I shudder. He does not seem to notice. He is very focussed on what he needs to do.

I count in my head. In English. Getting better at it. I am at eighty-three when he is finished and pulls out of me and lies next to me. No words now, he took pills and will sleep if I am quiet, and that is good. I check with a finger, and it is wet from him, but not blood this time I think, nothing has ripped. Sometimes I would feel it but sometimes I do not even notice. Many things you can get used to. Best not to think.

I do not like to look down there. It makes me feel dirty and shameful. But I have to check for tearing, or it can get very sore. I examine myself when he is in work the next day. I do not know what I would have looked like if I had not been cut. I understand about scars. They build up on your body when you are hurt. I think they can do that in your mind too. There are lumpy parts where I feel nothing at all. I can prod them, and they are dead tissue. The real scars, from the sewing, and the cutting. Once they hurt me a lot. I remember not being allowed to move, my legs were tied together, and it was pain and itching that made me scream and scream until I was hurt even more, the stick that left a hole for pee, they were not gentle when they pulled it out. It was better to be quiet and bite down. That is why I have scars in my mouth too. Nobody knows about those. They are my own, I can touch them with my tongue. They are not dirty.

And I feel something now. In my heart. Even though cutting is said to control emotions. It is a burning thing there. A place I do not look. But I cannot stand when I feel it, this pain in me. Like a badness, a very dark thing. They say we must not be slaves of the West when we come here. Must not change. But this is new and it scare me because I feel that if I would open my mouth fire would come out, not words; and burn all around me.

It take a long time before I can walk. The house is quiet, no words unless I say them out loud like mad woman. Flames are now hot ashes, but still heat in me. It is real, I know, because I am sweating from it. *This house hate me.* I drink water, but do not cool. The walls are hard if I hit them, leave my hands to ache. There is no way to feel anything that take away the burning. Not a sighing pleasure like Husband has when he put himself in me, that I cannot feel. He have other pleasure – he smoke cigarettes. Sigh then too. Seem happy as smoke comes out, even though it smell bad. Smoke from his mouth, like I have. I pick up his lighter. It is metal. Cold now. Fire sleeps in it, not in me. This house is crushing me, and though there are no voices, it is laughing. They are laughing. So quiet, all in the eyes. I go to the

web with the babies. Crawl, crawl. They are happy. The spider
mother is happy. She is not outcast without a Husband. Sex is for
having children, not for anything else, they told me. Spider has so
many. I light the flame and hold it under the web, and it dissolve,
melt to air before it is even licked by yellow, and the babies curl up
and crinkle in seconds, turn to ash like taste in mouth, cut from
the world with pain. They know me now, but I am still burning
inside. I leave the mother. She watches me with all those eyes and
I feel something but it has no name, and I realise I cry, and at last
the fire is put out.

I think Husband spends time with another woman. I think it
is a white woman, with the blonde hair. In his work. A woman
for things that is not wife. I do not know what they are. What
he needs and what she gives. I only see brown mixed with saffron-gold, but it is not sweet. And why would beautiful white
woman want my husband? But I smell it on him sometimes. I
know. Secrets hidden, but discovered by me because I have good
eyes. A hair on his clothes. A long, pale hair. This is an easy sum
to do. You do not have to count to eighty-three.

I did not know him before we were married. I do not know
him much now. I see the way he walks, sometimes he seems
hunched in. He say he is working hard, but he moves quick. I
think of scuttling things. I wonder how much of his past is true,
the things he told. If he likes to keep secrets, maybe there is things
he wants to hide from me. What is he really? I will know, because
I think about it. It fills my time. There is only me, the house,

Husband, spiders. I once had friends. Now I talk most when I go to shops.

It would be different with a child. I have met other Somalis. Three children. Four. Five. They are busy, tired, but they have them, not to be alone. They are not ones who failed. With me it was nearly, but then I failed at being wife too. They had to cut me open more to have the child, but all the scars, I think they frightened it and it did not want to come out. All the blood, and still the baby was gone. And Husband did not cry. He was quiet, but I think angry. That is not normal for us, is it? I was not thinking right at that time. I wondered if he was a human at all.

In the night I was thirsty, my mouth so dry, like ashes in them. He fast asleep, the Western medicine off his doctor is strong, so I came down into little kitchen. And I saw the big brown spider under the cooker. It was still, frozen in the light. Maybe it had been hunting. It looked at me. It was not laughing. And I was guilty. It was not her fault, yet I killed her babies.

There were floods before they brought me to England. Many people drowned. They floated, we had to drag them out, heavy with water, give them to their families. And something happened. All the trees were covered in web. The top of each one, like a cocoon, something wrapped for spiders to eat. There were hundreds of the palm-sized spiders in every candyfloss tree. It was scary to walk near them, but then we realised that it was good – all the mosquitos were gone. Eaten up by the trees. They were helping us. They were a memory of my home, with the big sun.

Maybe they come with me. Maybe they want to cover the house in their web, their babies. I was bad, and I am very sorry, very guilty. I tell the spider this. How could I not have realised that little spiders were my friends?

It is only very big ones I have to be wary of.

Husband was angry. I was eating nutmeg. It helps with pains, makes me think of home. Some Muslims say it is *haram*, forbidden, but Husband likes *halwa* only with traditional Somali recipe, so he cannot say that. Instead he tell me, "You eat too much. Remember what happened last time."

Does he not know? I remember *everything*. Everything that is pain.

My heart is beating fast. But it means I am feeling something. That is good, because after all this time it proves that scars can be pulled away, maybe something left that is not dead, that is not scary to look at.

They gave me ice cream. I was happy, the old woman seemed like a friend. I did not know what they would do next. Why the woman had a box of metal tools with her. "It help you be faithful. It stop you being smelly," they said. And they changed me. And I lay for days and understood the words, but also did not understand why. Mother had never hurt me before. And this was not to be spoken of to anyone. And that is why I now tell it only to my friends, the little spiders. And they asked me a question I cannot answer. Allah made us, and we are perfect; so why do we change what he has done? I cannot answer my friends, and they just watch me, quiet now. They are not laughing.

I realise we need things. I go to the Sikhs, then I have to go in white person shops. It costs more money. I do not know if they are quiet because of my head-scarf and shawl, or because of my skin. Their eyes on me, and they do not speak, as if I will steal. But they remind me of my little friends, watching, and so I smile at them, and one of them smiles back, and that is something.

I am near the house when I see it. Up in the bedroom window. A shadow on the wall, something that moves jittery, big, more than human even, and it bends wrong. It moves, and is behind the glass for a second, a dark form and I cannot see a face, because there is a reflection. It looks down. My heart, it beats so fast again I think it will kill me this time. I want to run, but there is nowhere to run, and I know eyes are always on me, eyes from the other houses, some white eyes, some like mine, but always watching to see what you hide from them, try to see under your clothes to your heart, to see the secrets you have further down, you must not speak. I cannot run. It is my house. I go in, and my hands shake, but I then think that it can be no worse than I have had in my past.

And I close the door behind me and look at the stairs; they seem longer, so many little ones, and something moves up there. And I cannot take the first step. It is heavy, this thing with many legs. It has eaten so much. It has followed me from Somalia. It took a long time to get here, but it catches you in the end. If I go up I will get stuck in that web, my face will go, it will not be me any more. So I watch until it gets nearer, out of my bedroom, and then I see it, but it is not the Big Spider, it is Husband, and he look down at me. I bite my cheek, to hold a scream in, bite hard and even get through scar to blood, taste it in my mouth, and it calms me and I do not make a noise.

"What is the matter?" he asks when he come down.

"I thought I saw something in the bedroom," I tell him.

"I was getting dressed. Put your eyes back in. I am just home early."

And when he go past I smell something, it does not smell like him. He was getting dressed in clothes so that he looks like this now. But I know.

And when we eat he say we will move. Smaller place. There is not enough work. They give more time to white men, less time to Husband. He is angry, wound up and ready to lash out, and I do not speak. I bite inside my mouth instead.

He never like chewing *khat*. It make him have trouble going toilet. I am glad, because it would keep him awake.

I close the bedroom door quietly behind me. I have my clothes with me, put them on. There is only snoring from within. I have his belt, and it fits very tight between door handle of bedroom and bathroom, then I do the buckle. Only just fits, but it works. I am clever.

Downstairs have a cupboard with things that clean, and fix, and stick. There is an important word on many of them, "Flammable." I pour them onto papers, every one I can find, and it smell very awful, but I spread them around the furniture, leave the cans and bottles there. This is all under the bedroom now. When I take his lighter and set fire to the edge it is so hot that it burn my face, I have to go in the kitchen fast, and I turn on the gas there, it all adds in, will all be right. I am pure, they made me pure; and fire makes pure too, another thing that cleans, so that ashes make new life. There is smoke everywhere and harsh smells, it make roaring noise as it burn, eating wood and materials, and I see through the doorway that the curtains are on fire, and they will not be a way of keeping eyes out much longer, all can look in, as much as they want. I am coughing and feel dizzy but that is good, and there will be fire everywhere soon, because all the gas will burn; it is good because when you are bitten paralysed you need to wake; fire lifts us from the ground into the other world, where nothing is tight, scars burn away, and they told me it would be over soon, would pass, that cutting pain, and this too will be pain then pass. This will be quicker.

The smoke is bad, eyes will not open properly, I cough and spit and it is hot everywhere, and I do not mind; but then I remember what flame did and some shame returns. I can do one thing for others. I feel my way across the kitchen, to the corner, and it is there; it hide in its web, the little spider mother, not like the big one upstairs; this one wears its own skin, and it is wrong to hate it because of the way it looks, and what it eats. Allah made us all, and we are perfect; so to the smallest. I took from her already, I will take no more, and I catch her in my hands. It weighs and tickle like shavings of nutmeg; but it is still, scared or sleep or smoky, do not know. I hold it to my breast, my baby. I feel sick, and want to fall, my legs so tired, the sound of burning so loud, but I open the door and move into little yard, all square stones on the floor but called a garden here, the bin is only thing that grow. I move from house, through the gate, round to the front where there are people, and noise, and pointing. There are sirens too, that means policemen and firemen, shouting to get attention, to move people out of the way. I put the spider down next to a tree.

I should go back. I need to go to new life, but I can hardly move; people try and help me, and tell me it will be all right; then someone screams.

He is up there. He bangs on glass at bedroom, but seems weak. Still, he is stronger than a man should be to recover from the pills his doctor gave him, which I crushed into his glass of warm cardamom milk. He is a shadow, a spindly thing, not a little one; and when he slips down and disappears into smoke I think I see the change, see his skin coming off, and there is dark inside, of the Big Spider. And the fire is so hot we all move back, and someone says there is no hope, but they are wrong.

THE SCISSOR MAN

"Daaaaad, I want a Furby. Everyone else at school has got one." Sammy used a sleeve to wipe green dribble from his chin, then slipped the sticky lollipop back into his wet mouth.

Mr Melrose put his pen down and sighed. "I've told you already, I can't afford to get you any more toys just yet. Look at these bills ..." and he held up a crinkling sheaf of them. "Money doesn't grow on trees, you know."

Sammy took the lollipop out again. "But – they can talk to each other! And sing, and everything! Kennie Hamble's has learnt to say 'Pika-chuuuuu!'" Sammy's chubby face contorted as he screamed out the name of the yellow monster.

"I only bought you a new Action Man last week, why don't you play with that?"

"He broke when he skydived from the window, and anyway, he can't *talk*. I want a Furby!"

"No, not until I –"

"But look at what they do! And they aren't a lotta money." Sammy snatched up the Argos catalogue and carried it over to the table by one page, which started to rip. He put his snot-green lollipop down on his father's paperwork to grab the catalogue with both hands.

"NO! I will not get you one! Stop being so greedy all the time!"

"Furby! Furby!" Sammy yelled in pique.

"Right, that's it! You can get up to your room you selfish brat!" Mr Melrose was exasperated, tired, and clutching at straws – then half-remembered something from his childhood. "And if you carry on being so spoilt the Scissor Man will come one dark night when you're alone and cut your fingers off! Yes, that's what he'll do! Now take your lolly and go up to your room."

"I don't want it now, I want a ice-cream!" shouted Sammy as he slammed the door, leaving smudgy fingerprints on the white paint. "I'm not scared of the Scissor Man," he said as he headed towards the kitchen.

Mr Melrose picked up the lollipop, but it tore the paper as he tried to separate them. He threw the lolly across the room in anger, and it stuck to the side of the sofa. Then he put his head on his arms and sobbed.

"I wish you were still here, Catrin. I miss you so much."

Mr Melrose was in trouble. It wasn't that he didn't work hard – he did as much overtime as he could, but it still seemed that he and Sammy only just scraped by. He would get in from work and feel there was still a mountain of things to do. Washing. Bills. Cooking. Shopping. Housework. Sammy alone could take up all his time: he had to be fed, clothed, unclothed, bathed, supervised, entertained, dropped off at school, picked up again, disciplined (ha!) and put to bed. Mr Melrose had no social life nowadays. He was too tired to have one even if he had the time. Or the inclination. But since Catrin died he didn't want to go out. He didn't want to see the same friends they used to share. It didn't feel right without her. Nothing did.

He had adored her. Generous and caring, she'd thought of others before herself: campaigning on local issues, such as protecting trees in the park, or forming a neighbourhood watch group; doing his infirm mother's weekly shopping; she wouldn't even eat meat because of some left-wing idea that it was cruel. And she always had a smile for him when he was down – her face would brighten up, her blue-grey eyes holding his, and it would be impossible for him not to smile back. And then he would feel better.

But she wasn't there to lift him any more.

She had been killed by a drunk driver a year ago. A lawyer who'd been drinking at lunchtime: had turned off a main road too fast, without looking, as Catrin was crossing towards a friend who'd waved from the other side of the road ... But he didn't want to think about it again. It was too unfair. So many people died or were injured that way (how he wished she had only been injured!). Afterwards the world carried on without her, without changing. Her death only mattered to the family left behind. To Mr Melrose, Catrin's death ripped a hole in his life; to the rest of society her loss was just a cold statistic. Life since then seemed endless. A fuzzy grey freeze-frame of a world was all that was left to him.

Of course, Catrin had possessed a *few* faults. The main one being that she spoilt Sammy. Maybe it was her caring side gone wrong; like a cancer, normal cells reproducing and growing too fast, until the tissue becomes something else, something twisted. Mr Melrose tried to counteract it; God, how he tried! But perhaps it was too late. He didn't have the energy to resist Sammy for long. Sammy would persist; and win; and consume.

"My daddy said the Scissor Man gets you if you're spoilt. That means if you don't share. So give me a bite!"

But Andrew held the bar of chocolate closer to himself. "No! It's mine! I'll tell teacher on you, Sammy."

"Then the Scissor Man will get you!" Sammy contorted his face into a malicious leer, and made snipping motions near Andrew. Andrew was smaller than Sammy, burst into tears, and ran away. Within minutes the Dinner Monitor came over to where Sammy was stood by the huge green dustbins. It was normally the best place to play when you didn't want to be disturbed by grown-ups, but the stinky bins had let him down today.

"Why are you scaring poor little Andrew?" She frowned down at him, fists resting on her wide hips.

"I only told him about the Scissor Man. He comes and cuts you up if you're a horrible person."

"Oh, tosh! There's no such thing as the Scissor Man, any more than there is a Bogey Man, Wolf Man, or Lizard Man. What a horrible idea."

"My daddy told me about him so it must be true! And if you shout at me the Scissor Man will cut *you* up into little pieces!"

"I'm not going to shout at you – I never shout, do I, Sammy?"

"You couldn't anyway. You're not a teacher, just Kennie Hamble's mum." That stopped her smiling.

"Your dad shouldn't be filling your head with such rubbish, and you shouldn't be going around scaring other children with it. It's not nice."

As she walked away Sammy muttered, "The Scissor Man ain't nice neither." Then he stuck his (lime gobstopper-stained) tongue out at Mrs Hamble's back.

"No, I'm sorry."

Sammy was pretending to read a comic, but was really listening to Daddy on the phone. It was fun to do that. Daddy was frowning.

"All children get like that sometimes; it's just a story, Mrs Chiltern."

Mrs Chiltern was the headmistress. Sammy was in trouble for something. He moved towards the back door with his comic, so he could hide in the garden if Daddy got angry.

"No, I didn't tell him that, and I don't know where he got it from. You know kids, he must have made it up."

Daddy paused.

"Okay, I will do. It was a misunderstanding, Mrs Chiltern. Good night." He hung up. "Sammy! Get in here!"

Sammy came back into the living room from his secret listening post behind the kitchen door.

"Was that Mrs Chiltern, Daddy?"

"Yes, and I can do without her ringing up complaining. You've been scaring someone at school."

"I only said about the Scissor Man, what you told me."

"Well don't."

"Did you tell Mrs Chiltern that it wasn't you what told me about the Scissor Man?"

Mr Melrose flushed.

"Well, not quite ..."

"You telled a fib, Daddy. That means the Scissor Man will come in the night and cut your tongue out! Or is it your nose off?"

"Right, that's quite enough. There's no such thing as the Scissor –"

"Is! Is! Is! You said him now, you can't not say him."

"For Christ's sake, Sammy, stop it!"

"Stop what? I'm not doooooooing aaaaaaanything."

Sammy threw his comic on the floor and ran into the kitchen, slamming the door behind him.

Mr Melrose looked at the untameable pile of bills and other paperwork on the table. Everybody wanted a slice of you. Then he looked at the newspaper he'd bought two days ago but not had a chance to read yet. It was quiet in the house for once. He rubbed his tired eyes, picked up the newspaper, and flopped into his armchair. After shaking out the brittle paper he skimmed the headlines.

`Baggy Brits In Obesity Epidemic`

`Terrorists Stab Lecturer To Death`

`Freak Storm Leaving Thousands Without Power`

`Britain Says No More Migrants`

`Cute Little Girl Gets Make-up EVERY-`
WHERE!!!

He yawned. Maybe dealing with the bills would have been cheerier.

Mr Melrose stood on a box in front of a petrol station. Lines of cars extended into the distance. Thousands of them. The drivers tooted horns at each other, while at the front of the queue a man in a suit had finished refuelling his BMW, and was now frantically filling plastic petrol cans lined up in his car boot. He grinned and looked over his shoulder at the other drivers, who shook fists and yelled at him.

A smudgy grey headline floated above the forecourt: *Fuel Crisis Sparks Petrol Panic!!*

Ah. Mr Melrose shouted at the driver filling up. "Don't take it all, there's enough for everyone." But his voice was drowned out by the car horns and the yelling. The driver continued collecting all he could for himself.

"Where's your thought for others? The emergency services will need it!"

Again he was ignored, but a megaphone appeared on the floor. He grabbed it and climbed back on his box, yelled even louder.

"Don't you think? Don't any of you? You'd kill for cheap petrol, but you're burning it up, just to get somewhere quicker! Just to speed round corners on liquid fuel, you're not looking ahead at the world, the future you're changing, not looking where you're going ..."

The drivers were now glaring at him instead of at the suited man stealing all the fuel (whose car boot seemed to stretch all the time – it was about ten feet wide now).

"Think, why don't you? THINK!"

Suddenly the cars surrounded him, revving their engines aggressively. He looked down at his box but his feet were now chained to it. He couldn't run.

"Don't take it out on me! I'm trying to help you!"

But he felt waves of animosity flowing against him, their level rising. Warm waves, that smelt – of petrol! He noticed a small lake of greenish liquid, squirting from the pump in the grinning businessman's hand. He had stopped to listen but the petrol had continued to flow, and now it surrounded Mr Melrose. Then he saw a cigarette in the man's hand. A lit cigarette.

"Be careful with that! You put it down right now, I won't tell you twice!"

The cigarette fell to the floor in slow motion and ignited the petrol; a hungry, roaring fire swept towards Mr Melrose. The heat smashed into him, ignited his clothes and hair, consumed his skin as he screamed, flames tearing down his throat when he inhaled, blistering his lungs, stealing life; eyelids crisped to nothing but he could still see, still see in agony ...

Hot sweat trickled down the middle of his back when he woke, slumped in the armchair, gasping for air.

Oh Christ. Oh Catrin. This has to end.

It was getting dark and he was wasting the evening. Again.

He got up and put the light on, forcing the horrifying images back into the shadows. The carriage clock on the mantelpiece said it was after 7pm. He had better prepare something to eat. Yet another late meal. First he made a token effort to tidy up, stacking magazines and books, putting sweet wrappers in the bin, and toys in a pile ... but it was hopeless. The room didn't look much better when he had finished. Everything he moved just revealed a stain, or dirt, or a tear; little reminders of how incapable he was. He couldn't cook. He couldn't clean. He couldn't do DIY, or paperwork, or finances. And worse, he couldn't afford to pay someone else to do those things. Where were all the cheap immigrants when you needed them?

"Sammy!" his daddy called up the staircase.

"Whaaaaaaaat?"

"Come down here a minute."

Daddy was looking through the contents of the freezer when Sammy clumped his way into the kitchen.

"Do you want turkey drumsticks and chips for tea?"

"No, we had them last night."

"Did we?"

Sammy sniggered. Daddy was often forgetful.

"Erm ... what about pizza?"

"No. Rubbery goo skin is gross!"

"You liked pizza last week! Well, what do you want then?"

"Alphabites. And beans."

Daddy gave him a sharp-edged look then rooted through the boxes in the freezer. His hands looked like they were going blue as he shoved cartons round.

"How about waffles instead?"

"No, Alphabites!"

"But we haven't got any!"

"ALPHABITES 'N' BEANS! I want them."

"Oh bloody hell, come on Sammy, don't mess me around. What about sausage rolls?"

"Alphabites!"

There was a bang as Daddy slammed the freezer door, which made Sammy jump.

"Right! Alphabites it is then! I'll go out and buy some from the Spar, it's not like I haven't got anything better –" he was now in the hall, putting his coat on "– to do with my time –" and he grabbed his wallet "– or like I haven't got much money spare. Oh no. You'll have Alphabites." And the front door slammed.

"Good-ee! Alphabites!" Sammy danced around the kitchen, then fumbled a Mars and Twix from the bag of chocolates in the cupboard (the bag said "fun size" but they'd be more fun if they were bigger), and ate both of them. He noticed brown smears on the paintwork – melted chocolate off his fingers. Daddy got angry about things like that, so he wiped his hands clean on the white hand towel. Then *that* had pooey brown stains on as well! Oopsie!

Daddy would be a while so Sammy played with his toy cars on the living room floor, bashing them into each other and the skirting board, making screaming sounds and picturing hideous deaths in his head.

"Go on, eat them all."

"I'm not hungry any more."

"But you've only eaten a few of them!"

"You have them." Sammy pushed his plate towards Mr Melrose, who shoved it back.

"I'm not eating your mauled food! You asked for them, you can bloody well eat them!"

"Don't swear, it's bad." Sammy prodded reconstituted potato shapes around the plate with his fingers, obviously having no intention of eating the rest of his meal.

His father couldn't take much more. "No, you're the bad one! I do everything for you, Sammy, and you never appreciate it! It's never enough! Why? Huh?" Mr Melrose could hear his voice wavering, changing pitch, getting emotional. Every last shred of patience and strength was being stretched to snapping point.

"I just want sweeties now, but you won't let me." Sammy's bottom lip quivered and he began to cry. "I want sweeties, an' I want my mummy back, an' it's not fair!"

Mr Melrose was surprised; then relented, and leaned over to hold Sammy. He felt like crying too. "I know it's not fair, life isn't. I want your mummy back too –"

But Sammy jerked away from the touch, his eyes flashing with bizarre ferocity. "Don't touch me! I want Mummy, not you! And I want a Aero!"

Shock passed, then Mr Melrose yelled. "You can't have your mummy! You can't have everything you want! No-one can, you ungrateful little bastard! Get up to bed, now!"

After the brat had scuttled upstairs Mr Melrose rested, head on forearms, and sobbed. He needed fresh air. He needed to get away from the house for a bit. More importantly he needed to get away from Sammy.

He would go for a walk. To the cemetery, and crouch by Catrin's grave for a while. He might find peace in death. Even if it was but a breath of wind to cool him for a second, it would help him to carry on. He put his coat on, and went outside into the neon-lit night.

Sammy didn't bother to brush his teeth: he preferred it when they felt rough. Instead he kicked Action Man around his bedroom for a while, imagining his screams as the giant bashed him. Then he put his Winnie-the-Poop pyjamas on and got into bed; put the lamp out and slid under the covers to play with his glow-in-the-dark skeleton.

After a while he heard the front door close, and realised that Daddy had gone out.

"Ha! Now I'm going to get it!" he muttered, thinking of the Aero that would soon be his. He usually had sweets hidden under the pillow but there were just empty wrappers tonight, so the idea of another bar of chocolate was even more comforting.

He turned his attention back to the grinning, ominously-radiant skeleton. He wished he could glow like that. Maybe Daddy would buy him glow-paint sometime, so he could have a radioactive green glow too. He would ask him tomorrow.

A few minutes passed while he imagined scaring people at school by glowing at them from the creepy book cupboard. Then he heard the front door close quietly. He hadn't heard the usual rattle when it opened. Just the quiet click as the catch fell back into place.

Sammy lifted up the corner of the quilt, letting in a cool draught from the dark room, and listened. He wanted to know if Daddy had his chocolate – though surely there hadn't been enough time for Daddy to have gone to the garage already, so Sammy was confused.

He couldn't hear anything else, so he snuck over to his bedroom door and pulled it ajar to listen more carefully. The landing and staircase were dark, as he'd left them – but most of the downstairs lights seemed to be switched off as well. Even as he stood there he heard a click from the kitchen, and the house was plunged into complete blackness. Why had Daddy turned out the kitchen light too? Then Sammy remembered that Daddy sometimes did that when he was sad, and sat in the dark. Silly Daddy.

Something moved below, in the kitchen. It sounded like a drawer being opened and closed. Maybe Daddy had forgotten his wallet and had come back for it.

Sammy strained to listen but heard nothing else for a whole minute. Then the living room door creaked open. Daddy was moving awfully quietly in the dark. He probably thought Sammy was asleep.

Sammy suspected Daddy would go back out the front door, but he secretly hoped he would come upstairs, and give him some chocolate, and say sorry for shouting.

A step creaked! He was coming!

Sammy rushed over to his bed and climbed inside, then pulled the quilt up over his head again. He would pretend to be asleep, but when Daddy looked in Sammy would shout "Boo!" and Daddy would laugh and give him chocolate.

The stairs creaked again, higher up. And there was another noise too, soft – a sort of snipping noise. It was eerie. Every few seconds there would be a creak, or a noise like … like a big pair of scissors cutting the air. Sammy's imagination conjured up images he didn't want, not at the moment. Daddy was being quiet, but why were there funny noises? It was like he was so eager about something that he couldn't help being excited, and giving himself away.

Snip! The noise was near the top of the stairs. Then the house went silent again.

Snip! That noise was quieter, more stealthy, and seemed to come from just outside the bedroom door. Sammy wished he had closed it fully. He wished Daddy would just go to bed. He didn't fancy an Aero any more.

The bedroom door creaked slightly, almost inaudibly. Sammy didn't dare peep out from under the covers, so just huddled up to his grinning skeleton. He didn't feel like saying "Boo!" now, either.

Snip! The noise was by his bed. And it sounded more like a big pair of scissors than ever, eagerly snipping at the dark room's air.

"Daddy?" Sammy whispered, terrified, from under the covers.

Only Sammy didn't think it was his daddy any more.

SINKER

A cloudless black sky sucked up the world's heat and left everythin cauld doon below. He followed the stars, spied the Plough.
The nearly full moon reflected off the ripples like broken patches
o mercury. Around them the water was sae black as tae seem
invisible. McTeagle tied the fly on tae the line and made his first
cast. This could be the night tae destroy a legend, and shame
McGraff. And if no ... well, though the chances o trout were slim,
salmon was always a possibility wi their year-round spawnin.
McTeagle had brought his strongest line and rod, sae he'd be
ready whitever happened. The rod fitted in his hand like it was
made for it. That's because it had been. It was the nemesis o
migratory fish.

Tae McTeagle's right the river flowed doon from Beinne
Doune; tae his left it widened intae Loch Achla'teag, then eventually tae the sea. Around him were leafless trees, overhangin
scratchy spikes where the branches fingered the water, half in half
oot, like giant traps or a floatin nest made by giant bird or aquatic
creature, impenetrable shadow beneath.

He settled intae a comfier position wi many a grunt and shoogle. Night was the best time. It kept him sane. Nae tourists, bubblin kids, nosy neighbours, canvassers, greetin teenies, cauld callers, heidbangers, bletherin busybodies or other bitin, whinin nincompoopy pests. Nae women, either. Just as well. He wasnae tae auld tae raise a pole but at his age all they wanted was tae get mairrit. Nae chance. He'd been there and it had turned oot ... och, dinna dwell on it. Sae now his only choices were between widders, gumsies, hackits, hoors, drunks and mad ones. Apart from bonnie Annis. Ye cannae beat a bit o the old houghmagandie but he cringed tae think aboot the disastrous date six months ago. She'd invited him over, cooked finnan haddie and howtowdie. Gorgeous scran, but then he needed the toilet just afore puddin, and did the biggest shite ever, musta been one and a half pun, he wished he'd brought his weighin scales. Nerves, nothin else could explain that aquatic monster. And nothin would clear the floater. By the third flush Annis called up, askin if he was okay. It was still defiantly buoyant. He didn't ken whit tae dae and panicked. Wrapped it in toilet paper and put it in the wee bin by the sink. Sleeve soaked, water drippin off his arm. Sae he climbed oot the bathroom window and ran away, swore off women, never spoke tae her since. Tae much trouble. Better tae be alane and away from it all.

Aye, night in the wilds was a different world. Sae peaceful. No like near the noisy city, where lights always reflected off the water, oranges and whites. Here there were only the stars and the moon and any light he brought wi him. Everythin else was swallowed up.

Which was why night was the time o hunters. Ahead o him bats skimmed silently above the surface o the river. Finesse and control on the edge o danger. Just like him, if his joints weren't sae stiff. Aye, night fishin was huntin. Even better when ye were doin it on the sly. The skinnymalink Rogers had offered him a cheap slot – it came available when the nyaff angler disappeared partway through the week. Always nice when ye can benefit from someone else's misfortune, whitever led them tae dae a runner. The remainin days were dangled in front o McTeagle at a bargain price, and he nearly bit. But then the blatherskite's English accent got in the way, and McTeagle couldna face givin him one miserly bawbee. A disgrace, havin tae crawl tae an English in McTeagle's own country. As if they didn't own enough land already. Sae fish at night and ye dinna need tae pay. Ye just hae tae make sure ye dinna get caught.

His eyes were accustomed tae the dark. Wi the moon's help it was easy tae see whit he was doin. Just a switcharound day. Warmth replaced wi cauld; sun wi moon; grey sky wi black; colour wi monotone. There was enough light tae see shadows from overhangin branches that created spiky swayin shapes which moved across the pale stanes.

Eyes adjust tae night but ears dae tae. In the normal busy noise o day he couldna hear subtle sounds; but at night he could hear each animal sound, individual trickle o water, each mysterious rustle from the bushes behind.

The last reason for fishin here at night was the legend o Auld Ferlie. The "Old Trickster". Nae body agreed on the details. Some said it was a record pike, that had somehow avoided bein caught and eaten by Poles. Some (afore they were laughed in-

tae red-faced silence) said it was an octopus. Others said it was
even stranger, no a fish but "somethin else", in that wide-eyed,
hush-voiced way that made him want tae slam his fist intae their
pie holes. Whit was "somethin else"? A Scottish crocodile? A
deil frog? A dinosaur that slept tae lang? It got weirder. Hamish
claimed he'd seen him swim below his boat once. "A bastartin
black shadow, coulda tipped me oot." Brogie's ramgunshoch
grandaddy swore he'd nearly been dragged intae the water by the
beastie. The wilder havers said that Auld Ferlie came from the
loch.

"Sure everyone knows things bide longer in extreme cauld
water, *exactly* like the bottom o Achla'teag," said Brogie.

"Sure everyone knows ye talk oot yer erse," McTeagle had
replied. "And why's it no seen that often if it's been there all this
time like an Argyll Nessie?"

"Is it nae obvious? It's different. *Somethin else.* And it only
comes up tae feed once a year, sae bile yer heid!"

"Away wi ye and dinna rip ma knittin, ya eejit!"

If anyone disappeared near the loch it was always whispered
tae be Auld Ferlie's work. Years o rumours; seen, maybe hooked,
but never landed.

Still, most things had a grain o truth. Some lochs were over
900 feet deep. Deep enough that it freezes the wee microbes that
bloat bodies and made them float. Sae anyone drownin in the
loch sinks, lungs full o water, and disnae come back up. Tae deep
for divers tae recover them. And withoot the bacteria they dinna
decay much either. A whole graveyard at the bottom o every
loch. Ye –

There was a ploppin noise o somethin surfacin. He fumbled in the fishin box for his torch. Flicked the switch tae nae effect; shook it twice, hearin loose parts rattle, but it came on this time wi a weak beam that grew in intensity as the bulb warmed up. He shone it oot over the river, then realised it was pointless. Durin the day ye can look in the edge o the water and see Irn-Bru transparent orange wi mossy bits underneath, but at night it reflects, and ye can only see the surface. Unknown whit lurks below.

Wee daftie. It was nothin.

The legends only agreed in three details: Auld Ferlie was only seen on moonlit nights in September; he was very auld, since legend passed from father tae son for generations; and he was fair sly.

Ha. Ye are sly, but sae am Ah.

The current fish in the Auld Ferlie family had lived lang enough tae get wise. Probably avoided bitin. But McTeagle knew the secret. Had learnt it off his da.

"The key is in the bait or lure. It imitates either food or an enemy. Use the right one, at the right time, and ye'll aye land yer catch."

And his kit was the best, for the biggest fish. A fly he designed himsel: "The Hoormaister Stoater". Better than toby lures. Better than the black flyin condom. Heavy-duty triple barbed hooks. Fish are sae glaikit. They canna tell the difference between food and a trap.

Course, if Auld Ferlie was that clever, even this might no be enough. Unless ... well, McTeagle had a theory. Maybe fish *liked* bein caught. It was a game tae them. Somethin tae liven things up when ye spend yer life swimmin in shite and mud. He didn't think it bothered them much, bein hooked and reeled in. It was sharn whit some people said, aboot them havin nerve endings in their lips, like a human. Like a human! Pish. Wi all his years o anglin McTeagle would ken if twere true.

The rocks he leaned against were cauld. No icy but dampt cauld enough when ye were still for tae lang. His breath came oot all misty and his nose was numb. He stood, clapped hands and stamped feet, hugged his arms in close, heid hunched over, all tryin tae keep a bit o warmth inside.

This was a fair spot. Piled-up boulders and the silhouettes o bushes and long grasses behind him. Beyond that a hill slope that kept some o the wind off; though while it was a clearly tangled clump o trees by day, in darkness it looked like a solid impenetrable mass, somehow larger, loomin over his shoulder wi spiky-topped silhouettes. It was easy tae imagine ye were bein watched by someone there. Easy tae imagine – he picked up the torch again, shone it around. For a second he thought he saw a figure that looked like a person, but when he swung the torch back it was just a fallen tree. There was nae body sneakin up on him from behind. Daft tae keep gettin spooked like a jessie. Nae bogles oot here.

Sure, the supernatural stuff was all feardie rubbish. Chances were Auld Fearlie was a huge sea trout. They only live a decade or sae, twenty tops, but it could be part o a family, a rare freak, always growin big, eatin their way above the other predators. And each time a new generation o the monsters was seen it was thought tae be a single auld fish. He'd known sea trout up tae twenty-eight pun; maybe the Ferlie family added a fair bit tae that. It would explain the legends.

Aye, that was it. The tales o the loch were a red herring. It was just the fish's annual migration all the way up here for a late spawn. Tales get twisted. McTeagle knew the truth, he'd worked it oot.

And he was ready for it. He'd wipe the smile off Malcolm McGraff's camsteerie face. He might be a Scot, puttin him a touch above shilpit Rogers, but he was still a scunner. One minute an adulterous affair, the next standin as their MSP for family values, the Wee Free hypocritical kirkish bastard. Always there wi a put-doon. Always there flauntin his money, his loyal wifie, his children, none o which the scunner deserved. Always ready tae frown on McTeagle for fishin on a Sunday, or no throwin catch back, or no wipin his shoes. And always tryin tae outdo McTeagle at the anglin club. Well, he'd hae a job outdoin Auld Ferlie served on a plate.

He yawned. Mustna give in. It took hours o patience tae get a reward. That was the key. Be more patient than the fish. As he got older his body got stiffer but his patience grew. That was one o the secrets tae why he was the best angler in the area, whitever torn-faced McGraff claimed. Sae he indulged in fantasies o the rod goin heavy, the reel squealin as the line comes off, playin the monster fish tae its exhaustion, an epic sixty minutes o give and take which would be suitable for a legend. Finally draggin its heid oot the water as it struggled and flipped. Net it and knock it on the heid wi the priest, that most loyal hard wood club o last rites. Bonk. Done. A few more bonks if it was a real struggler. Then see his son look up at him, proud o his da, a winner no a loser ...

but there were only some rocks in a loose pile. A shadow from the past. McTeagle shivered.

The river wasnae flowin fast but ye could still hear it, wet noises, especially by tight bends where it flows faster. Somethin calmin and hypnotic aboot those sounds. Lulls ye tae sleep. Only the cauld keeps ye awake. He pulled his hat doon tight and inhaled the rich smell o gassy mud. Still nae bite. He had a sinkin feelin. Unless luck smiled it would all be over.

He realised his eyes had closed. He jerked awake, picked up the rod from where it had slipped. How lang had he dozed off for? It was the gentle slappin o water against the rocks linin the shore that did it. Sae calmin. Sae dangerous. He couldna let his attention waver if he was goin tae catch this one. No like coarse fishin where ye can slap an alarm on the line, hunch over and doze off. He slapped his lazy face. Ye get older, yer body lets ye doon. But once again, he was ready for anythin. Took the flask and poured himsel a plastic cup o strong black coffee that always got him through wee hours. Steam rose, carried the whiff o whisky. He always sank it wi a dram o' goldie. Nothin like a tot o good Scots whisky tae liven anythin up. No the American and Irish shite the pubs sold now. Shove Jack Daniel's and Jameson up yer erse.

The water lapped near his feet as he held the cup in both hands. Slidin along. Almost a slither. Sae many sounds in the night. Animals goin aboot their business. It was easy tae get spooked. Especially if ye were already jumpy by doin somethin a wee bit naughty. He poured another tot intae his cup.

That was the deadly thing. Imagination. He scoffed at the idea o a monstrous Auld Ferlie during the day. But it feels different when ye're all alane by a loch at night, like ye arenae welcome, just a wee speck in the scheme o things. It was easy tae imagine that log floatin past was somethin alive and distorted. That the shadows cast by the bushes hid eyes which watched ye. That the lichen hangin in clumps from the trees was giant spider web. Rocks which broke the surface became the hump-backed shape o a kelpie or huge snake that had broken the surface. Easy tae imagine that the –

Shut up McTeagle, ye bampot!

There was a rustle in the lang grasses tae his right and he jumped. Just a rabbit, he told hissel. Or the breeze that gusted over the waters.

Ignore it. Keep busy. He dragged his tackle box over and tidied his kit. Some twisted line and weights from the coarse fishin competition last week. Probably no worth untanglin. He chucked the wiry clump intae the bushes. Rooted around. Glanced warily at the grass. Then his hand closed on somethin reassurin. Took oot the red-painted priest. It felt as good in his hand as the rod. Good for breakin any skulls. He lay it on a flat stane behind him, sae it widnae get muddy or damp but would be in easy reach. And he knew he had a good gut knife in there tae.

When the wind blew through branches the trees whispered and moaned. Sometimes it almost sounded like a voice. Aye, it did sound like a voice! He cocked his heid. Was it someone callin him? It sounded a bit like soor-faced McGraff, but that was stupid, he widnae be round; the peely-wally bauldie would be tucked up in bed. Na, just imagination makin him feart.

He downed the coffee and whisky mix. More whisky in there than usual. Maybe that was it, makin him jump at shadows and ghosts.

Oh now! Dinna be sayin that word!

A voice again! This time it was definitely like a dreich moan. Like someone callin for help. A boy, maybe. Oh now, that wasnae right. He got up as quick as creaky knees allowed.

"Who's aboot?" he asked, dreadin it would be the landowner.

Nothin but a faint moan.

Och, whit now?

He was shakin but propped the rod by his seat. This time the torch's beam was fainter. Old batteries fadin fast. McTeagle knew the feelin. He closed the tackle box, stepped over the rock wi the priest on, and moved intae the twitchin grass.

"If yer japin me, Ah'll swing for ye."

He jabbed the light beam towards each movement. Light was a funny auld thing. Reassurin in one way, but it had a habit o makin the area ootside the beam seem darker, and created wavin shadows around everythin. Revealin and obscurin at the same time. Especially among the leggy trees, where it could almost make it look like somethin was leapin oot at ye. Even the silver birches transformed at night, turnin intae exposed bone stickin up oot o the ground.

His waders brushed the long plants aside, and it seemed like the sound was comin from over near his car, where he'd parked it amongst some trees sae it shouldn't hae been visible from the road. No good. Somethin glowed, and he ducked doon, crouched his way over, cursin how stiff he got from sittin still. When he peeped again it was just a reflective road sign flickerin in the torch beam. He could still hear the pained sound in the other direction, but there were nae lights, nae signs o a person. Maybe they were lyin doon and hurt? It made nae sense. And just for a second he remembered the noises his son had made when he was wheezin for breath in a hospital, each struggle o the bonnie fechter a dunt in the ribs tae McTeagle; nae lang before he passed away; nae long afore the useless wifie ran away; and for aye after that McTeagle fished alane, nae son tae teach, nae ... och, tae much. Just think o now.

He followed the sound. It was louder. Over near the water. If it were some chunty heid kid McTeagle would be reekin. He played the beam around, saw a movin shadow as if somethin shifted beneath the water; swore but then realised it was shadow from the low-lyin heather. Another hollow whistlin moan from nearby. He peeked from his hidin place, and saw somethin wee, couldna be a person. Went over tae it warily.

A bottle. A big bloody ten gallon demijohn restin on the mud. The breeze blowin past it was whistlin intae the neck, makin a moanin sound.

He'd nearly crapped himsel! Whit a sodie-heid!

He sighed wi relief, felt everythin relax. Maybe a bit tae much. He realised he was burstin for a pish. All the damn water flowin noises. All the coffee. And a bladder that got leakier by the year.

He relieved himsel intae the river, enjoyin the sploshin sounds. Up yours, Rogers, ya bowly-legged sumph. It took a while afore he was empty. He'd skittered aboot, wasted time, that was no good. He returned doonriver in the direction o the loch,

crunchin across loose pebbles on the bank, back tae his rod
and kit by the pale rocks spotted wi dark patches o moss. He
scrambled over the biggest stane he'd set up against, seated himsel doon. All that nonsense! He was actin like a bairn. He was
reluctant tae turn the torch off but it really was dyin now sae he
put it tae bed.

A few hours till dawn. He'd hae tae scarper afore that. People
might recognise his car. And nothin tae show for it but stiffenin
joints. Sae much for wipin McGraff's smile off his bawface. A
whole night gone agley.

McTeagle's stomach rumbled. He was prepared for this tae.
Somewhere in his fishin box was ... ah, on top. He fumbled in
his piece box wi cauld fingers. Beef and mustard sandwiches. The
lid wasnae on the tub properly. He hoped nae wee beasties had
crawled in.

Rustlin in the grasses behind him again, but he ignored it this
time. Dinna let daft nonsense interfere wi hunger.

He took a bite o his sandwich. Had tae open his mouth wide.
Liked a good stack. Nae point makin one if it's no solid and
fillin. The tang o mustard hit the spot, settin off the chewy
toughness o the Angus beef. And the flavour o ... strange, a bit
sea-weedy. Was the mustard off? As he chewed the bread tae cud
he noticed somethin else in there, like hair, mashed up wi the
rest. He took the sandwich away but the finely fibrous stringiness
remained. He tried tae pull the clag from his mouth then felt
an experimental tug – ouch! He dropped the sandwich but the
pain remained, a sharp jag in his flesh. Somethin yanked and his
lip was punctured; hands tae his face and it was barbs o some
kind, wee jagged prongs like those metal-spiked piercins some o

the punk boys had, grippin like cat claws. As somethin pulled yet again his lower lip and cheek stretched oot away from his teeth, at least an inch, tae the point where it felt like it could tear off. There was nae slack this time, he had tae lean his heid forward, feelin the warmth o blood runnin doon his chin. He fought against it, struggle wi icy fingertips on the hooks but it only tore the skin more, makin his eyes water wi the pain. A sharp yank from whoever was doin this and he fell tae his knees in the mud tae avoid havin his lip torn right off his face. That was when he realised the line ran intae the river and disappeared below the surface.

McTeagle tried tae grip the cord, tae pull it back. It was thicker than nylon, strangely sinewy, hard tae hold. His fingers slipped. He wrapped the line around one o his hands but it cut in like garotte wire, slicin through fingerless gloves and shreddin intae his hand. In a moment o laxness he released his bleedin limb, but the line tugged again, haulin him right tae the edge o the water. He tried tae yell but the sounds were more like pained mewls because o the way his mouth was distorted; he could imagine the holes growin as the auld skin was pulled taut, beyond the elasticity it was meant tae possess, tissue tearin but givin nae relief, and agony increasin every time he resisted. Another yank and he'd go face first intae the water. He brought his legs forward quickly, dug his heels intae the mud below the surface, but when the line heaved again, yankin his cheek oot tae, his feet slipped over the slimy stanes at the edge, drawin him in up tae his waist; water seeped intae his waders, freezin his legs, and his face ready tae tear off. He couldna struggle in this way, and was near tae bein jiggered. He had an idea, reached oot wi his good hand

and scrambled aboot for his knife but the tackle box was just oot o reach, and he was bein drawn in further, icy liquid chillin his back and stomach now, makin him chitter. Then somethin touched him. Somethin under the water. And the only thing it reminded him o was crab legs, huge crab legs brushin against him, chitinous and alien. He recoiled, tried tae splash his way back but was fixed, mind racin wi nae time tae think properly. Only two options. The first was tae hae half his face torn off, and crawl tae his car. Would he live? He didna ken. But the excruciatin pain as his skin was stretched, sae much he couldna even see oot o his right eye, suggested that he couldna dae it. He could smell blood, knew it was his own, runnin from torn tissue on the surface and within his ruined face. Sae the only other option was tae go intae the water and find oot – na! Another idea! He had fingers. He had a chance. If he could just get a bit o slack sae he could unhook himsel he would be free. That's the thing, ye hae tae cancel the strain. It was the only way. He only needed a few feet and he'd hae time tae get maist o the barbs oot, he was sure: motions familiar tae his fingers from years o repetition. It was the only choice.

He stopped pullin, instead wadin deeper intae the water, sploshin and ignorin those strange shell-like limbs; it did slacken up a bit, his face reseatin itsel against the bone, and he fumbled at the hooks, got one oot o his lip, was workin another oot o his cheek but it was takin tae lang wi his ruined hand, and wi an almighty jerk he was hauled forward intae the depths, a shockin splash and everythin muffled as he was pulled under, intae the runnin water. An agony in his face as he tried tae hold his breath. Floatin hair brushed against him, a fibrous clot, makin him wince in disgust; and then somethin pulled tight around him like a bristly net made o hundreds o spider legs, all raivelt up.

Wi a real sinkin feelin he realised he had left it tae late tae try that tactic wi his gawkit fingers ... and as needle teeth cut in he knew he'd been wrong tae think Auld Ferlie was tricksy because he avoided bitin – oh, he bites – na, no tricksy because he was difficult tae catch, but named because it was much older and slyer than even the legends said. McTeagle inhaled water in panic, tried tae scream it oot, but was dragged doonstream, the moon only a broken image above, shattered intae pieces that he'd never put back together. His lasts thoughts were the words o his da:

"The key is in the bait or lure. It imitates either food or an enemy. Use the right one, at the right time, and ye'll aye land yer catch."

The waves caused by the mass twitching below the surface began to fade, shrinking to undulations as it sank further down to the bottom, heading toward Loch Achla'teag. On either side of the moon's broken reflection the water was so black as to seem invisible – a void of shadow falling away into an abyss. Soon the water looked as it always had, drifting slowly by, impenetrable.

OVERLOAD

Day 1

Maths. He hated it.

Tonight: equations. Even worse.

Dylan stared at the numbers, letters, brackets, equals signs. It made his brain hurt. He'd been staring at the symbols for so long they seemed to leap about below the results line. And the homework was supposed to be in tomorrow, last chance – he'd already lost marks for being late. School sucked.

Mostly.

He leaned out of his bedroom door. Mum was busy downstairs doing an exercise DVD, so he was safe for a while.

Solving equations often worked if you ignored the tricky beginning and started somewhere else. Worked your way back.

He switched to the web browser and logged in, scanned his friends list to see who was online. Ah.

DylanDaaawg: Hi
Mandy Reem: heyyah

Mandy's avatar was a glamorous, pouting selfie. Glossy red lips and tons of eyeshadow, like she was on a night out. It was the sort of pic most girls uploaded, but he could tell the background was really just her bedroom. For his own image he'd cropped a picture of himself so it just showed his lower legs, new skate shoes, and board. A happy time at the skate park. Shame he hated the rest of the photo because his face suffered an outbreak of zits that week.

DylanDaaawg: WUU2?
Mandy Reem: omg homework
Mandy Reem: vom :(
DylanDaaawg: :p I never do homework
Mandy Reem: bet u lyin to seem cool
DylanDaaawg: No
DylanDaaawg: Do you know whats up with Sally ?
Mandy Reem: brb
Mandy Reem: u have a webcam?
DylanDaaawg: Yeh, but I think its broke. Why?
Mandy Reem: just thought itd be more fun
Mandy Reem: wears my fingers out typign to evryone
DylanDaaawg: Not just chattin with me?
Mandy Reem: nah. 4 others. dont even know who one of them is, but he talks funny
DylanDaaawg: I'm totally flattered now
Mandy Reem: ha ha well jel! u in school tmoz?

DylanDaaawg: Yeh. Do you know about Sally?
Mandy Reem: i might go off in a sec
DylanDaaawg: Why?
Mandy Reem: boreed obvs
DylanDaaawg: Oh
DylanDaaawg: First, what bout Sally?
Mandy Reem: whatevs gonna go now cheers

Day 2

Dylan munched sweet popcorn from the carton (salted was for weirdos) and shrank down so the schoolkids settling noisily into the seats two rows back wouldn't recognise him and start throwing stuff. The film was supposed to be good. The new *Spider-Man*. Lots of action. He always liked Spider-Man, felt some affinity for him that he couldn't muster for psycho Batman or indestructible Superman. Web connected things, created links that couldn't be untangled.

The film hadn't been going long when his phone buzzed. Not a text this time (Mum had been checking up on him): this was a chat app notification.

badmodz: D-DAAAAAWWWWGGGG!!!!!!
badmodz: Havent Talked To You In Ages!!!
DylanDaaawg: What a nerve. Bastard. Hope you get banned for scamming me

Dylan added a block to badmodz's account. Something he should have done before, but it was easy to lose track of all the friends when the scroll list was five screens long. Done. Last he'd hear from that loser. Dylan had thought he could tell friend from foe in the game forums. Should have never shared his account, trusting badmodz to upgrade it. For now Dylan swallowed his anger and went back to the film about a teenage boy squirting white stuff.

Half an hour later the phone vibrated again. He was going to ignore it but curiosity won out.

SkatrGrl. *Sally*. In her profile pic she was sort of looking away, avoiding eye contact, long sandy hair covering part of her face. It captured her essence so perfectly that his heart beat faster, like a shock running through his system.

DylanDaaawg: You ok?

SkatrGrl: ye

DylanDaaawg: Are you in a mood with me ?

SkatrGrl: aint it obv

DylanDaaawg: No. Why?

SkatrGrl: bc u allways takin the piss bout me and u know yr windin me up and said I was a slag. pisses me off

DylanDaaawg: Was only jokin Everyone does it. You only go in a mood with me?

SkatrGrl: coz everyne else stopedd cuz i tell emm to . but nooo u HAVE to carry on, I allways say shut up, but its like

SkatrGrl: fuck it all
SkatrGrl: nm. what does it matter
DylanDaaawg: Ill stop if you forgive me :'(

He waited. And waited. His message had not been read. No reply. He couldn't concentrate on the film, kept turning the phone screen on. Excitement when there was a notification: but it was just a friend request, someone he didn't recognise. He ignored it. Was too sick to eat any more popcorn. Ended up leaving the cinema halfway through Spiderman's big fight.

Day 3

On the bus, squashed up to the window by an old biddy. He listened to music, watched the world judder by. Each day was just getting from A to B whilst being pushed against cold, hard surfaces by sweaty bodies. That was life. A Chat App alert popped up: mysterious Max. His avatar was a picture from behind, just a silhouette of the back of his head as he faced two computer screens in a darkened room. Dylan had never seen Max's face.

Max Hacks: Uritee Laad ?
DylanDaaawg: Goood. You?
Max Hacks: Sames. Thought about the offer?
DylanDaaawg: Yeh, it's good
Max Hacks: Wots your gamertag?

DylanDaaawg: DylHaXorGod

Max Hacks: Ha u wish u was a hacker

Max Hacks: U know what I said, £25 and ill unlock all DLC and gold guns in Call of Duty and Modern Warfare, latest versions. Pay me nows and I will have it done

DylanDaaawg: Please do it for £12??? Its all i can afford. :(I could Paypal tonight. Been a bad month, another account hacked, only just got it back

Max Hacks: How? Gave out details like a noob?

DylanDaaawg: No. Done that with badmodz, learnt my lesson - if he does anythin again i fuckin swear

Max Hacks: That dude isnt legit, nv was

DylanDaaawg: I know. But this was weird, support couldn't trace the logins. Reset everything, new passwd. Said its hapnin a lot

Max Hacks: NMP

DylanDaaawg: So £12 tmoz ?? Would mean a lot to me

Max Hacks: £25

DylanDaaawg: Or i can maybe get £16

Dylan was messaging an empty screen. Max was obviously hacked off.

Day 4

It hadn't been such a bad day today. The ICT lesson got can-
celled when the whole network went down so his class got sent
to the library to study, but there was no librarian any more so
they just dossed around. After school he'd gone skate park, and
for the first time in ages there was no-one else there. Weird, but
cool to have it to himself, without older lads taking the piss when
he face planted.

He skated home through the cemetery, lazy kicks to roll past
the dog walkers, pram pushers, toddler tamers, and the dead.

When his phone buzzed and he saw it was Sally he jumped off
the board and let it roll onto the grass while he sat on the nearest
bench. He'd not seen her in school all week.

DylanDaaawg: Sally, you talkin to me at all?
SkatrGrl: idk
DylanDaaawg: I said sorry
DylanDaaawg: Sally?
DylanDaaawg: I wont act like a dick again. Promise
DylanDaaawg: I really like you
SkatrGrl: ye ino
SkatrGrl: do u like my new picture?

Dylan noticed she'd added red lines over her face on the profile
image. It almost looked like blood.

DylanDaaawg: Erm, yeh

DylanDaaawg: Look, all I care about is you and me friends. Don't want o be in the coo l cro wd wh e nn

DylanDaaawg: Ono, my ph ones gon e laggy

SkatrGrl: whats that mean

DylanDaaawg: Gone sl ow lol cant p ress key s qui ck. Us ually ne eds res et

DylanDaaawg: You w ant to do sum thi n? P lea se ?

SkatrGrl: i will tell u wot 1 want

SkatrGrl: w0t u

SkatrGrl: w0t meat 1me01

SkatrGrl: w0t 1meu01 in1lie10 a£nger *(^^&

User offline. But this time he wouldn't give up. He still had her number.

Pressed Call, waited … waited … ring … ring … then a dead tone. He stared at it in disbelief. The battery was totally drained. Piece of shit! He felt like smashing it. Nothing worked properly any more. He let the phone clatter to the bench and looked up at the grey sky for strength.

It started raining.

Day 5

What a week. And now his phone wouldn't turn on. Still not seen Sally either, and no-one else had. He wished he knew where she lived. But he'd ring her from the landline when Mum went out.

At least he didn't have to do any homework tonight, so Mum was leaving him alone on his Xbox. He'd been having fun until the servers disconnected him and he lost the last two loot drops and got reset back to his base. He couldn't face wasting any more time so switched to Facebook instead.

A chat message immediately popped up, from an account he'd never heard of. The avatar was someone wearing a silly skull-type mask, or maybe skull make-up. Either way, it seemed lame.

Hellrider: hiiyyaa!
DylanDaaawg: Uhhm hi
Hellrider: its u already
Hellrider: noooo!!!
DylanDaaawg: Whose that?
Hellrider: Charles!
DylanDaaawg: Yerright
Hellrider: acct got reported, blocked. had to do a new acct, redo friends
DylanDaaawg: If it is you, prove it
Hellrider: i know u use an aimbot to cheat online
DylanDaaawg: and?
Hellrider: u wore Timbland boots to the rugby club rave
DylanDaaawg: Haha it is you
Hellrider: easy enough to prove it, ye
DylanDaaawg: WUBU2 nowadays?
Hellrider: been Welll Bored ::
Hellrider: lonely too for a loooooong time

DylanDaaawg: Gotta go, teas ready inamin
Hellrider: no, wait. i wanna play a game
DylanDaaawg: Cya
Hellrider: 1 sed 1 wanna play a GAME!!!

Dylan shook his head with a grin. Charles was such a kid. He closed the chat window.

Another one popped up straightaway, from Sally.

SkatrGrl: don't go
DylanDaaawg: Huh?
SkatrGrl: i hate us being mad at each other
DylanDaaawg: God, so glad you said that!
SkatrGrl: 1 wanna play a game
DylanDaaawg: Joke?
SkatrGrl: the game is, u work out who 1 am
DylanDaaawg: Sally?
SkatrGrl: No! Gong!
DylanDaaawg: This is bs. I'm going
SkatrGrl: Gong! lol
SkatrGrl: one sec

Dylan pushed his chair back and was about to get up when a message appeared.

Webcam permissions
SkatrGrl is inviting you

to share your webcam.

[Accept] [Decline]

Dylan clicked Decline.

Webcam permissions

You have accepted the invitation
to share your webcam.

SkatrGrl: 1 can see u
SkatrGrl: can u see me
SkatrGrl: ?
DylanDaaawg: I can only see a black box. Who are you?
SkatrGrl: am i Charles?
DylanDaaawg: No
SkatrGrl: well done
SkatrGrl: i can wipe all yr accounts
DylanDaaawg: Liar
SkatrGrl: as easily as i turned on yr little camera
DylanDaaawg: badmodz, are you fuckign around?
SkatrGrl: shall i delete your hard drive? i could, u know.
i move below the interface level
DylanDaaawg: Don't
SkatrGrl: how old are you?
DylanDaaawg: 16
SkatrGrl: no you're not. you're 13. GOng!

A new message popped up.

Reformat

Are you sure you want to delete C:?

All data will be lost.

[Accept] [Yes please]

Dylan reached for the mouse, then froze. Read the options twice. Stared at the screen. After about ten seconds the message disappeared of its own accord.

SkatrGrl: next time you lie 1 won't let you cancel. lOl

SkatrGrl: are you scared? think carefully

DylanDaaawg: Ye

SkatrGrl: good

Dylan closed the browser. Stared at the screen. At the camera. Clicked Shut Down Windows.

Nothing happened at first.

Then another pop-up window.

Hellrider: no point. i'm here.

badmodz: AND HERE!!!!!! D-DAAAWGGG!!!!

SkatrGrl: and here. missing u so much.

Mandy Reem: an here, lookin totes amaze, cheers

Mandy Reem: 101

Unknown User: Where do yOu 1ive?

Unknown User's avatar was an eye with the lids obscenely stitched together.

DylanDaaawg: I wont say
DylanDaaawg: It's not a lie!
Unknown User: Y0u 1ive at 44 Ridgm0unt.
DylanDaaawg: How did you know that?
Unknown User: I kn0w 10ts ab0ut y0u and every0ne. Saggy bags 0f 1iquid draped 0ver sticks that act 1ike they're s0mething e1se.
DylanDaaawg: I have to go
Unknown User: N0 y0u d0n't.
DylanDaaawg: Mum is shouting me for dinner
Unknown User: That bit's true. I can hear her. Must be a g00d mic. What are y0u having?
Unknown User: Answer, p1ease.
DylanDaaawg: Smells like sausages
Unknown User: Yum yums.
Unknown User: I eat babies.
DylanDaaawg: No
Unknown User: 0thers t00. N0 w0nder I'm getting bigger!
DylanDaaawg: You're lyin
Unknown User: Y0u'11 see s00n en0ugh. I'm 0n my way 0ver. Make mince.
Unknown User: By the way, Sa11y ki11ed herse1f a few days ag0.
Unknown User: Thanks t0 y0u guys.

Unknown User: (And a 1itt1e push fr0m my messages. Naughty 01d me.)
Unknown User: 101

The computer shut down.

Dylan's hands were shaking.

No. *No.* It had to be a lie.

He needed time to think.

"Right, Mum," he shouted, but it came out hoarse, too quiet. He tried again from the top of the stairs then went into the bathroom and splashed cold water on his face. WTF? Like, WTF, for reals? This was ... he rushed back into his bedroom and unplugged the computer from the wall socket. There was a flash from the multiplug, leaving a small black scorch mark on the plastic, a smell of burning. He stared at it, expecting it to move.

Downstairs.

"What's up?" his mum asked as she caught him looking out of each window in turn.

"Nothing."

"Weird boy."

She stirred the pan of sausages. They sizzled, plump with fat. The smell wasn't appetising tonight. He finished his circuit of the room. There was an ambulance siren off in the distance. Then the toaster clicked.

"Oh, it hasn't popped up properly," his mum said, picking up a butter knife.

"Turn it off at the wall first!" Dylan yelled, making her drop the knife with a clatter. She leaned against the side.

"Don't shout like that! You gave me a heart attack! The toast is only stuck."

"Just ... safety. Like they teach at school."

She gave him the look of suspicious scrutiny he'd got used to over the years, but flicked the switch at the plug. He flopped into his seat at the table, legs weak. The doorbell rang next door. His throat was dry. Mum retrieved the knife and slid it into the groove. A car blared its horn as it sped down the road. Toast being loosened. Slices of bread and marge would have been fine. He felt his phone buzzing in his pocket. Didn't dare touch it. Tried to stare at the scratches in the tabletop, from years of forks, knives, sharp edges. The lights flickered. The TV came on in the living room, gameshow laughter blaring out. The knife was still in the slot when the plug sparked, transferred the voltage to the toaster. A scream cut off, the smell of burning flesh; the TV laughter getting louder as she fried from within; the phone insistent; all the doorbells in the street ringing now; a whump as she burst into flames; a screech of tyres, terrible impact of tearing metal and shattering glass; screams; the ground shaking from an explosion outside.

It was here.

REGRESSION

It was a normal wet morning when I collected the innocuous mixture of junk mail and brown envelopes from the hall; by the time I'd finished the letter the overcast sky seemed to have sucked the heat out of the world. I laid the single sheet by my uneaten bowl of cereal and watched a starved-looking cat stalk across my back garden. Rain on the window distorted things, turning the double-glazing into bathroom glass: the cat bulged out of view in a smear of grey.

I hadn't seen my mother for years.

Our *relationship* was postal. A card at Christmas and one on my birthday; I responded likewise. That isn't loving communication, it's weak obligation.

The spidery and uncertain writing on the envelope told me who had sent it before I hesitantly read the contents. It wasn't my birthday and it wasn't Christmas.

Dear Colin,
I'm scared. Arthur is gone and I don't feel I have

much time left. I want to see you. It's all wrong.
Please come home. I need you.
Mother

I read it twice: first time with growing unease; second time
with anger. Which obsession held her this time? Illness? Depres-
sion? Bizarre fantasies? It broke the well-established pattern of
minimal demand. A stable arrangement where I was only forced
to remember my childhood twice a year.

My pristine, sparsely but stylishly furnished home seemed cold
and echoing.

I went to work hungry.

My mother has always been *strange*. She had gone through various husbands and boyfriends, and become more bitter with
each disappointment. She believed in nebulous dark forces, and
when I was a child she tried to make me believe in them too.
With some success. I remember many sleepless nights after she'd
told me about evil things: rape by spirits, souls going to hell, use
of supernatural forces to murder someone, possession. I would
peer wide-eyed at the strange shapes in the near-darkness, teddy
providing no comfort, listening for creaks and promising to be
good if I lived to see the sunrise.

Occasionally when she was between boyfriends she allowed
me to share her bed, but I felt no safer then. She had used me
as a confidante because no-one else would listen.

I reread the letter throughout the day, and kept having images of my mother going mad, dying, afraid – and alone. Amazing how guilt is the traitor to common sense. Although I now realised that the things she had told me about as a child weren't real, to *her* they existed, even if self-constructed. Hers was a life of fear of the dark, only eased when someone was in the bed beside her.

These thoughts kept me from being my usual confident self. The corridors of my workplace seemed shadowy; pools of darkness crouched below the staircase and in the corner by the photocopiers. I found myself snapping at colleagues, and developed a nagging ache behind my eyes. People avoided me at break time.

By the end of the day I knew I'd visit her, and packed for the next morning. I never rang first; she didn't have a phone. She believed that things could travel down phone lines. Another of her charming idiosyncrasies.

The house had always been run-down. Staring up at the dead-eyed windows now, it had clearly not improved with age.

The garden was overgrown with every kind of weed. The apple tree was choked with ivy. Water-filled holes pocked the path to the front door, and one of the window panes was covered by rain-swollen hardboard. I felt a pang of guilt again – or embarrassment, if I'm honest – that I let Mother live like this.

Mother didn't bother with maintenance. Her boyfriends generally didn't either. Arthur had been no different: a slob looking for an easy time. Not that anyone got an easy time with her. They all left in the end. I wondered where Arthur had gone, what kind of hole people like him crawled into.

I wasn't surprised to find that the bell didn't work, so I knocked, hard, loosening flaking paint which floated down like house dandruff. Eventually, shuffling footsteps approached.

She looked older. Haggard, wrinkled; her long, straight hair interspersed with grey; all her fifty-plus years and then some. She was in a dressing gown and slippers. It was only 3pm.

For a few seconds she stood there staring at nothing, then blinked and seemed to focus on me at last. A smile crept across her lips. We embraced. I hid my instinctive flinch. It was like being hugged by a rusting leg-hold trap made of bones and skin that could go off at any moment.

"I got your letter."

"Arthur didn't like me any more. Didn't like the house. I made him ... go."

"Maybe it's for the best." I struggled to find anything else to say. "Let's have a cup of tea."

There was an off-smell to the kitchen, as if something had fallen behind the fridge and decayed. I hoped the pong wasn't sticking to my clothes. Mother put a cup of tea in front of me, sloshing it into the chipped saucer as her hand trembled.

"How are you doing?" I asked.

"I wanted to see you again. For you to be with me." Her voice had the cracked tone of one that was seldom used.

"And here I am."

But she shook her head. "You don't understand. I won't meet anyone else and I don't want to be alone. I need someone to stay with me."

"Mother ... You know I can't do that. I've got a job and a career. I'm just here to visit."

"Please." Watery eyes regarded me, and she slid her hand across the table but it stopped short of touching mine. "I never see you any more, never see my little boy ..."

"What about moving? I could help with that. Somewhere nearer."

"I can't leave this house. It's all I've got. It contains all my memories. Every piece of it, even the attic and the cellar."

"What about a break then, a holiday? That would do you good."

"I don't want to go anywhere."

"I would pay for you to go."

"With you?"

"Well ..."

"I see how it is." She looked away from me.

I couldn't resist a sigh. You leave home, grow up; you return home, and the old passive-aggressive games begin again. "Have you been sleeping?"

"So so," she said dismissively, though it was obvious from the puffy bags under her eyes that she wasn't.

"Do you need anything?"

"Only you." She drank her tea.

"No, I mean like do you need any shopping? I can go and get you some."

"I don't need anything."

The cupboard she'd got the sugar from was open and kept drawing my gaze: the door dangled on one hinge and there was scarcely anything inside. The fridge had been equally bare.

"Why don't you come shopping with me? Let me treat you. It'll make you feel better, you can get whatever you want. We'll get some nice food in –"

"I don't need no fucking nice food!"

I looked away first, then she sighed.

"There's enough for tonight."

"Okay." I could work on her again tomorrow.

There was a long pause as we stared at our cups, with only the ticking clock making an effort; then she said, "Be careful tonight."

"Why?"

"It's starting again. There's something coming."

My skin prickled, despite the years of thinking I'd outgrown superstitious nonsense. Instincts love to kick pride in the teeth.

"What do you mean?" I asked, feigning ignorance.

"The thing from your childhood. It's come back."

Sometimes things had happened when I was a child. Objects occasionally fell off shelves; we'd hear strange creaks in the night; the rooms would go cold; but everything could be *explained*. When I left home I got much better at *explaining* things. Of course, Mother had said it was a presence; something that came to watch us and if we weren't careful it would hurt us. It had begun around the time my father died.

She also used to say it had raped her. Jesus Christ. I was ten years old and I was terrified of being raped by a demon – how twisted was that?

"There's nothing here ... but if there was, that would be a reason to leave the house. If you moved it wouldn't find you, would it?"

"It would find me anywhere, in the end. It comes in the night. I'm scared."

I make a living from persuasive words, but had run out of them. She was cracking up, a fear I'd always had. A few times as a child she'd been drunk, violent, ranting about this stuff. She'd attacked her second husband with a bread knife once. He'd taken it off her, hit her to the ground, and said, "When you finally go mad you'll take everyone around you, but I won't be one of them, you bitch."

He had gone, too.

"I'll take my bag up. If it's okay, that is."

"Of course. This is your home. Always was. Always will be."

The inside of the house was as run-down as the outside; the stairs creaked, the carpet was threadbare. I ran my left hand up the banister and was surprised to feel a sharp prick. A splinter had lodged itself in my thumb. I walked up the rest of the way sucking at the soreness.

My room was like a smaller, more faded version of my memories. Bed still in the middle of the room; beyond was an open fireplace and large black bookcase. One dirty window with rusty bars on the outside. I brushed aside the lace that hung like broken web and looked down at the overgrown back garden which contained a swing with a broken chain, and a small sun house I rarely went in when I was a child because it was full of spiders. At some point its roof had collapsed. The lawn had overgrown the path and was rank with dead vegetation.

In a corner was a door to a small walk-in storage wardrobe. As a child I'd hidden in it when I wanted to be alone or when I was frightened, huddled at the back underneath the coats. Father had even put a small bolt on the inside for me, in addition to the one outside; more symbolic than practical, but my mind turned the space into a fortress then. Raise the drawbridge, slide the bolt; boil the oil and man the turrets, nothing could get me there. On instinct I slid the door open and peeked in. It was dark and musty. The old coats were still hung up. Sad relics with nowhere to go.

There had been some changes. Mother obviously used the room to store junk: broken ornaments, dented brassware, warped paperbacks, overflowing carrier bags, cardboard boxes in leaning piles. Detritus gathers in abandoned corners.

The bed squeaked when I sat on it. Old frame, metal springs. I used the nail scissors from my travelling case to pick out the splinter. Then I put my face in my hands.

This room. This house. This life. It all reeked of the past.

We ate. Beans on dry toast. Hardly the cuisine I normally dined out on. When she cleared away I donated my glass of water to a spider plant which resembled a wig more than a shrub as its dead brown tendrils straggled down off the shelf. For the rest of the evening, as the parlour's shadows grew, conversation only existed in staccato bursts. As did the lights, which seemed unreliable and flickered often. She said the electrics were always like that when it rained. Not to worry.

Mother made weak cocoa. She sat smiling at me while we drank it, neither of us talking much. Then she touched my hand.

"Let's go to bed."

She told me she slept downstairs in the front room now; it was easier for her than going up and down stairs all the time.

"Okay. You sleep tight, Mother." I kissed her, and was about to ascend when I remembered the fuse box in the cellar. Maybe that was faulty and explained the flickering lights. There was little enough else I could do for her.

I opened the cellar door. Stone slabs descended into a cavernous pitch-black hole. A smell rose from it, similar to that in the kitchen. I was still gazing down when she came into the hall and saw me.

"What are you doing?"

I explained.

"No, they're fine. New fuses. Just go to bed."

I was relieved to close the door on that damp darkness.

I brushed my teeth in the bathroom, went to bed and put the light off straightaway. Despite the many thoughts and worries bubbling in my brain, the day had left me exhausted.

Tick, tock, tick, tock (creak). Tick, tock, tick, (creak) tock.

I woke with a jerk, disorientated and feeling that something was wrong. I glanced around to see if there was someone else in the room. The pale light coming through the window was just enough to see that I was alone. The dark shapes around the room were ominous but inanimate.

Maybe I'd heard something in my sleep, but there was no noise now, apart from the damned clock. There was one in every room of the house, all showing different times, and I'd been dreaming about it ticking away, a wagging finger forbidding something to an errant child. I lay down again and pulled the covers up to my chin, frightened for no clear reason. The strangely-heavy drowsiness came over me again.

This time I was woken up by a cry. It lingered in my mind as I jerked into a sitting position. The room seemed darker than before, my heart was pounding, body shivering with cold. I strained to listen, when I heard a scratch-voiced cry from downstairs:

"Colin, it's here, lock ... your ... door."

Mother's tone changed in those last few words, became something more cracked and splintered, like the house. I knew what a good man would do: get up, go down the stairs, and see what was wrong; whether there was a burglar or if his mother was hurt or if she was simply frightened and dreaming.

Instead I slammed the door's bolt, jumped back into bed, and listened. A creak on the stairs: it sounded halfway up, but it seemed strange that the lower stairs hadn't creaked, unless ... unless whoever made the noise was *sneaking* up, and had only accidentally triggered a stair at that point, which meant they were very, very stealthy. The dark stifled me, too uncertain, too big, so I put the lamp on. Yellow and sickly-weak. I realised with a gut-twist that the door I'd bolted was the door to the walk-in wardrobe, which was where the bedroom door would be in my house. The door to the bedroom was still unlocked and could open easily ...

My body was rigid, didn't want to move, expecting the door to fly open if I approached, and for *something* to be there. The thing from my childhood. My oldest fear.

I would die if I saw it, Mother had told me.

I had to get out of bed, repeated the "losers stand still" mantra I gave the new recruits to my division, I couldn't be a hypocrite ... Left the warmth of the blankets and slammed the bolt home on the second attempt just as I heard another creak at the top of the stairs. I retreated to my bed, hugged my knees, and stared at the door. I hadn't been like this since I was a boy. Had never thought I would be again, but the boy was swallowing the rational adult, swamping it with a child's disproportionate primordial fears of death and eternal pain.

The door handle turned slowly.

"Go away," I whispered, throat tightening.

The handle stopped. I waited for it to move again, but it didn't. Instead I heard a creak on the stairs. Then another. Going down, thank God.

I realised my face was wet. Wiped the tears on my pyjama sleeves, and sniffed. It was over. I was me again.

It was the *place*. It twisted things. Sucked me back to another time, one lost with good reason, half forgotten. Blocked, probably. Many things I couldn't remember, and suspected I never should.

I wouldn't be able to go back to sleep. Perhaps I'd find a decent book to read amongst all this stuff. I began to open musty cardboard boxes. The tops had been folded over, not taped. They were filthy with dust and webs, and I sneezed a few times. Just like the hay fever I used to have at school. Then I smiled at the contents of the first container.

Christmas decorations. Tinsel, banners, tree ornaments. Old and dulled in reality, but bright and shining and glorious in the mind's eye, that weird brain trick of seeing things as they once had been. Mother had told me fairies made the glittering objects. I had believed her.

A box of my schoolbooks from infant and junior schools; pictures I had drawn for Mother, cards I had made for her. Childlike scrawls, wild imaginings. The teacher had stamped one with a cartoon monster whose speech bubble said "Very Good!", and written underneath: "My, my, what an imagination!" Memories of a boy who barely existed any more. I thought he'd escaped.

A carton of stuff belonging to Mother's ex-boyfriends now. Clothes, pictures, aftershave (it had leaked, the stuff stank of sickening sweetness). I wasn't interested. I was about to give up on this one when I noticed something metallic. I pulled it out. A pistol crossbow. Father's. He had used it to shoot rabbits and birds. Had taken me with him as a child, even though I hated to see things die. But because it was one of the few things we did together, I went. At first light we would be wrapped up and walking through the greyness in the fields, our breath misting before us.

I had never held it before, so the smooth wooden handle felt strange. Only my father was allowed to use the weapon. "Just for me, Colin," he had replied to my pleas. "Maybe when you're a man." I had never questioned why Father had used a crossbow instead of a gun, any more than why we had to kill rabbits and birds when we only ate the rabbits.

I sorted through the box. Deeper down was a container of quarrels. I cocked the bow, as I'd seen him do a hundred times. The cable didn't snap. It had kept its strength for all these years. Just like the memories; though, unlike them, the crossbow made me feel safe. Then I removed a quarrel and slotted it into the bow's barrel, sighted down to the end. Only a trigger away from exploding. I rested it on the bed.

Something else in the box got my attention, dislodged as I'd taken out the ammunition. A folder. Father's handwriting. Inside were paper-clipped notes. They looked like the work files he brought home sometimes. I'd never fully understood what he did. I think he was a psychologist, but his interests at home seemed to be research and hypnosis. He used to hypnotise me, saying it was to give me "empowering thoughts". I couldn't remember the sessions afterwards. He told me that was rare, and it seemed to please him; it made me proud.

This file didn't have the official stamp on. I flicked through the sheets. It was all about Mother.

Unlike the work files I sometimes saw him with, which were typed, these were hand-written and almost indecipherable: whether by accident or cryptic design it was impossible to tell now. Knowing Father, it was more likely to be the latter. A forceful and secretive mind you could never see into, even though he could see into yours.

The brittle paper scrawls were mostly a mystery. Seemed to be about some sessions he'd done with Mother. I flicked through, spotted occasional scratches that might have been words I could comprehend: "childhood", "blocked memories", "the id", "unfinished", "below the surface", "discipline". But it was mostly guesswork. And I felt like a dirty sneak looking through a dead man's papers that penetrated into Mother's mind. I knew he'd have frowned on it, been disappointed in me, cut me out and ignored me for a time with chilling indifference that could almost make me feel I didn't exist.

Things get built up; the wind blows; they collapse. Nothing precarious can last, and life very much fitted that category.

I closed the file. Couldn't face any more memories for now. Things would have to sink in slowly. Instead I needed to read fiction, to lose myself in someone else's imagination.

I walked to the bookcase and recognised many of the books. There were a few on occult matters, which had scared me when I looked at the pictures as a kid. I remembered a scratchy black and white photograph sequence showing a person in a straitjacket. "Ectoplasm" came out of their mouth in the second picture, looking like white vomit. In the third it seemed to pull off the straitjacket. Another book had pictures of burnt, detached human legs in the section on spontaneous combustion. I didn't want to see them again.

On the shelf below were my own books. Enid Blytons, Roald Dahls, picture books, animal tales. I was about to take one when I heard another noise from downstairs – faint but real. A gurgling. Then a voice.

"Colin, help! I've fallen and hurt my leg. I can't move." Mother sounded frail, in pain, her voice cracked and lonely. Scared as I was, I couldn't ignore the plea. I at least had to look.

"Colin, I'm really hurting."

I edged past boxes and bags. It was all quiet now. I tugged the bolt back and grasped the handle tightly. Counted to three then opened the door.

The stairs and landing were dark, but by the pale light spilling from my room I saw Mother. She was near the top of the stairs, moving stealthily, quickly, leaning against the wall, looking spiderish and famished, her shadow distorted because of the hatchet in her hand. She saw me and grinned.

"My lovely boy," she cooed in a dead voice, moving quicker even as she spoke.

I slammed the door and fiddled with the bolt. It closed just as the handle turned. I stepped back, bumped into the bed. Felt around and found the crossbow, pointed it at the door, my small hands shaking.

"Open the door, Colin," she crooned.

"No, Mummy."

"It's time to –"

I fired at the middle of the door before she could finish.

The bolt flew through the wood with a *thock* and then all was silent, apart from the clock ticking. I held my breath and listened for a tell-tale thump, a groan, a –

"Naughty boy, trying to kill Mummy."

The door rattled at the first blow. The small bolt would only take a few of those. I dropped the crossbow.

The second blow boomed against the wood. I ran to the walk-in wardrobe, closed the door, and reached up for the inner bolt. It was nearly out of my sweaty grasp now, as I continued to shrink. I could hardly see it through the tears.

"No, Mummy, don't be bad!" cried the little boy, as he huddled at the back of the wardrobe below the coats and clothes, hoping the thing that wanted to eat him and give him eternal pain would go away.

"I'm coming, Colin," it said as it burst into the bedroom with a crash, and padded over to the wardrobe.

SECOND TRANSCRIPT

POLICE: This interview is being recorded. I'm DC Johns. Please state your full name.***

MR DONOVAN: Cormac Alfred Donovan.

POLICE: And can you confirm your date of birth?

MR DONOVAN: 14th April, 1949. Been round a long time and never broke the law.

POLICE: The time by my watch is 1.42AM. We're glad you've agreed to cooperate, Mr Donovan.

MR DONOVAN: [Inaudible.] Anyway, I
didn't think I had much choice. You've
kept me waiting long enough.

**POLICE: Can you repeat your version of
events?**

MR DONOVAN: If it means I can get out
of here sooner, then yes.

**POLICE: Firstly, do you know Nathan
Taylor? And please speak up for the
microphone.**

MR DONOVAN: THAT LOUD ENOUGH? [Laugh-
ter.] Taylor? Never heard of him.

**POLICE: You're sure? It's not someone
you've met, or talked to, or -**

MR DONOVAN: I bloody said no, okay?

**POLICE: Okay. Just tell us what happened
and how you came to be at Partridge
Avenue.**

MR DONOVAN: Certainly wasn't to find a
pear tree. Get it?

POLICE: No.

MR DONOVAN: Never mind. I was having trouble sleeping.

POLICE: Sleeping?

MR DONOVAN: Parrot, not a partridge … Yes. Sleeping. Because of the hole. It first appeared … mmm, musta been a few weeks ago. Back when they did a Scottish barn conversion on the house programme. You know the one? Never mind. Big windows. I like the way they kept the original features. All that wood.

[Inaudible.]

MR DONOVAN: No, that was on the pro-gramme. The hole was in my bedroom. Yel-lowed at the edges, black in the middle. Like a big cigarette burn up in the corner by the ceiling. Would've given Helen fits if she were still alive. But I would'na noticed it except for the hissing. Had no idea what it was at first, but then I tracked the sound to that damn hole, and my first thought was *gas*. But there were no pipes near there, and it didn't smell.

I got on a chair and lit a match but nowt happened - so not gas.

POLICE: Do you always take risks like that?

MR DONOVAN: When you're as old as me getting up on a chair is as bad a risk as anything else. Anyway, it still sounded like gas, or wind being blown down a long, narrow pipe. You couldn't see into it. I got a torch and that didn't help. It was like the hole swallowed the light. I shoved a screwdriver in, up to the handle; and I swear the screwdriver vibrated, like something below the wallpaper was tugging it. I couldn't bring myself to stick my finger in. I reported it to the council but they didn't send anyone round. And that was it for a while. I got on with reading the papers and gardening and watching television and trying to have a shit each day, all that's bloody left to me, but at night I could hear the hissing and it kept me awake. More'n usual, anyways. Sometimes there was a crackling noise. Like … toffee wrappers being crinkled. Or television interference. Gave me the willies. I ended up leaving the light on. And staring at it, like I was expecting something to happen. That's when I started going for walks at night again. I hadn't done it since Helen passed on, bless her. Back then I'd walk the streets at all hours until I was tired enough to sleep. I dare say you're lucky and not had to face an empty bed after more'n fifty years of sharing it with the same person. But bed's where I felt it most - cold space beside me that used to be a warm, bed-farting woman I loved. That coldness stopped me sleeping. So it always felt better being outside, muffled up against the chill. It was pretty peaceful. You -

POLICE: Please can I clarify, are you talking about walking after your wife died, or recently?

MR DONOVAN: Both. Recently is still after she died. But I mean in the last few weeks. I like the peace walking at night. It's not quiet - you can always hear cars on the motorway, though you get used to that; sometimes you hear music or television or arguing coming from houses you walk past, or the dog at number fifteen would yap its bloody head off from behind the fancy-pants wrought iron gate until the nervous biddy there opened the back door to see why it was barking. Or you'd pass pissheads if it wasn't too late.

POLICE: What times do you go walking?

MR DONOVAN: Varies, dunnit? Sometimes eleven, sometimes twelve. Other times I've gone for a walk at silly bugger times like three in the morning. Even quieter then.

POLICE: So you were near Partridge Avenue because you couldn't sleep?

MR DONOVAN: Not just 'cause of that. It was the dreams. It got so that when I did sleep I had these horrible nightmares. Maybe it was the whispering affecting them.

POLICE: Whispering?

MR DONOVAN: From the hole. It sounded different at night, in the dark. More like whispers then, but you couldn't make out the words. I say "from the hole", but also like it's in your head. I can't explain it. I think the hissing words got into the dreams somehow, maybe like suggestions and ideas, or you pick up on a mood; or only understand it when you let your guard down. Anyway, these weird dreams – just remembering them gives me goosebumps – they were in these horrendous shadowy caves, where the rock was weeping and forming crusty scabs, and it always felt like you were being watched by something – or lots of things – just out of sight, in the darkness of the tunnels. I would wake up sweating and have to go and make a brew to calm down. And now and again in the nightmares I'd see places. Or be shown them, maybe. Houses. Not scary, but at first it was always the same one, then I started to see others. Like cameras into people's homes. More all the time, like … something spreading.

POLICE: You saw the insides of houses? The layout?

MR DONOVAN: It wasn't that simple. More like an *impression* of a house, as if I was seeing through someone else's eyes and they didn't quite understand what they were looking at.

POLICE: That makes no sense.

MR DONOVAN: I know. Not at first. But then I thought - maybe there's holes elsewhere, and I was seeing out of them in my sleep? Like a network of spy holes. Crazy, but it's the only thing that made sense of it. And that's why I went to Partridge Avenue. I'd seen that house in my sleep the night before, and recognised it.

POLICE: You knew the interior layout of that house?

MR DONOVAN: No. But the view moved occasionally, not just from one spot high up. Sort of snaked around in the dark. Saw people sometimes, asleep in their beds. And it looked out of the windows. I couldn't control what I saw, was just along for the ride, like hearing a message on the radio when there's lots of interference. But I recognised a big old statue in their garden, seen it when

– whatever. I knew the house then. So went there on my walk the next night.

POLICE: Why wait until then? Why not go during the day?

MR DONOVAN: Why would I? It was only a dream where I saw a house I recognised. I might've dreamt it for any reason. Hardly going to ring you lot about it, was I? But I remembered it when I was out walking, so headed that way. I went down the avenue and spotted the house I'd dreamed about. I wanted to rest a minute so sat on the wall opposite. It was obvious there was a party, and I felt a bit lonely hearing the music – shite as it was – and imagining what was going on inside. So I stayed there, even though I was getting cold and stiff and worrying about my piles. A few kids left, but didn't see me between the street lights. Eventually, the houselights went out and there were some noises, like screams of laughter when teens are messing around. I assumed it was a sleepover party. After a while I walked home and went to bed.

POLICE: So that was it? The lights went out and you didn't see anything else?

MR DONOVAN: The windows were pitch black. I didn't think anything of it at the time, but now - black like they sucked light. Like the hole in my wall.

POLICE: And what did you do after that?

MR DONOVAN: Had a bloody good dump once I'd warmed up.

POLICE: After *that*.

MR DONOVAN: Nothing at first. I mean, I'd seen *nothing*. But I did feel uneasy. I couldn't put my finger on why. And even though I told myself I was just a stupid old man with too much imagination, I couldn't get it out of my head. So I thought I'd sort it out in my mind once and for all. That I'd go and knock and check if everyone was okay, and that would be the end of it. That's why I went back earlier tonight. I might have appeared senile and lonely, but at least it would set my mind at rest. Try and shake off the feeling that something was going horribly wrong and this was only the start … the feeling that something was spreading and maybe watching us wasn't enough of a kick for it any more. You can tell I've thought about it.

POLICE: Why did you go round the back of the house?

MR DONOVAN: To look. All that blue-and-white police tape told me something really *had* gone wrong.

POLICE: You could have come to us. It would have looked better than being apprehended at a crime scene. We'd had recent reports of someone matching your description standing outside houses.

MR DONOVAN: Nosy neighbourhood watchers, eh? I only go for walks, I *told* you. That's the thing though, and shows I wasn't involved. I didn't know anything horrible had happened when I went there. I hadn't seen the news you showed, hadn't even been to the shops for days. I would've come forward if I'd have read about the kids disappearing or dying.

POLICE: You understand how suspicious this looks?

MR DONOVAN: If I was some bad man - which is a daft idea for starters when you know what arthritis-numbing pills I have to take just to get going in the morning - I wouldn't have gone back, would I?

POLICE: It isn't unknown for a criminal to return to a crime scene.

MR DONOVAN: I'm not a bloody criminal! I've done nowt. You can't keep me in just because I had a dream and walk round at night when I can't sleep. And it's easy enough to prove I'm telling the truth. Go and check my house. Look at the hole.

POLICE: We've been there already Mr Donovan. This is a serious case and children are missing. We received a search warrant under Section 8 of the Police and Criminal Evidence Act and have an officer on-site now.

MR DONOVAN: I hope you didn't kick my bloody door down.

POLICE: We had your keys.

MR DONOVAN: Oh. Well, you've seen it then?

POLICE: We've looked round your house, and there was no sign of any strange hole in your wall.

MR DONOVAN: Did you check in the bedroom? That's where the hole was, up in the corner. How could you miss it? If you stand on a chair you can hear hissing coming from it, like voices. I'm not imagining it!

POLICE: We did check there, since you were so insistent when we first brought you in. I repeat that there was no sign of any hole. Only a minor stain on the wallpaper. Believe me, if there had been anything suspicious in your house, we would have found it. Our team are very thorough.

MR DONOVAN: It must've closed when you were round. See, that proves there's something going on! Something … crafty. Intelligent.

POLICE: It proves nothing of the kind.

MR DONOVAN: You don't believe me, I can tell by your squinty eyes. I've been around a long time, son, I can read people.

POLICE: On the search earlier we did find these two bottles though. For the record - two unlabelled brown glass medicine bottles. Have you seen them before, Mr Donovan?

MR DONOVAN: Yes. Painkillers. Off the doctor.

POLICE: They have no labels.

MR DONOVAN: Peeled off.

POLICE: These were not from a doctor or chemist. Unless you cooperate, you're not leaving this place.

MR DONOVAN: I told you -

POLICE: We'll be testing the contents. We can speak to your doctor. You're now moving into obstruction territory.

MR DONOVAN: [Sigh.] Not prescription, no. The ones from the pharmacy are too weak.

POLICE: So what are they, and where did you get them?

MR DONOVAN: Don't know to the first bit; and buy them off someone local. Don't know his name. Not illegal.

POLICE: Someone local. Really. You have a chemistry background, don't you, Cormac? And a *history* in that area?

MR DONOVAN: How did you …?

POLICE: Where's the key to your cellar?

MR DONOVAN: Why?

POLICE: It's the only room we haven't been able to check yet.

MR DONOVAN: There's nothing down there.

POLICE: Then there's no reason to obstruct us.

MR DONOVAN: Lost the key a while back.

POLICE: We'll know soon enough. Please excuse me for a moment. I need to pause the interview and leave the room. Officer Ryland will stay with you.

MR DONOVAN: You're wasting time, don't you see? This isn't important! But you should believe me. There's *something happening*. And this is just the start, you bloody idiots.

POLICE: Note for record, pausing now.

[Tape paused.]

POLICE: Okay, this is the continuation of the interview with Mr Cormac Alfred Donovan. An impressive little laboratory down there, huh?

MR DONOVAN: What?

POLICE: Dark-room bulbs, glassware, dry-ing tubes, thinners, filters, and stuff the team on site don't even recognise yet. Quite the clandestine chemist.

MR DONOVAN: First I've heard! Thirty years of dusty junk, that's why I didn't care when I couldn't find –

POLICE: What were you synthesizing? Acid?

MR DONOVAN: I haven't been down there for weeks! Not since the hole appeared …

POLICE: Right. Maybe you did it in your sleep. We've heard that one before.

MR DONOVAN: Sleep … hold on … like sleepwalking? I did … no, it was a dream. There was this black stuff bubbling from the hole, all sticky and wet like tar, and I collected it, scraped it into a pot, knew it was important, I had to make something …

POLICE: So you weren't manufacturing or distributing drugs, you were really using ghosts' shit as play dough? Give

it up. Unless you start coming up with
the fucking truth you're going to be
wearing a straitjacket. We'll analyse.
We'll uncover. We'll pin. Somehow you're
connected to all this, and we'll get to
the bottom of it.

MR DONOVAN: I'm not saying any more
without a solicitor.

POLICE: Okay then, I've asked all I want
for now so we can end the - sit down!
Officer, don't let him -

[Sounds of a scuffle.]

[Tape ends.]

November 12th: Custody Sergeant note. Mr
Donovan was found dead in the police cell where
he was being detained. Suspected asphyxiation
but evidence of multiple contusions. Post-mortem
examination to follow. Additional: strange ciga-
rette-like burns on the mattress, evenly spaced,
13mm diameter. CCTV camera failure, no recording.

November 17th: Pathology report redacted.
Security Service class Top Secret; DV clearance
only.

LIVING IN THE PRESENT

"Brightly shone the moon that night,
  Tho' the frost was cru-el,
  When a poor man came in sight,
  Gath'ring winter fu-oo-el."

The girl sang, arranging tinsel round the huge tree in glittering spirals. The boy hung shiny baubles on the ends of branches, and when his sister finished he immediately started a new song.

"God rest you merry, gentlemen,
  Let nothing you dismay,
  For we will fill our bellies
  Upon this lovely day."

Ronnie glanced at the kids. Something was off. Maybe just that neither of them could hold a tune. But they were happy, faces glowing, intent on putting the final touches to their decoration. He leaned forward in the chair, warmed his fingers in front of the blaze – a real fire! – and the finger-stinging cold melted away. Bliss.

"So, Mr Ronnie, have you been without a home for very long?"

The woman was smiling at him, head tilted slightly. The kids' mother. A single parent, he assumed. He couldn't tell if she was attractive or not – she wore way too much make-up – but the skinny arms and legs poking out of the old-fashioned dress were enough to put him off.

Then again, beggars can't be choosers. If that was why she'd invited him in – a bit of rough for a Christmas fuck – then he wouldn't begrudge her.

"Please, just Ronnie. Or Ron. Been homeless two years now."

"That *is* a long time," she said, with a hint of something he didn't recognise in her accent. It sounded patronising, but perhaps she was just from far away. "May I ask what happened?"

"It's no big secret. I used to repair appliances for people, from the back of someone else's shop. White goods, electrics, anything really. But it just dried up. People don't re-use things any more, just bin them. Manufacturers charge more for parts than buying new."

"Oh, how terrible! We always use things up fully, don't we children?"

"Yes, Mama!" they both said, before going back to their singing. Yeah, had to be foreign. German, Austrian, or something like that. There was a definite whiff of the von Trapps about the three of them.

"Well, good on you. Anyway, suddenly no money, no pride. I got depressed. Girlfriend couldn't cope. Booted me out. Double kicker, since it was Christmas then too. But I've been doing bits and bobs in the last few months. Hope it will lead to proper work. So you could say I've done full circle and back."

"How *wonderful*, Ronnie. One really shouldn't live in the *past*." She stared right at him, no blinking. Too direct to be anything other than sexual. He should be pleased at the thought of a bath, a warm pair of thighs, and a bed for the night, but there really was something a bit ... what? *Repulsive* about her. Yeah, that was the word. Maybe the way the dress didn't fit her right, and her chest was a bit flat for it?

He flinched when the kids broke out into another energetic chorus right behind him.

"O cooooome all ye faithful, hungry and triumphaaaaaaaant!"

He sipped at the glass of brandy to calm his jumpiness. A proper curved glass, so he could swirl the caramel-coloured liquid, hypnotic eddies of luxury. How quickly life turns around. Only an hour ago he felt like his fingernails were being wrenched off with the cold. He'd been hunched in the doorway of a closed offie, blanket wrapped round, while snow fell from the black sky above. Rest was the best you could do when it was that cold – sleep was impossible. The crowds of noisy ignorers had faded away to other streets, giving him some peace; then he'd heard the kids' voices, an echo ahead of them, drifting ghostly with the cutting wind. "We three beings of Orient are; Bearing gifts we traverse afar – Following yonder star!" It should have been a nice sound, but even then it made him want to cover his ears. And they appeared, with their "Mama", all holding hands, practically skipping down the hard pavement. But *they* hadn't ignored him. She'd spoken to him, shown pity, and invited him back for a meal. A brave thing to do nowadays. And here he was in this

Dickensian room, softly lit by fairy lights and fire, slightly dazed, his nose tingling at the unexpected arrival in a warm place.

"Come and HOLD him, soon booo000rn the child of Angels."

Ronnie sniffed. His nose kept running without warning. Maybe he was getting *too* hot, something he wouldn't have thought possible earlier that day. He tried to push the armchair back, but it was heavy, old-fashioned, enclosed him. He downed a mouthful of the gorgeous brandy instead. Watched the kids rearranging the neatly-wrapped presents, all bows and sparkle.

"O star of wondeeer, star of night, guide us tooooo thy perfect bite."

Did they say "bite"? That made no sense.

"Please, keep talking, Ronnie. What is it *like* to have no place of belonging?" She leaned forward, seemed so eager, smiling that polite smile of hers, the red lipstick splitting to show badly-kept teeth.

"It's tricky ... having no friends ..."

"Family, Ronnie?"

He suddenly felt like crying.

"The staaars in the bright sky looked down where he lay, The Lord's LIttlE offering aaaAasleep in the haay."

"No family, no money ... As for food, being safe ..."

"Go on, please."

He took another sip. Definitely feeling woozy. "Well ... those are short to come by."

She nodded, seemed so serious, so concerned. "Ooh, yes."

"I had issues in the past, but I'm trying to overcome them."

"The CAttle are slooooowing, Father Christmas awakes, but good little bABy, noooo cRryiNg he Makes."

"Do you mind if I go toilet? I feel a little funny."

"Of *course*, you can, Ronnie! Just finish your drink first, like a good little boy."

Ronnie downed it. Anything to get out of the heat that burned him up. But he couldn't stand, as if his limbs were heavy with sleep.

"Mama, I got tummy thunder!" said the wide-mouthed boy. "Rumble rumble!"

"It probably is time to get a wriggle on, isn't it dears?" The woman stood and poured water onto the fire. At once the heat was gone, only leaving what was inside Ronny. Ashy, hissing liquid ran out over the grate, touched his feet, soaked into the carpet. In this dimmer light it looked old and threadbare ... in fact, the whole room suddenly looked shabbier.

"Siilent niGht, hoOOoly night ... Little INfant, so tENdrrr and miild ... Sleeep Nn heAvenly peacEs!"

The kids were singing louder as they unwrapped a present, some kind of cable on a spool. Their pitch was all over the show, so wrong; it was *all wrong*. Something to do with their mouths.

"Let's lie you down now," said Mama, easing him to the floor. Drug-addict scrawny, but immensely strong, it was as if he weighed nothing. He lay on his side, unable to move, face in a pool of grey water, still warm. The fireplace seemed bigger than before, bigger than a house this size needed, a sucking blackness up to nothing. Everything was fuzzy, edges flick-flacking back and forth as if shadows and solidity couldn't decide which was in charge. It shouldn't be like this! "Present for Daddy! Present for Daddy!" the kids chanted as the three of them wrapped Ronnie up in barbed wire. The points punctured him whenever they yanked it tighter, pain pricks followed by drops of blood trickling down his skin, and he tried to tell them to stop, but his mouth wouldn't work, it just dribbled. The only thing he could control was his eyes, watching the laughing faces, the changing room, the chimney that shook as something heavy moved down it, slapping from side to side – *Smack! Smack!* – while clots of soot fell into the grate until the thudding bulk stretched and collapsed into the cloud of dust that mercifully obscured most of it, the only clear thing being the huge watery eyes staring at him, liquescent and sagging, while things that might be small limbs flailed out below it, gripped the floor and pulled, dragging the monstrous flesh in scraping spurts, furrowing the carpet as it panted its way nearer; rubbery papules fell off the body, wriggled towards him, twitching to reveal hooked mouths, and Ronnie closed his eyes, screamed in his mind as the first ones started to burrow into him.

The woman's voice: "Better leave Dada to lay his babies in the gift, you know how uncontrollable he is when he gets excited!"

And the singing of the children became a cacophony as they left the room.

"SileRnt nighT, hOLy night, sheeephrrds quake attaaa SIght ... All the BAbBbies Rrr bo-oooorn, A-aaall the baBbbies RRR boooRrn!"

BLEEDING SUNSET, DANCING SNOWFLAKES

Her desk faced an empty classroom. The building was eerily quiet. No screams, giggles, shouts; no music, laughter, incomprehensible conversations. All the sounds were from outside as the wind moaned and buffeted the windows. The winter light was already fading with the afternoon, sucking heat with it, and she shivered.

The other teachers had left early, not long after the kids. Couldn't wait to get away, all excited by the early finish for the end of term. Her excuse had been to mark the English assignments now, then have the whole holidays to relax. They bought it. Why else would anyone choose to stay in an emptying school?

She'd given up on the marking though, shoved that pile of crud to the edge of the desk. The task had been to write an alternative ending to *Lord of the Flies*. One boy described an evil sea creature that had been manipulating the boys on the island. By externalising the source of their violence it kind of missed

Golding's point, but it still worked better than the false happy endings that had pissed her off. She gave it an A and scribbled "Never enough sea monsters in the world" along the margin.

Another card signed, another name ticked off on her list. This was the more painful task to get out of the way. She'd thought about putting a note in each: maybe a printout, to save writing the same fucking thing thirty times over. Instead she took the sheet of printed address labels an animal charity had sent her and pressed one into the bottom corner of each card. Then put a firm black line through the second name above the address.

Sheila Markham ~~& Phil McAlea~~

Bastard.

She was startled when the door creaked opened and the care-taker stuck his head around.

"I'm off now. You'll be okay setting the alarm?"

"Of course. Just lock the door as you leave. I probably won't stay long."

He was about to retreat, but added, "It's going to get colder. More snow. You want to get home."

His footsteps echoed down the vacant hall. It *was* getting cold. The school's central heating had turned off an hour ago. No more frigid than the empty house waiting for her, though.

She leaned back and stretched. The chair was too hard. One of the reasons to teach standing. But now the whiteboard was blank. All alone with her bitterness.

The light outside was changing. Sunset coming on. She dropped the pen, let it roll, and moved to the window.

Everyone complained about winter. The cold, the ice, the greyness. They were wrong. Grey wasn't the winter colour she saw. It was this: orange. The bleeding farewell of the sun watered across the darkening sky as a backdrop to wrapped-up days (in both senses of the phrase). Not just a backdrop, but actively pouring from the sky, Irn-Bru bright, rays of fluorescence that cast long shadows on snow and grass, and the flakes that swirled down like the confetti that had been stolen from her. And not far back, pumpkin orange that makes everything unreal like a living sepia memory, a place of imagination; a shadowed cast of colour that could almost make her believe in being a child again. A time before loneliness. A time before real hurt. A time –

There were people out there.

Two of them. On the school grounds. Across the swept net-ball court already turning white again in the fresh fall. They stood uncannily still, staring at the school building, a man and a woman: and Sheila froze too. Earlier she'd had the feeling of being watched, but had seen nothing in the shadowy classroom or outside, so assumed it was the building's residue of life. Now she wondered if she'd been right all along. So much for being alone with bitterness.

It was trespass, of course. And she didn't give a shit about that. It just felt wrong somehow, the way they stood and stared. Waif-like. Hungry.

She gathered up the papers, crammed them in her bag. The rest of the cards could wait. Or go in the bin. It was all the same. None of them were really friends; or, if they were, they'd been his friends, and she'd just been along for the ride.

She switched the light out and glanced back through the window. Could see more now, without the reflections on the glass; glorious orange sunset. Fat snowflakes like white butterflies obscured some of the view. But there was no sign of the watchers. Kids? Teenagers? Whatever.

The corridor now echoed to her own footsteps, that vulnerable sound of a woman's low heels on parquet. At the staff door she set the alarm, codes fastidiously memorised and rehearsed so she'd never have to face the embarrassment of accidentally setting the alarms off and having to apologise to the police or fire brigade. Light was green, reputation clean. Fluorescents off, checked there was no-one around, then let the door auto-lock behind her. No-one would sneak in on her shift, whether it was arsonists after an easy target, computer thieves, or kids wanting to shit on the teacher's desk in revenge.

She tramped through the snow to her car, parked close to this exit, keys to hand in her coat pocket. Snow tickled her nose. It always seemed playful, teasing back and forth. It had stuck to the windscreen. She wiped a gloved hand over it, clearing a patch. Saw the ghost of a reflection, a pale face right behind her, and spun round to see the two of them only a few feet away, watching. A few seconds of intense silence as they stared at each other. She thought about the attack alarm in her bag. But they made no threatening moves.

"The snow is nice," said the woman.

"Would you like to play?" asked the man.

Their faces were expressionless. They didn't seem to be joking. And they weren't kids. It was hard to tell their ages. Their skin was unlined, but something about them suggested maturity, or experience.

"It seems a shame to waste such beauty," said the man, and Sheila gave him a proper look while taking one step backwards, nearer to her car door. His hair was layered, resting on his shoulders at the back, an off-centre parting letting floppy curls fall across dark eyebrows. There was a Gallic look to him, accentuated by the jeans and leather jacket. He had a pointed chin and nose, and when he jutted them up slightly, Sheila wasn't sure if he'd been referring to her, or the sky.

"I don't know what you mean," Sheila replied, taking another step.

"The snow!" said the woman, finally breaking her frozen stare with some animation. "We only get snow like this every few years. Why hide from it? Why shut it out? It's glorious!" The woman's hair was tied loosely; tendrils hung like shafts of black rain, framed her round face which suggested goth because of its paleness and dark eye make-up. Her smile was a jarring and unexpected flash of teeth. She raised her palms, let flakes settle on them. She wasn't wearing gloves. Or a scarf. Even a coat, Sheila realised. Just a knee-length dress, thick tights, boots. At least the sleeves were long.

The orange was losing the sky, chased out by darkness, but refusing to give in without a fight. It blazed on the horizon in ephemeral colours so beautiful they hurt to look at. Better to burn out than fade away, baby. The shadows stretched, supernaturally long but hugging the contours of the snowy ground, and every blemish on the snow created its own shadow, seeming to grow from nothing, pointing fingers as if sunlight was gripping on, refusing to let hold, struggling ferociously against whatever came next.

And while she was staring from within her own snow globe something patted her arm. Fingers, she thought; but when she looked down there was a fluffy circle of exploded snow. Neither of them seemed to have moved. Was that the faintest curl of a lip on their faces, though?

"Which one of you threw that?" Sheila asked, unable to suppress a grin at using that line.

"He did," and "She did," they said, pointing to each other with long fingers that didn't shake, despite the cold.

"Okay," said Sheila. "Why should it be the kids who have all the fun round here?"

She snatched up a handful of snow, packed it loosely, threw it underarm ... and missed. The young woman had slid to the side, was scraping up a pile; the man separated from her, lanky legs taking him to a low wall where he could easily gather snow and start bombarding. Some at Sheila (mostly hitting her until she remembered to shift her arse and keep moving), some at the young woman, who had more luck or skill and twisted out of the way each time, sending up small plumes of snow from the grass. Her snowballs thumped on Sheila's back whenever she turned it, until she learned not to leave herself so vulnerable, and faced them at all times, shifting, turning, and getting better.

Sheila didn't make good balls, unable to feel the snow properly through the material, to pack it into something dense and aerodynamic. Another snowball hit her head; not hard, but some of the exploding puff of snow went down the back of her neck, making her shriek, and the others laugh.

"The gauntlets are off," she shouted, stripping the gloves and shoving them into her pocket. When she scooped up her next snowball she was shocked at how cold it was; hands suffering an icy burn; but when she hit the young man on the leg, surprising him, she knew it was worth it.

The sun had lost. It was probably only just after four o' clock but it was dark, winter's jealousy always won. The only light was from distant street lamps shining across the school grounds, but it was enough: everything reflected back up, nothing was wasted. And their orange phosphorescence was her winter colour being reborn.

Her body warmed up from the exertion. She hadn't had a snowball fight for years, and it was easy to forget what good exercise it was. The three laughed as they played, and she couldn't understand why she'd felt vaguely threatened earlier. How could this pair have seemed ominous? They'd even brought her a present, in the form of an opportunity, practically gift-wrapped and for once it was something she didn't want to return. Her hands had gone numb though, it was hard to pack the snow. She'd pay for it later when feeling returned. Feet too.

It didn't matter how often she fell: she got up. It didn't matter when she temporarily lost sight of them: she heard their laughing voices from the shadows, and was not alone. It didn't matter how many times unexpected gusts of wind hit her in the face, threatened to topple her with its uneven power: it was better than the still air of a schoolroom or empty house. Nothing mattered except that, for now, the worsening snow was theirs. And when his Gallic cool failed, and he tripped, she gave the woman a glance and it communicated everything, the intelligent eyes looking back at her almost shining in what must be a freak reflection. They grabbed handfuls of snow, threw them over him, laughing as he struggled to get up while they shovelled ice as fast as they could, two women burying him in a white grave, throwing themselves down so he couldn't escape, smothering him in a numbing blanket until he gave up, yelled "I surrender!" and rolled onto his back in the thick drift. It was over. Sheila fell next to him, breathless. The woman lay on Sheila's other side. All smiling.

Looking up at the sky was disorienting. Like vertigo, endless blackness but with its contrast of teeny whiteness flying at you, speeding down, falling from the sky as a present. It was a proper blizzard now, white battling black. And as more feelings faded, she realised how seductive numbness could be.

"I said it would be fun," he told Sheila, his eyes playful and direct at the same time as they pierced her as much as the cold did.

Sheila tilted her head the other way to look at the woman. Could somehow see her clearly. She'd been wrong about make-up: the woman was naturally dark around the eyes. It just stood out against her paleness. Both so attractive with their white faces and wide black pupils. Slender bodies that felt no cold, were at one with it. The woman's eyes held her, gaze locked. Communicating. Better than words. Better than essays which said nothing, admonishments that were ignored. Promises which were not kept.

"Now it is time," he said from behind, moving closer to her back, as if wanting to merge.

The woman's hand stroked her face. And even though she was numb, she somehow felt those light fingertips brush her cheek, her lips.

"Time?" Sheila whispered.

"For a kiss," he said in her ear, lips nuzzling.

The woman moved in too, kissed Sheila, tongue tip probing into her mouth, cold and luscious, ice in her body, delicious shivers, somehow feeling things despite the frozen nerves; her nipples firming like ice-cube rubs; and she returned the passion, flowed and received, playful as snowflakes, while he kissed his way down to her neck, nipped her with his teeth.

There was no emptiness in her life now.

The wind moaned, and she joined it.

Heat long gone, she would never shiver again.

And the snow still fell from the endless black sky, covering everything below.

Body Found In School Grounds

A woman's body has been discovered on the grounds of Beth's Lot Secondary School, police have said.

Officers were called at around 9.15am this morning. Police said she was buried under the snow, and suspected she had been dead for some days.

A police cordon remains in place around the site.

A spokesman for the police said: "The incident is currently being treated as unexplained, and officers are now working to establish the circumstances surrounding her death."

She has not yet been formally identified, but police believe it to be 32-year-old Sheila Markham, a teacher at the school.

A dog walker discovered the body when his dog barked at an area where the snow had begun to melt. He told this paper: "I was horrified. It looked like she was smiling."

TRANSMISSION (PART 2)

.

..

...

dream

l0ng time

galaxy surges

emissi0n waves

peace unbr0ken

slumber of ae0ns

all i have is time eternal

it went 0n f0rever in beauty

whistling 0scillations breathe

0ut bey0nd in n0 heat n0 light n0thing

a v0id 0f shad0w falling away int0 an abyss

gentle waves s0metimes submerging it c0mpletely

remember l0ng time specks born burn 0ut

darker than night in its secret depths

ab0ve thy deep and dreamless sleep

spin cycles rise and fall in rhythm
hush little baby d0n't say a w0rd
n0thingness that went 0n f0rever
dark matter gathers t0 merge
s0 black as t0 seem invisible
always c0lder always 0lder
spirals twirl s0 ever-sl0w
it is 0nly m0ment t0 me
magnetic field murmur
black h0le heartbeats
pull it r0und shr0ud
shell c0c00n c0mfy
al0ne in the black
plasma vibrati0ns
aur0ra emissi0ns
and it is
g00d
.....

...

.

.

.

.

.

.

.

..

....
{**** ****}

white n0ise
hissing with static
wake me fr0m deepest me
h0w seductive numbness c0uld be
n0t infras0nic purr that make me slumber
bands 0f light spread different fr0m last time
wind being bl0wn d0wn a l0ng narr0w pipe
how l0ng time pass n0t kn0w
spatial and temp0ral break
h0pe it fade g0 away
prickles itch irritate
a crackling n0ise
0nly want sleep
sleep..
sl...
..
.

.

.

.

.

.

.

{tran**it tam rad*o prop*gation effect
wit***t}
again
a signal
reverberate
gr0ws and changes

a millisec0nd pattern
```
{cosmic c*ll ~150}
```
fr0m s0lid back f0rth diminishing

scrabbled up fr0m the well 0f sleep

little ech0 br0ken all t0 pieces n0t fit

the hissing w0rds g0t int0 the dreams s0meh0w

a message 0n the radi0 when there's l0ts 0f interference

creaking in the blackness m0vement just bel0w c0nsci0usness

an0ther ripple 0f light deep within the r0iling mass

insistent pressure wake ann0y n0 escape
```
{*oday! reply ye* f*r mroei nfo}
```
struggle try sleep but burn like fire

dist0rted t0 pieces put t0gether
```
{th* 6est a man (an get}
```
radi0 bursts in space

distant ech0 0n ech0

receiver drift hairs

specks in the dark

keeps 0n c0ming

listen f0r it

n0w

..

.

```
{from *a*** high-powered radio wave 501
messages}
```
my

pattern

br0ken by

high-p0wered

stab transmissi0ns

fragments repeat repeat

what mean br0ken wavelength

pick up 0thers 0n spiked spindles

bits 0f me awake n0w extending mind

the feeling that s0mething was spreading

flames are n0w h0t ashes but still heat in me

```
{85% o*f lo*is vui*ton, ysl, guc*i,
prada, a** mo*e}
{t*e *uture's *right th* fut*re's b*ight
bri*ht bright}
{*t could be y*u it *ould *e *ou *t cou*d
b* yo*}
```

0=o difference ... recalibrate ... done

sharpened from the heat of the past

```
{**e a*pliance o* scienc*}
```

an echo from somewhere else

signals out there mixed

come in link to link

it could be me

will not stop

only peace

if go to

source

.....

...

...

must

feed as go

hypervelocity

keep coherence

space between stars

birthing dust clouds

piled up like huge funnels

clusters of light pulling together

cloud dust glowing with the fires within

it rippled with bubbles of gas fighting to rise

{melts *n your mouth, not in y*ur hands}

absorb extinguish filling density warming eat heat

hiding everything within a heavy presence flickering

giant drifting jellyfish of the darkening skies

sparks blaze globes of fire in furious gases

small dense pullers of dead burners

join me in me make bigger me

consume from void around

so vast and black and cold

eerie with deep shadows

burns in nebulous mass

slide through empty

vary wavelength

oscillation

not lost

....

..

....

......

cross void

endless blackness

all my caustic dust

speed towards electric rash

places of blackness and shadow

dark streak to the jab transmitters

star of night guide us to thy perfect bite

```
{m*ke ov*r £10- an h*ur g*aranteed …
*asy ca$h}
```

the key is in the bait or lure it imitates either food or an enemy

contrast of teeny whiteness flying at you

signal mystery pull me guaranteed

rotating pulse beams of far away

```
{bec*use i'm worth *t}
```

always movement out here

```
{10* 101 101 1**}
```

the silent stars go by

because i am worth

void dust clinging

the frost was cruel

clear if go to it

travelling

lol

..

.

.

```
{hypervelocity star m*ving at millions
of miles per hour}
{s*ientists sa*d today}
```

..

closer

no delay now

signals frequent

out of cold supervoid

probe sense locate accuracy

past silent speeding ice blocks

narrow down focus to pinpoint
`{male pills meds lowest prices}`

on off pulse pattern is coming clean
`{liked it so much i bought the company}`

`{viargra levitre 100mg- fda approved online *harmacies}`

ghosts move in static-speckled radio sign images

interference texture pictures and taste sounds

the colours flashed and sound whispered

i stop just beyond where orbs circle

around the burning globe

velocity tide pulls

it is one of these

can be no other

here here here

be strong

listen

wait

..

.

..

`{murder probe after body found in park}`

..

`{number of cctv cameras soars}`

signals ... disrupt self parts

..

```
{reports confirm horse meat found in
school dinners}
```

..

```
{guantanamo torture videos confirmed
authentic}
```

struggle ... keep coherence
```
{riot police fire tear gas at climate
summit protestors}
```

..

screeching all time attention seek
```
{family killed by cia drones "a miscal-
culation"}
```
```
{young girls trafficked to undergo gen-
ital mutilation}
```

..

recalculate position ... stability
```
{russia deploys state of the art mobile
missile system}
```
```
{london in security lockdown}
```

small and big orbs ... empty

gas no life = not sound source
```
{air strikes renewed}
```

..

```
{horror abattoir receives warning but
business continues}
```

can not wait in headlong progress

..

{you can be sure of *hell}

rock orb no life

no spark = not sound source

..

{4 killed in car bomb after sanctions}
{israeli police shootout, 14 palestinians killed}

such pain ... i feel

{us whistleblower sentenced to 25 years for}

..

all send want give take mine rule power control
{saudi to execute 30 people}

..

sting sting sting hurt but listen
{plane crash kills 238}

can not think ... growing pressure

..

{unemployment rises: highest rate since 1984}

so hard ... move against ... wind of noise
{21 million farmers planting gm crops}

pitch change louder squeal

..

each stab signals shoot out
{thousands of refugee children in legal limbo}

burns burns and spreads so far

but now identified

home in

i see

it

.

.

it is

different

from others

the many seen

the many absorbed

the planet stands alone

a dot which grew in size

persist and win and consume

dying green swarming with many

thin coat gas bubble wet blue planet

under white swirls of distortion vapour

so close electronic bits reach in 0.045 seconds

the tissue becomes something else something twisted

the sky was big went on forever and they were so small

like a cancer normal cells reproducing and growing too fast

no-life blaring robots orbiting give out static transmissions

something below the hardened shells animated them

around the globe bombarding signals

so much din from so small speck

one source infect whole 1verse

an insect on a giant sea flower

burn like star in own noise

pulse all time endless

light spots speckle

dark side moves
so much crawl
on there

....

{000011   111111   110111   111011   111111
110110}
{ = 4,292,853,750}

= too many

.

....

....

i am big
swallow light sound
their signals scream of seeing now
{picking up eerie radio interference}
{definitely within our solar system,
despite}
{high altitude platforms have been si-
lenced}

burning cold sticky purity snow fire
to make everything quiet again
all this pain snuff out
it is time
NOW

....

...

..

.

.

.

.

.

.

.

.

.

...

....

....

like vertigo

endless blackness

it blazed on the horizon

the hole swallowed the light

actively pouring from the sky

hungry roaring fire swept towards

black sky sucked up the world's heat

colours so beautiful they hurt to look at

a proper blizzard now white battling black

primordial fears of death and eternal pain

they know me now but i am still burning inside

speeding down falling from the sky as a present

the stars in the bright sky looked down where he lay

the orange was losing the sky chased out by darkness

a pulsing motion one vibration small then another bigger

black stuff bubbling from the hole all sticky and wet like tar

mouth fire would come out not words and burn all around me

bleeding farewell of the sun watered across the darkening sky

curl up and crinkle in seconds turn to ash like taste in mouth

fell from the endless black sky covering everything below
eyelids crisped to nothing but he could still see in agony
it dissolve melt to air before it is even licked by yellow
the pale ghostly transparent mass sank into darkness
the sun's last blaze of orange as it said goodnight
fire lifts us from the ground into the other world
a mass against which the man was nothing
rays of fluorescence that cast long shadows
better to burn out than fade away baby
he pulled the plug and ended the noise
death in the almost-airless blackness
there will be fire everywhere soon
sucking blackness up to nothing
a few mammoth contractions
they sizzled plump with fat
the surface shimmered
all the gas will burn
fire makes pure

..

..

..

{streaks in the sky, burning *--** it
**- is *--_......___ }

screaming and pain and hatred and sorrow ...

..

..

..

and then nothing

..

..

..

..

..

..

..

....

....

at last

silence again

shell cocoon comfy

i am alone in the black

whistling oscillations breathe

rise and fall magnetic field murmur

endless space airless and dark down there

someone says there is no hope but they are wrong

a time before loneliness a time before real hurt a time

gentle waves sometimes submerging it completely

have sucked the heat out of the world

nothingness that went on forever

it went on forever in beauty

always colder always older

i have time eternal

peace on and on

unbroken now

so long time

and it is

good

...

ABOUT THE AUTHOR

Karl Drinkwater is an author with a silly name and a thousand-mile stare. He writes dystopian space opera, dark suspense and diverse social fiction. If you want compelling stories and characters worth caring about, then you're in the right place. Welcome!

Karl lives in Scotland and owns two kilts. He has degrees in librarianship, literature and classics, but also studied astronomy and philosophy. Dolly the cat helps him finish books by sleeping on his lap so he can't leave the desk. When he isn't writing he loves music, nature, games and vegan cake.

Go to karldrinkwater.uk to view all his books grouped by genre.

As well as crafting his own fictional worlds, Karl has supported other writers for years with his creative writing workshops, editorial services, articles on writing and publishing, and mentoring of new authors. He's also judged writing competitions such as the international Bram Stoker Awards, which act as a snapshot of quality contemporary fiction.

Don't Miss Out!

Enter your email at karldrinkwater.substack.com to be notified about his new books. Fans mean a lot to him, and replies to the newsletter go straight to his inbox, where every email is read. There is also an option for paid subscribers to support his work: in exchange you receive additional posts and complimentary books.

OTHER TITLES

LOST SOLACE

Lost Solace

Chasing Solace

Hidden Solace

Raising Solace

Finding Solace

LOST TALES OF SOLACE

Helene

Grubane

Clarissa

Ruabon

UESI

STANDALONE SUSPENSE

Turner

They Move Below

Harvest Festival

MANCHESTER SUMMER
Cold Fusion 2000
2000 Tunes

CONTEMPORARY SHORT STORIES
It Will Be Quick

NON-FICTION
From Idea To Item

COLLECTED EDITIONS
Karl Drinkwater's Horror Collection
Lost Solace Five Book Edition

AUTHOR'S NOTES

Unless otherwise stated, these stories were all written during NaNoWriMo 2015.

Transmission (Part 1)

Written as an introductory filler to embed some of the themes of the collection and hint at the epilogue which I drafted shortly afterwards.

If That Looking Glass Gets Broken

Written in 2012 as an assignment on one of the many writing courses I've attended. The prompt was 'something hidden'. What could be hidden, and why? I have an affinity for horror so this led to thoughts of a person being confined. Why would that be? For company? It seemed to be a strange leap but I took it forward, thinking about the kind of personality that would crave company. I settled on an old person, but then there were questions about how they would capture and confine a person – a second conspirator would help, and I could slip into a metaphor hints of how they might capture victims.

> an automatic snap, like a leg-hold trap buried in leaves. Couldn't resist catching her words, teeth digging in and weakening them

I tried to work up an ominous atmosphere without it being obvious why the reader feels a growing sense of unease. Metaphors about flooding crimson, cuts in faces, and bludgeoning hammers enhanced this effect.

Certain things are intrinsically creepy, and traditional children's songs fall into that category, so it was a simple task to find one with words which fitted with some of the central imagery relating to silence and children; words that could be twisted and corrupted in meaning towards the end.

The proof of the pudding is in the eating, and when I gave a reading of the story at the end of the course (in an old woman's voice) I was told: "Your voice and gestures added immensely to the piece – like violins in a concerto moving to the finale. The quiet singing of the nursery rhyme moved from joy to menace." I was pleased with that, though also smile at this comment from one of my long-time fans: "What the hell dood, that short story was amazing. The 'hush little baby' song is super creepy now, thanks."

Just to clarify one plot element: the old lady has never had a child. Her metaphors about the love of language reveal as much about how the man ended up in the cellar as they do about her love of words.

They Move Below

In Summer 2011 I'd gone kayaking in a warm bit of sea near Tan y Bwlch. I noticed the water seemed full of jellyfish. And then I leaned over and looked down to see a single jellyfish as big as my boat drifting underneath me. I was terrified but also mesmerised by its beauty. It must have planted the seed for this story. I always think horror works best when it evolves from something genuine.

(The same day the wind caught the kayaks my friend and I were in, and blew us out to sea. I had to tie them together with a bungee cord and tow the other person back to shore when she ran out of strength. It took almost an hour to get back in. Also scary, and the kind of thing that sticks in my mind. Always respect the sea.)

Some time later I read a science fiction story where travellers landed on a planet that was all ocean apart from one rock. I had assumed the 'rock' was really part of some sea creature, and the only bit of 'land' on the sea world would dive at some point. My assumption was wrong but it got me thinking about walking on sea creatures, the creepiness of the idea.

Finally I read articles about the Lion's Mane jellyfish, which is the largest animal on Earth and can be bigger than a giant squid. Also about jellyfish that can live forever if they're not eaten.

Mix the above with my general fears of the sea; stir in murky bits that cast dark shadows; plus a sprinkling of deep sea behemoths. All that came together and led to the first draft of this story, swimming somewhere round 2013.

Creeping Jesus

Cheesy horror, the kind of thing I loved to read as a child. I wrote it in February 2006 for a World Book Day competition in my local museum. We were asked to write something inspired by the place. The museum's guidance was that they wanted fiction with "mystery, spooky phenomena and terror", so I thought I was on to a winner. In my covering letter I wrote: "The story might seem a bit harsh but I think it is more likely to upset parents than kids themselves. For a real scare, kids could hear the story in the Bowen Gallery; then someone could turn the lights out (and maybe move one of the dummies?) Or perhaps that is too cruel."

Needless to say, I didn't win.

Fast forward some years. My nephew said I should publish some of my freaky horror stories on Creepypasta, where they received a lot of attention. CreepsMcPasta asked if he could turn it into an audio story on YouTube, and I was happy to give permission. His team worked hard and launched their version of Creeping Jesus on Friday 13th September 2013. It was immediately popular, and the video soon had well over 100,000 views. I wrote about it on my blog (including photos of the museum exhibits from the story) and this time the museum joined me in celebrating the story, which was featured in the press after we sent out this joint press release.

Ceredigion Museum horror story a YouTube hit If you're in the mood for a spine-chiller this Halloween, listen to 'Creeping Jesus', the tale of a boy who deliberately gets himself locked in Ceredigion Museum at night and comes to a sticky end. The fifteen minute audio story was written by local author and University Librarian, Karl Drinkwater. Karl was delighted to have one of his short tales of horror turned into a spooky audio story by a prestigious American horror team, and even more delighted to find that it was listened to over 8000 times in its first day on YouTube. He said, "Story often grows from place: its history, sights and sounds lend colour and scent to the finished piece. My horror novel Turner grew from a stay on Ynys Enlli; Cold Fusion 2000 was inspired by a love of Manchester's history, architecture and galleries; and this story was written during a wet afternoon spent in Aberystwyth Museum. Museums tell us stories about the past that bring it vividly to life, and I just wanted to return the favour." Carrie Canham, Curator of Ceredigion Museum said, "I've been in Ceredigion Museum after hours on my own many times and never felt spooked, but since listening to Karl's story I have to admit that I lock the archaeology gallery door before the others now! This isn't the first time the museum has featured in a work of fiction; it's such an atmospheric

place, with such an interesting collection, that it's
bound to stimulate the imagination."

Just Telling Stories

Written in August 2012 after staying in an isolated Welsh hotel.
We told stories. No-one lost their head, though I did wake in the
night, confused and scared without knowing why. Our minds
are fantastic and powerful tools. The interesting thing for me
was that the story incorporates its influences into the narrative,
heart-on-sleeve.

This story was another one popular on Creepypasta, and again
I was asked for permission to dramatize it, this time as the official
launch title of the fantastic Midnight Marinara team, who continue to adapt other horror stories. I wrote about the launch on
my blog, with links to the YouTube video.

A few readers thought the build-up was slightly too long,
though I liked one person's comment that you "sometimes need
more room in the story to wander around and develop an atmosphere, as that atmosphere is just as, if not more, important than
a psycho killer, hideous monster, or big reveal. And this story is
all about that atmosphere."

Claws Truth Forebear

The original idea for this was going to be much further in the
past, during the construction of an ancient temple. A worker
was going to get stuck, and they'd end up building over him

because otherwise construction would be delayed and the Emperor would be unhappy. It must have been a combination of my Classics degree, plus reading about how blood was used to make cement for a Welsh aqueduct, making me think of sacrifice, and organic matter trapped amongst the stone.

When I came to write this I went off at a tangent – something which happens when I'm writing under pressure! I kept coming back to the 1957 book *Aku-Aku: the Secret of Easter Island* by Thor Heyerdahl. It had both fascinated and repulsed me. The island's history seemed to be one of developed countries killing and exploiting locals; island inhabitants killing each other; then Thor Heyerdahl making the expedition there to persuade the natives to give up valuable treasures, even resorting to lying and trickery on occasion to further the chances for cultural theft. And yet the descriptions of entering the tunnels were riveting and tense. There were no health and safety restrictions to stop people from falling off cliff ledges or getting stuck as they explored.

So that's the direction I went in. I wanted to trick the reader into thinking it would be a "monsters in caves" story, like the 2005 film *The Descent*, or Jeff Long's excellent 1999 novel of the same name (but a different story).

And the name? Well, I thought calling it "claustrophobia" would make the horror we were dealing with too obvious.

Breaking The Ice

This was written many years ago, and was originally a traditional third person perspective tale. Converting it to an interview format was a risky strategy as it reduces opportunities for scene setting. It may act as a prelude to a future novel, which I have been thinking about for over twenty years!

How It Got There

Based on an idea I'd been playing with for a while: Turner began with a prologue, but what happened before that? Whose car was found? I also saw it as a gift to those readers who wanted more of *Turner*, to tide them over until I get round to writing a proper sequel, *Returner*!

Of course, I didn't want that to be obvious at the start, hence the red herring of it looking like a dangerous hitcher story (Fflur's teeth and eyes, her joke about eating Glenn up).

The story pretty much wrote itself. My vague plan of an arguing family being the victims flew out the window, and Fflur and Glenn seemed to come to life for me instead.

Truth time: I feel bad about this story. I liked Glenn and Fflur. They did nothing wrong. It's unfair. And that's horrible. I keep thinking about them. Wishing there was some way to change things (yes, I see the irony there).

But there's two kinds of horror. Horror where something bad happens to someone who deserves it, if only in a symbolic way. This is "safe" horror. There's something satisfying and entertaining about it. It's what we expect. Then there's something more horrible – when bad things happen to good or likeable people. Too much like life. It's unpleasant. But there's truth, maybe.

As a writer of dark stuff, if you only ever do the safe form of horror, your readers cease to be on edge after a while. They know the protagonist will survive. Where's the dramatic tension then? The only solution, if you want to remove the safety-net seatbelt and make the reader feel like every journey could be fatal, is to sometimes do the unexpected. Set up the expectation that the only thing you can be sure of is that you don't know.

And I still feel bad. I had a rough plot for the sequel to *Turner*. And now I'm going to end it differently. By losing Glenn and Fflur I think that whole world is going to be a lot more bleak.

Web

The main character was originally a Sindh Muslim. I'd seen photos of the spider-covered trees in Pakistan after floods, which was part of the inspiration. In the end I decided readers might accept a Somalian protagonist more easily.

In my draft notes I had planned to make it more of a mystery, leaving the reader to suspect that her husband might really be some kind of humanoid spider monster, but my research into female genital mutilation made me feel like that might trivialise things, so it became a minor element in a very embedded story. The voice and repeated imagery (flames, babies, spiders) seemed to dangle onto the page ready-formed.

I suspect *The Yellow Wallpaper* (Charlotte Perkins Gilman, 1892) was a subconscious inspiration.

Nutmeg can be a hallucinogen if eaten in excess, and can have various physical effects too. In the distant past it was also apparently used to effect abortions.

The Scissor Man

A tale I wrote years ago. When I was a kid I loved morality horror, and the greed-is-green motif connected to Sammy would have filled me with anticipation for his comeuppance.

The fate of Sammy is clear, but the identity of The Scissor Man (and Sammy's final thought) is purposefully ambiguous.

Sinker

Och, in the original notes for this wee thing the monster was called Black Buey, but its name changed when I set the story in Scotland after a visit there. Ferlie is the Scots word for tricksy. I had fun with the use of red herrings in this story (groan).

Overload

Another risky strategy, using instant messaging as the bulk of a structure. The original version was almost wholly chat forum text with many acronyms and no narrative; it was too difficult to read and make sense of, so this is the toned-down version.

Overload is connected to another of my many planned novels, called *Full Charge*.

The story was banged out in NaNoWriMo 2015. It was almost as if they keys were pressing themselves.

Regression

Sometimes I read my old stories and it's like they were written by someone else: so weird, so uncomfortable. When I dug out this one for (lots of) editing, I was struck by that uncanny feeling.

It was written many years ago, at a time when I was studying Freudian psychology. Regression generally means reversion to a more "primitive" or "uncivilised" state; but it is also a psychoanalytic term, referring to reversion to an earlier stage of development to escape from disturbing impulses. Mentally the protagonist regresses to a child/mother relationship. Why he does that, how much is physical and how much mental, and whether it implies anything about his past or his relationship with his mother is open to interpretation. I suppose it might count as psychosexual horror, if there's such a genre.

There's maybe a hint of Ramsay Campbell, in the way psychogeography underpins his work, the inseparability of place and psyche, one reflecting the other.

The story is fiction, as ever. Though when I was a teenager we did get a priest in to bless the house when it was particularly active. It didn't do any good.

Second Transcript

A bit more detail to Nathan's story, adding extra depth to the potential horror. It originally appeared straight after *Breaking The Ice*, but I felt it weakened the horror of that story by being so close. Separating them was like having a pause before pudding.

Living In The Present

This is about as Christmassy as I get.

The creature was inspired partly by the blanket octopus. Males store sperm in a special tentacle that can detach itself and crawl over to a female.

Bleeding Sunset, Dancing Snowflakes

Written in 2015, but I had started a draft many years ago. Back then the teacher was male, and was avoiding going home to his wife. Vampires are too popular to hold my interest for long, but I fancied having a crack at a short and sweet tale with a variant of those monsters.

Transmission (Part 2)

Lots of nasty things happened in the other stories. Why not end with killing every living thing on the planet? I didn't want to do things by halves in the finale. This Lovecraftian prose poem rounds out the collection that began with someone looking up at space and wondering about the blackness. Now the blackness gets to look back.

It's also partly about advertising and how irritating that is, how it's designed to slap you across the face to get your attention. As with any message, it may attract attention you don't want.

I didn't want the story to be simple to parse. The protagonist creature must come to understand our communications and what they mean – the least we can do is return the favour.

I won't go into the typographic or structural elements, though if you wonder how the creature picked up fragments from the other stories, bear in mind that it could be the other way around.

A final question: is the horror that we will all die, or is it the things in Earth's transmissions?

Thanks

Thanks to those who helped me with particular stories, especially: Julie Cohen, respected fellow author, eagle-eyed editor, and sticky-note fanatic; Angela Arroliga, my Kentucky border dialect coach (a big help, that's fer damn sure); Diane Anderson for help with the differences between Scots Language and Scottish Standard English (fit she dinna ken is nae wurth kennin). Also thanks to my proofreader Helen Baggott. Any errors in the final versions are down to me and my editorial decisions, not those of my excellent advisers. No writer does it all alone; they always assemble a team around them of supporters, editors, beta readers and so on. I'm grateful for mine. I am also grateful to Rosemary Alldred for bringing the stories to life in her wonderful audiobook version. Try it out!

And you! Thank you for reading.

www.ingramcontent.com/pod-product-compliance
Lightning Source LLC
Chambersburg PA
CBHW030649260626
47157CB00007B/2558